HOPEFUL HEARTS AT THE WARTIME HOTEL

MAISIE THOMAS

B
Boldwood

First published in Great Britain in 2025 by Boldwood Books Ltd.

Copyright © Maisie Thomas, 2025

Cover Design by JD Smith Design Ltd.

Cover Images: Shutterstock and Paul Thomas Gooney/Figurestock

A CIP catalogue record for this book is available from the British Library.

Paperback ISBN 978-1-83633-252-7

Large Print ISBN 978-1-83633-253-4

Hardback ISBN 978-1-83633-251-0

Trade Paperback ISBN 978-1-80635-284-5

Ebook ISBN 978-1-83633-254-1

Kindle ISBN 978-1-83633-255-8

Audio CD ISBN 978-1-83633-246-6

MP3 CD ISBN 978-1-83633-247-3

Digital audio download ISBN 978-1-83633-249-7

This book is printed on certified sustainable paper. Boldwood Books is dedicated to putting sustainability at the heart of our business. For more information please visit https://www.boldwoodbooks.com/about-us/sustainability/

Boldwood Books Ltd, 23 Bowerdean Street, London, SW6 3TN

www.boldwoodbooks.com

In memory of my father's beloved aunts,
Nelly, Annie, Minnie and Jessie Harrop

1

MARCH 1942

Kitty made her way around the first and second floors of Dunbar's, unlocking the old guest rooms for all the contents to be cleaned. It wasn't that she didn't trust Lily, the cleaner, with the keys, but she liked to perform this duty herself, partly so she could tell her clients that it was her responsibility and also – well, frankly, because she enjoyed doing it. She loved the feeling of being in charge. Bill had never let her go out to work because it would have made it look as if he couldn't afford to support his family, and he wasn't having that. No husband would have put up with it.

Kitty smiled to herself as she sorted through the keys on the ring and selected the next one. She possessed a master key, of course, but she liked the ritual of using the individual keys one at a time. Just look at her now, not just working but actually running the business. Not only that, but she had set up the business herself. It might still say DUNBAR'S HOTEL over the handsome double doors at the front of the building, but the business inside was now Dunbar's Storage, providing secure accommodation for what was left of people's furniture and household goods after they had been bombed out.

She opened the door and peered inside the old guest room. Everything in here belonged to the Hepworth family. They had lost everything upstairs in the fire that had broken out when a pair of incendiaries penetrated their roof. Fortunately for them, the fire brigade had been just up the road and had quickly dealt with the flames. Once the house had been declared safe, the neighbours had mucked in to carry everything outside from downstairs.

The Hepworths, five of them plus the budgie, were now squeezed in with Mrs Hepworth's mother in her two-up two-down. When would they get a place of their own again? Since they had a roof over their heads, they wouldn't get priority. Presumably they'd have to wait until after the war. Thousands of new houses would be needed.

Kitty's glance travelled across the Hepworths' belongings. Many were tucked away safely inside tea chests, which Kitty supplied for a fee. Any doubts she had entertained about requiring her clients to pay for extras had long since been quashed. She was running a business and she had to make money, though her charges were always fair.

As well as the chests of smaller items were the Hepworths' dining table and chairs, their sideboard, armchairs, the hall stand and their old upright piano. The family had paid for tea chests but not dust sheets and the scent of Lily's furniture cream, which she made from turps, linseed oil and vinegar, lingered in the air.

The piano caught Kitty's eye. Should she offer an annual tuning? And what sort of person did that make her, profiting from other people's personal tragedies? She stiffened her spine. A businesswoman: that's what it made her. A businesswoman and a mother, who not only wanted to take care of her beloved daughter but also wanted to show her that, even though the traditional tasks of women were cooking and cleaning, they were capable of so much more.

Mind you, Abbie only had to look around her to see that. Women were working in all kinds of jobs now so as to free up the men to join the services and fight for their country. Instead of a postman and a milkman, they now had a post-lady and a milk-lady. Kitty had made a journey by train the other day and the ticket office clerk, the ticket collector, the station porters, the train guard and even the ticket inspector had all been women. There were women in even more obviously masculine roles too – operating heavy machinery, working in telegraph gangs and all kinds of maintenance; driving lorries and tractors, operating cranes; repairing electric motors and undertaking all manner of skilled factory work.

On top of that there was also the splendid work done by the WVS, the Women's Voluntary Service, of which Kitty was a proud member. Lily was too, and so was Beatrice Inkerman, Kitty's dear friend, who also lived here in Dunbar's. The WVS did all kinds of work. During air raids they were in the thick of it, driving their mobile canteens to the worst hit areas, providing sandwiches, cigarettes and numerous cups of tea to civilians, ARP wardens, rescuers and firemen. They staffed the rest centres where bombed-out folk went for help and information as well as a change of clothes and some toiletries. And they provided more day-to-day services than you could shake a stick at: advice centres, clothing exchanges, mobile laundries, friendship clubs for foreign servicemen, knitting and sewing circles, jumble sales, toy collections at Christmas... Basically, if something needed doing, you just asked the WVS and it got done. They even made camouflage nets for the army.

Before Kitty had finished unlocking all the doors, Lily

appeared, carrying her housemaid's box with its brushes, cloths and polish. Lily was a sweet girl and Kitty's heart ached at the thought of what she had had to go through at such a young age. She looked better now than she had when Kitty had first known her. She could still do with more flesh on her bones, but her blue eyes had lost that bleak look. Mind you, it was anybody's guess whether she was actually feeling better. Lily kept her cards close to her chest.

'You're quick off the mark,' Kitty said. 'I haven't unlocked everywhere yet.'

'Being prompt is part of the job,' Lily said.

'Don't tell me.' Kitty smiled. 'It's the Dunbar way.'

Lily smiled back. 'Funny you should say that.'

Lily had started working at Dunbar's Hotel as a fourteen-year-old school-leaver and had been trained in 'the Dunbar way' by Mrs Swanson, who used to be the housekeeper. Kitty felt a stab of regret. Telling the loyal, hard-working staff that the hotel would have to close, and that they must look for new jobs, had been one of the most upsetting things she had ever been called on to do. The only consolation was that in wartime, there was work for everyone.

Leaving Lily to get on, Kitty unlocked the rest of the rooms, then returned to the family flat, where she lived with Abbie. It had been a rather grand set of rooms when Bill's late Uncle Jeremiah and Cousin Ronald had lived in it. Now it was sparsely furnished and Kitty tried not to dwell on that distressing day when the bailiffs had descended on Dunbar's. She had begged them to leave Abbie's bedroom intact, and they had – not out of kindness to a child, but because they had gathered items to the necessary value by stripping the rest of the flat, the guest bedrooms and the residents' sitting room and dining room. Honestly, Kitty could have crowned Bill for that.

But what had started as a disaster had ended as a success, namely Dunbar's Storage.

The bailiffs hadn't needed to touch the staff accommodation on the third floor – thank heaven. Lily's room was up there, and Kitty had given Beatrice two rooms after she was thrown out by her landlady. From the remaining rooms, Kitty had scraped together sufficient bits and pieces to make the family flat vaguely respectable.

Truth be told, she, Beatrice and Lily spent a lot of time together clustered around the big table in the basement kitchen that had once served the hotel. They sometimes had to watch what they said because Abbie liked nothing better than to sit there with her ears flapping. With her fourteenth birthday coming up next month, she was at that age when grown-ups' conversation was of consuming interest.

In the flat, Kitty titivated her dark hair. It was cut in a pageboy style, which she curled using rollers and sugar water. The curls at the sides she wore scooped away from her face while those at the back curled underneath in a plump roll just above her shoulders.

She already had on her green WVS uniform. Many women were in a position to purchase only the hat, say, or just the skirt, but that hadn't been good enough for Bill. Oh no, he'd just had to buy the whole lot for Kitty, hadn't he?

'I want you to have the very best,' he'd said, the same as he'd said every other time he'd spent money he shouldn't have parted with. He always made out that he did it to please her, but really he did it to please himself.

Kitty was due to work at the British Restaurant that morning, which could well mean peeling her way through a mountain of potatoes or carrots; but when she got there, she was put on pudding duty, helping to assemble and bake scores of bread puddings and cheese muffins.

'What's on the menu today?' she asked the head cook.

'Lentil and parsley soup or carrot croquettes to start. Then curried cod or veg casserole and herby dumplings. You know about the puddings. For tea, there's going to be kedgeree or macaroni cheese, then potato scones or fruit shortcake.'

Kitty nodded. Members of the public could have two courses plus a hot drink for less than a shilling, which was very good value, and all the meals were nutritious. Many people were eating better in wartime than they ever had before. The same could be said for school dinners.

As she worked on the dinnertime puddings, Kitty reflected on how good it felt to have things back to normal weather-wise after the dreadful conditions earlier in the year. For three whole weeks, the entire country had vanished under several feet of snow. Temperatures had plummeted and the residents of Dunbar's all slept wrapped up in blankets in front of a low fire in the family flat so as to save fuel. Numerous buildings had suffered burst pipes and Kitty had read desperately all through her insurance policy to see if she was covered should her clients' belongings fall victim to water damage. She, Abbie, Beatrice and Lily had turned on the taps regularly day and night to keep Dunbar's safe from burst pipes.

Outside, the snow had been so deep that channels had needed to be dug for people to walk anywhere – and these channels had needed to be dug again and again with every fresh snowfall. Trying to get anywhere by public transport took for ever and a day, and everybody knew somebody who'd had to get off the bus in order to help dig a path for it. In the countryside the RAF had dropped food parcels to villages that were cut off and to people stranded for days on end on trains that were blocked in.

After three long weeks of agonising cold, the snow had let up. The thaw had brought its own problems, but at least the end had been in sight.

Now, after finishing her shift, Kitty hurried back to Dunbar's. Ideally, she would arrive home before Abbie got in from school, but today wasn't going to be one of those days.

She ran up the steps and let herself in.

Lily was passing through the foyer. 'She got back twenty minutes ago,' she said without being asked. 'She's fine.'

Kitty grinned. 'Just when I could have done with her stopping to play on a bomb site.'

'Your sister is here too,' said Lily. 'I tried to get her to come down to the kitchen but she said she's family.'

'It's perfectly all right for her to go up to the flat,' said Kitty.

She went upstairs, eager to see Abbie and Naomi. They looked round as she walked in. They were both fair-haired, but Abbie was dark-blonde while Naomi's fairness was starting to fade. She was Kitty's senior by ten years and had always kept an eye on her, something Kitty was grateful for. Naomi was the person she trusted most in the world.

Kitty's heart melted at the sight of her daughter, but she couldn't have a proper conversation with Naomi while Abbie was here.

'Have you got any homework?' Kitty asked.

'Only spellings,' said Abbie, 'and I already know them.'

'She does,' Naomi confirmed. 'I've been testing her.'

'Then you may go out to play,' Kitty told Abbie. 'Don't be late back for your tea.'

Abbie kissed her and Naomi, and departed.

'I'm so lucky to have her at home,' Kitty said as the door closed.

'It's a double-edged sword,' Naomi replied. 'You must curl up with guilt every time there's an air raid.'

That hurt, but Kitty knew her sister meant well. Anyway, it was true. 'Yes, I do, but I also remember how it felt when she was evacuated. Once we brought her home, we knew we could never send her away again.'

'I'm not criticising,' Naomi said. 'All the mothers of servicemen know exactly how it feels to have their children away from home.' She gave a rueful smile. 'No matter how old they are, they're still your babies.'

Kitty touched her sister's hand in a gesture of sympathy. Naomi and Derek had three boys, who had all joined up as soon as war had been declared.

'I know how awful it sounds,' said Naomi, 'but I wish they were married.'

'They're nowhere near old enough to support wives and families,' Kitty said in surprise.

'I know,' Naomi agreed. 'Leaving the war out of it, I'd have been appalled if one of them had wanted to get married so young, but as things are, I would have loved a daughter-in-law or two, and maybe even some babies, just so I could feel my family hasn't vanished off the scene.'

'You've still got Derek,' Kitty said gently. Naomi's husband was a telephone engineer, and from the summer of 1940 until the start of this year he'd spent much of his time restoring communications after air raids. 'You're lucky to have him.'

Naomi sighed. 'I know that as well.' She smiled. 'I've got my dear husband and you've got your darling daughter.'

'I was thinking earlier today about how I want my setting up and running my storage business to set a good example for her,' said Kitty, 'so she'll know what women are capable of. But I also want her to keep her adoration of her father. They mean the world to one another and I would never want to take that away.'

'Even though you sometimes think Bill doesn't deserve it,' Naomi said, hitting the nail on the head.

'Family matters can be complicated,' said Kitty. She brightened. 'I'll tell you something I'm grateful for: the way Beatrice, Lily and I have grown so close through living together. We all help one another and they both love Abbie.' Emotion enriched her voice. 'We've become a sort of family.'

Up went Naomi's eyebrows. 'Really?'

'In fact, not a "sort of" family,' Kitty realised. 'Just – a family.'

'Oh,' said Naomi.

Too late Kitty saw that her sister felt snubbed. Drat. All she'd ever had from Naomi was support and now she'd managed to upset her.

'I never meant to suggest...'

'Suggest what?' Naomi asked, her tone light. 'There's no earthly reason why you shouldn't have friends.' She sounded amused. 'I'm just surprised to hear you refer to them as your family.'

'I didn't mean to suggest they're anything like as important as you are,' Kitty said quickly. 'They mean a great deal to me but you mean more. You've always looked after me.'

'A big sister's duty is never done.'

'And a little sister never stops being glad of it,' Kitty answered sincerely. 'You know how much you've helped me. Just think of all the years when I was worried sick about Bill's spending. Not even Mam knew about that.'

Naomi nodded, mollified.

Kitty still felt impelled to make amends. 'You've always been the one I turned to, Naomi, and I want to tell you something that must be kept a dead secret.'

Naomi's blue eyes widened. 'Has Bill done something?'

'No. I did it.' Kitty drew in a breath and said quietly, 'I got him called up.'

Naomi leaned closer. 'You did *what*?'

'If he'd stayed here to run the hotel, he'd have bankrupted us. I knew that and so I secretly added his name to the Congreve's call-up sheet.'

'You got him sent away...' breathed Naomi in a wondering tone.

'For all the good it did,' Kitty said drily. 'No sooner was he gone than the bailiffs turned up and the hotel ended up closing.'

'Why didn't you tell me before?' Naomi asked.

'I don't know. I was ashamed, I suppose. Ashamed of being married to a man who can't be trusted with money. But I had to do it, Naomi. You do see that, don't you? I also felt dreadful for sending away Abbie's daddy. She worships him.'

'I know she does.'

'Do you forgive me for not telling you?' Kitty asked. 'It was such a huge secret that I didn't dare say a word. But I've told you now – because you're my sister. However close I am to Beatrice and Lily, I will never be closer to anyone than I am to you.'

2

It would have been all too easy to wish it had never happened – easy, but superficial. While there were some things Lily Chadwick might willingly have obliterated from her past, she could never regret Toby. Her heart creaked at the thought of her precious, short-lived son. Losing him had ripped her heart straight down the middle, but she could never wish him out of her life. Holding him that first time had changed her for ever. It had turned her into a mother; and as she had discovered, that didn't stop even when you no longer had a child.

That was the difference between being a mother and being a wife. You could stop being a wife. She and Daniel had been deeply in love at one time and had truly believed they were destined to spend the rest of their lives together, but Toby's death had blown them apart. No, that sounded as if it had been a fierce and dramatic process, full of passion, and it hadn't been that way at all. Far from being fiery, it had been as if ice had descended, creating a wall between them. They could still see one another through the ice, through the despair, but they were for ever separated.

Would it have been different if Daniel had been on dry land when Toby had died? But he hadn't been and it was useless to wonder. He was in the merchant navy, braving the dangers of the Atlantic crossing to bring essential supplies from Canada and America to war-torn Britain, and he had been at sea not just at the time of Toby's birth and death but also for some time afterwards. Lily had never needed anyone more than she had needed Daniel at that time, but she'd been forced to face her agonising grief on her own.

She had hated Daniel at times, because he had no idea what had happened. In his imagination, he was the father of a new baby and he was happy and excited at the thought that he would meet his son or daughter when he finally returned to England. Lily would have given ten years of her life if she could have lived in a similar state of ignorant joy, if she could have occupied a world in which all was well and life was filled with hope.

Then Daniel had come home to the news that the child he had dreamed of had been born with a heart defect and had slipped away. Daniel's shock and grief had been too much for Lily to bear. The rawness, the *newness* of his feelings after she had spent weeks struggling to cope with her own grief had taken her breath away and overwhelmed her. That had been the beginning of the end of their marriage.

In a strange way it felt like fate. Lily had already been carrying Toby when they got married, so did that make it inevitable that losing him should spell the end of the union? Daniel's snobby mother had told her posh friends that her son had only married lower-class Lily because he'd got her in the family way, but Lily knew that wasn't true... though once things had gone so badly wrong for them, it wasn't always easy to remember that.

She and Daniel had finally separated last summer. Separated. It might sound sensational but it hadn't been, because they hadn't been living together at the time. No suitcases had needed to be packed. Neither of them had had to rush about, calling in favours, seeking a fresh billet. No doors had been slammed, no voices raised. Neither of them had been obliged to de-register with one butcher and re-register with another.

Instead, they had simply dropped away from one another. Daniel had been living at his parents' house, which was still his home; and Lily had long since moved back to Dunbar's, the hotel where she had worked ever since leaving school, though it wasn't a smart hotel now but a storage facility, thanks to the initiative and imagination of Kitty Dunbar.

So when Lily and Daniel had called it a day, they had both simply returned to their respective homes afterwards and carried on living their lives. Daniel had gone back to sea soon after that, which had left Lily feeling... well, she didn't want to think about that. There was no point. That part of her life was over and the sooner she got used to it, the better.

Daniel had come to see her in the early autumn when he had returned from the Atlantic crossing. By then, the air was developing a crisper edge and the early morning sun was lower and dazzling in the sky, but the leaves had not yet started to turn.

'How are you, Lily? Are you all right?'

She had nodded, too surprised and unsettled by this unexpected encounter to think what to say.

He had nodded, pressing his lips together as if he couldn't find any words either. Tears had risen in the backs of Lily's eyes. He had come to see her. Might this mean—?

Daniel cleared his throat. 'I just wanted to tell you that you'll continue to receive your allotment from my wages.'

Lily had stared at him. Was this why he'd come? To reassure her about money? After everything that had happened, did he think the money mattered?

'It's only right, when you think about it,' Daniel added, discomfort clouding his hazel eyes.

'Is it?' Lily challenged him. Instinctively she took a step backwards, wanting to distance herself from this situation. 'I don't need your money, Daniel. I've got a job and I get my bed and board thrown in. It isn't necessary for you to provide for me.'

Rebuffed, he said, 'Yes, it is. After everything you've been through, I wouldn't ever want you to find yourself in the position of worrying where the next few bob is coming from.' Forestalling her, he added, 'I'm just offering you a small piece of security, Lily. It's the very least I owe you. Please don't throw it back in my face.'

Before she could gather together the words to frame a reply, he had departed, leaving her feeling churned up.

'It got me all riled that he seemed to think the money matters to me,' she had said in the basement kitchen to Kitty and Beatrice, having first made sure that young Abbie wasn't there to overhear.

To start with, Lily had called the two women Mrs Dunbar and Miss Inkerman, as was appropriate, given that they were respectively about fifteen and at least twenty-five years older than she was. It had taken young Abbie to point out that such formality wasn't right, seeing as how they were all supposed to be living together as a family. Abbie was allowed to call Miss Inkerman Auntie Beatrice, and she used Lily's first name as Lily was like a big sister to her. Mrs Dunbar and Miss Inkerman were on first-name terms too, which had made Lily the odd one out when she observed the proprieties.

It had finally been agreed that Lily would use the other women's first names in private and call them by their titles and surnames in public, which was the same way they treated one another.

'I'm sure he doesn't think that,' Kitty had said in reply to Lily's remark about Daniel wanting to give her part of his wages. 'In any case, even though you're separated and the marriage is over, you are still legally married. I expect this is his way of fulfilling his obligations. He'd be a pretty poor sort of creature if he did anything less.'

Fulfilling his obligations. Was that what she was now, an obligation? Lily felt annoyed all over again.

'Anyhow, I don't care about the money,' she said obstinately.

'Lucky you,' Beatrice said drily, though not unkindly. 'It's only folk who know their position is secure who can afford not to care about money. When I lost my job and my home, I was frightened out of my life, I don't mind telling you.'

Lily felt an urge to give Beatrice a hug, but she kept her hands to herself. 'I'm glad you found a home here at Dunbar's. And I know I'm being unreasonable. It just rattled me to see him, that's all.'

If it had rattled her to see Daniel, it positively discomposed her when his mother had a go at her a few days later. Lily was on WVS duty at the time, serving in the British Restaurant on Market Street where many of the big shops were, when – oh glory – Mrs Chadwick and her friend Lady Ingrid Campbell walked in, each of them carrying a shopping bag. Mrs Chadwick's was made of cloth, her friend's of wicker.

Seating themselves, the two ladies had studied the day's menu. Lily had been clearing tables and was carrying a loaded tray. She could have turned on her heel and walked around the perimeter of the dining room so as to avoid them, but why should she? Instead she carried on. If her mother-in-law saw her, then so be it, but in her heart Lily hoped she wouldn't.

She did. Of course she did. Mrs Chadwick had a special antenna where Lily was concerned. She looked startled, but then her face settled into lines of disdain.

'Lily! What a surprise.' *And not a nice one*, said her tone.

'I work here sometimes,' Lily replied, wishing she'd skulked around the edge of the vast room after all.

'Jolly good show,' said Lady Ingrid. 'Where would the country be without the WVS?'

'Exactly,' agreed Mrs Chadwick.

Lily knew she ought to say something polite like 'It's nice to see you', but she couldn't bring herself to utter a bare-faced lie. Instead she nodded and moved on, her skin prickling all over in relief at having survived the encounter.

Just before she made it to the swing door that led to the kitchen, she turned to push it open with her bottom – and found that Mrs Chadwick had followed her. Her eyes blazed with anger as she regarded Lily.

'I told Daniel I wouldn't utter a word,' she said, her voice tight and clipped, 'but I made that promise never expecting to set eyes on you again. If you have no intention of living *with* my son, then you have no business living *off* him. I know your sort. You're out for all you can get and you have been right from the start: that's your so-called marriage in a nutshell.'

* * *

Lily's meetings with Daniel and his mother had both taken place last autumn. She hadn't seen either of them since, which suited her just fine, especially where Mrs Chadwick was concerned. That barb about being out for what she could get had hurt. It was so unfair. Lily had never viewed Daniel as a meal ticket. To her, he had been the handsome, caring young man she had instantly fallen for, but his mother was never going to believe that. Well, let her think what she wanted. There was nothing Lily could do about it.

Now, on a chilly, cloudy day in March, Lily was due to spend the morning on WVS duty.

'What will you be doing?' Abbie asked her at the breakfast table.

Lily gave the child a wry smile. 'I believe two of us are on nit duty.'

Abbie pulled a face. 'Nits?' Her tone expressed deep disgust.

'Nits haven't gone away just because there's a war on,' Beatrice pointed out.

'I haven't been on nit duty before,' said Lily, 'and I really could do with somebody to practise on.' She eyed Abbie innocently. 'Can I have a good old riffle through your hair?'

She made a pretend lunge for the girl. Abbie squealed and almost tumbled off her chair in her effort to duck.

'That's enough of that, thank you,' said Kitty. 'The table isn't the place for horseplay.'

But the words were spoken with a smile. Lily knew how much Kitty appreciated the family atmosphere in Dunbar's, which was of such benefit to Abbie. Lily could understand that. An orphan herself, she had been brought up by her uncle and aunt, and Auntie Nettie had always put the children first, something Lily had never questioned. It was only now, having been a mother herself, that she understood the powerful urge that made mothers do this.

In that instant the loss of her son swept over her as if it were brand new. She looked at her palms so the others wouldn't see the despair in her eyes as, heart thumping, she rode out the moment.

After breakfast it was her turn to clear away, then she got ready to go nit-hunting in one of the local elementary schools. She was to accompany Mrs McCartney, who immediately declared herself to be an old hand at it.

'And if anyone is upset at having nits, tell them nits prefer clean hair,' said Mrs McCartney. 'That might stop the other children being mean.'

Lily braced herself for a morning she wasn't exactly looking forward to. If her Toby had lived, she would never have let him catch nits. Then again, Toby alive and infested would have been infinitely preferable to reality.

At the end of the nit session, Lily caught a bus to visit Auntie Nettie. She and Uncle Irwin had taken Lily in when she'd needed it most. Even though they had very little themselves, they had welcomed her warmly and she became a big sister to their own five. She had lived with them, all squashed together in their two-up two-down, until she went to live and work in Dunbar's.

Auntie Nettie opened the door to her, her eyes brightening with pleasure at the sight of her niece. 'Come in, chick. Come straight from the WVS, have you? Let me pop the kettle on and you can tell me what you've been up to.'

Soon they were sitting together in the small parlour with its worn furniture. Tea and home-made ginger biscuits sat on the table in between them.

Lily told her aunt about nit duty.

'I was told to tell anyone with nits that they only like clean hair – you know, to spare their feelings.'

'And did it work?'

Lily smiled. 'Sort of. The first lad with nits was a scrawny little herbert with scabby knees.'

'A real boy,' said Auntie Nettie. To her, a real boy was a tearaway and a real girl was a docile housewife-in-waiting.

'When the others twigged this one had nits, the other boys in the line nudged one another and whispered, and some of the girls pretended to shrink away, so I tried to put the lid on it with the line about clean hair.'

'Didn't it work?'

'It did, but not in the way it was meant to,' said Lily. 'The lad gave me a huge, gappy grin and said, "Oh good. I'll tell me mam I'd better not wash ever again." We came close to having bedlam once that idea spread down the line.'

Auntie Nettie laughed. 'I can imagine our Harry or our Roy trying to pull that one.'

'How are they?' Lily asked.

'Dying to leave school and join up.'

'They do know they can't join the army at fourteen, don't they?'

'I keep telling myself it'll all be over long before they're old enough,' said Auntie Nettie.

'Goodness, I hope so,' said Lily. But Toby had died and that meant anything could happen. 'Look.' She picked up the cloth bag she had put beside her chair. 'I got these off the market. I thought they'd do for the girls.'

She produced a pair of cotton dresses and held them up. One was blue gingham, the other green with white daisies.

'They're lovely,' Auntie Nettie exclaimed. 'Thanks, chick. The girls will be chuffed to bits. You're so generous, Lily, but you don't have to keep turning up here with gifts, you know.'

'I know,' said Lily, 'but I like to. You and Uncle Irwin have always been good to me and now I'm in a position where I can give something back.'

'Oh aye? She must pay you well, that Mrs Dunbar.'

Lily bit her lip, then decided to come clean. 'I still get money from Daniel's wages.'

'You what?' said Auntie Nettie. 'Does he know?'

That surprised a laugh out of Lily. 'Of course he does. Don't be daft.'

'Well, I don't know.' Auntie Nettie shook her head, looking perturbed. 'It's a rum do, if you ask me. Does this mean you've called an end to the separation and you've gone back to being married?'

Heat flared in Lily's cheeks. 'No. We're still separated, but Daniel's a decent man and he wants to do right by me.'

'I don't call walking out on you doing the right thing.'

'It was what we both wanted.'

Did that make it sound as though there had been lots of discussion and decision-making? It hadn't been that way at all. It was as if the situation they were in had taken on a life of its own and somehow become stronger than they were. Or was that a feeble way of trying to evade responsibility?

'What you both wanted, my eye!' Auntie Nettie didn't often get vexed, but her expression was pinched as she tapped the arm of her chair with her finger. 'Times were when you couldn't have just called a halt to being married. Times were when couples stuck together through thick and thin. Folk are saying there are going to be plenty of divorces after the war – and I suppose you'll be one of them. Your poor mother would be that ashamed.'

'Are you ashamed?' Lily asked in a small voice.

'Well, I do ask myself how I'm going to explain it to the children,' Auntie Nettie answered. 'You're their big sister, as good as, and they think the world of you. I don't want them growing up thinking that divorce is somehow acceptable. You've got a lot to answer for, our Lily.'

3

During her dinner break, Beatrice popped into Ingleby's on Market Street. Ingleby's was a large establishment that had been there for decades. Unlike Paulden's, it hadn't been hit by a high explosive. Even so, the war was evident in the lack of goods available for purchase, just the same as in every other shop all over the country. Beatrice sighed inwardly. There were some shops that were real landmarks not just on the street but, possibly more importantly, in people's lives. For her, Ingleby's was just such a one. She imagined that many Mancunian home-dressmakers must feel the same.

Ingleby's had been a kind of department store even before such things were invented. What made Ingleby's different, and possibly not really a department store in the strict sense, was that the various departments were all to do with dressmaking. While there was nothing unusual in finding haberdashery and drapery under the same roof, Ingleby's had always had an accessories department, offering gloves, belts, handbags, scarves, capes and other items to enhance the garments their customers made. They also had their own dressmaking department for those customers who could afford to hand over the work to somebody else, though that department had been given over to war work. After several months of churning out blackout curtains, it had moved on to uniforms.

The other big change that Ingleby's had seen dated back to early in the century, when they had, as Beatrice's late mother had once put it, 'jumped on the ready-mades bandwagon'. 'Ready-mades' was the old name for clothes that were made in certain sizes, which seemed normal now, but only last week Beatrice had overheard a couple of old biddies in the grocer's queue recalling how bizarre it had seemed back in Edwardian times that women were somehow meant to conform to specific measurements.

Beatrice had come to buy darning wool and a reel of cotton. These things weren't on ration as such but, as with all everyday items, they were in short supply and it was normal for shop-keepers to limit how much a customer could purchase so as to eke out the stock for as long as possible and also to prevent hoarding. Everyone scorned hoarders.

After making her purchases, Beatrice spent a few minutes wandering around. She didn't have long because her so-called dinner hour was actually thirty minutes, but coming to Ingleby's had always been a treat for her. She'd never in her life had much money to spend, and certainly none to fritter, but she'd always enjoyed browsing.

Her education had been patchy at best because of constantly being kept home from school to look after her sickly mother and their home. That had led to a couple of dead-end jobs and then she had become an inco lady – an incontinence lady, delivering adult-sized nappies to families taking care of an infirm or invalid person who lacked the basic dignity of being able to control their bladder or bowels or, in the most distressing cases, both. Being an inco lady was an important and necessary job, but the fact remained that it wasn't exactly something that people queued up to do. Beatrice still felt a twinge of shame when she recalled how gladly she had left the post last summer – though the reason she'd left had been because of a wonderful new opportunity that had unexpectedly come her way.

After pausing to look at a board on an easel, advertising Make Do and Mend classes, she walked slowly around the accessories department. Many of the items these days had been made from what remained at the end of a bolt of fabric after all that could be sold had been. Beatrice thought of the ranks of seamstresses in the sewing room. After a week of churning out uniforms, was it a treat for them to make simple needle cases, pin cushions and decorative flowers to pin on hats?

A little flash caught her eye – silver? No, metal. She stepped closer. A dainty pair of scissors. Not for embroidery, but manicure scissors, proper ones with gently curving blades. Next to the scissors lay a pair of tweezers, a nail file and a nail buffer.

Beatrice turned to a middle-aged assistant in a plain black dress with white collar and cuffs, who was standing nearby, ready to help.

'Are these new?' she asked, hearing the wonderment in her tone. It was like discovering treasure.

'Yes, madam. Ingleby's does not deal in second-hand goods, especially not when the item is something as personal as a manicure set.'

'Then why hasn't it been snapped up?' Beatrice asked.

The assistant smiled; not a wide, friendly smile, but a discreet, professional one. 'Because it only went on display ten minutes ago. I put another set out earlier this morning and it was sold almost at once.'

'I'm not surprised,' said Beatrice.

She bent closer to see the little white label, knowing even as she did so that the price didn't matter. She didn't care how expensive it was. She had to have it – not for herself, but for Abbie. What a magnificent birthday present! Abbie was going to be fourteen, just the age to appreciate a grown-up gift like this.

'I'd like it, please,' she told the assistant.

'Thank you, madam. I have to point out that this set is incomplete. There ought to be a pouch or a case to hold the pieces.'

'That doesn't matter. I can soon make one.' And that would add a personal touch to the gift. Beatrice felt a little flutter of pleasure, but it was instantly followed by anxiety. 'The only thing is, I don't have enough money on me at the moment.'

'If madam would care to write a cheque…'

Goodness, did she look like the sort to carry a cheque book around with her? 'Could you please put it on one side for me while I go home and fetch the money?'

The assistant looked doubtful, as well she might. It wasn't as though she was going to have any trouble selling this pretty little item.

'I haven't got far to go,' Beatrice said quickly. 'I know most folk don't live in town, but I do – on Lily Street, in Dunbar's. Maybe you've heard of it.'

'Everybody has heard of Dunbar's.' The woman looked wistful. 'When I was a child, my godmother used to take me there for afternoon tea as a special treat. Their Victoria sponge melted in the mouth.' She looked at Beatrice. 'I thought Dunbar's had stopped being a hotel.'

'It has. It's a storage place now – you know, for when folk are bombed out. I live there with Mrs Dunbar and her daughter. If you'll put this behind the counter for me, I'll hurry straight there and back.'

The assistant nodded. 'With pleasure, madam. One old established family business supporting another.'

* * *

By the time she reached Lily Street, Beatrice was too puffed to run any further and she proceeded along the road at a swift walk, once or twice breaking into an undignified trot. She mounted the steps to Dunbar's handsome double doors. No one passing by for the first time would ever imagine that this wasn't a hotel any longer. One of the stipulations laid down by the Corporation at the time when the storage business was set up was that Dunbar's had to appear from the outside to be as it had always been, so as not to lower the tone for the other hotels in the street.

Beatrice let herself in, calling, 'Only me!' in case Kitty or Lily heard her. She hurried up the stairs all the way to the third floor, where the former staff accommodation was. Lily had a bedroom here and wanted nothing more, while Beatrice had both a bedroom and a small sitting room, which was a grand name for a simple room with a chintzy armchair that had seen better days, a set of shelves, a cupboard, and a table and chair. It might not be much by many folks' standards, but to Beatrice it represented security, friendship and a bright future.

Diving into her bedroom, she wrenched open her bedside cupboard and pulled out her piggy bank, upending it to turn the knob in the ceramic tummy and gain access to her money. After taking what she needed, she set off down the stairs again.

Kitty had appeared in the spacious foyer. With her was her sharp-eyed mother-in-law, Mrs Ivy Dunbar.

'Sorry, but I can't stop.' Beatrice's breath emerged in a series of tiny gasps. 'I'm in a tearing hurry.'

'So I see,' said Kitty. 'Anything I can do?'

'No, thank you,' Beatrice answered, then had second thoughts. 'Actually, if you don't mind, could you telephone the Town Hall and leave a message for Miss Brewster in Welfare to say I may be a few minutes late?'

Kitty nodded. 'Consider it done. Now off you go.'

'Thanks.' Beatrice was already halfway out of the door.

She rushed back to Market Street, past all the sandbagged shopfronts and anti-blast-taped windows. What if the Ingleby's assistant had given up on her and let another customer buy the manicure set? But she hadn't. Beatrice handed over the money and placed the little items in her handbag. Long gone were the days when shopkeepers wrapped your purchases for you. That was officially a waste of paper now, and nothing could be wasted in wartime. It was even the done thing, when buying cigarettes, to empty the packet straight into your bag or your pocket and hand back the empty box immediately.

After that, pleased with her purchase but aware of her undoubtedly rumpled appearance, Beatrice set off at a smart pace for the Town Hall and Miss Brewster. She didn't have an appointment with that lady as such, but Miss Brewster kept an eagle eye on her. Beatrice had spent a lot of time in her company in recent months and, to be honest, didn't care for her. She much preferred Miss Fay Brewer. From time to time it caused confusion having both a Miss Brewster and a Miss Brewer in Welfare, but such confusion was only ever to do with their names. Nobody who had met them would have any trouble whatsoever telling them apart.

Middle-aged Miss Brewster had very fixed ideas about what she deemed right and what she would permit to happen. Fay Brewer, on the other hand, was a good-looking young woman of around thirty with gorgeous dark-red hair and, best of all, an open mind and the ability to be flexible. She was guided more by individual circumstances than by preconceived ideas. It had been she who had found a way for Kitty to change Dunbar's from a hotel into a storage business. She had also championed Beatrice and got her the Welfare post she now loved so much.

But because Fay Brewer had recommended Beatrice, the powers that be had decreed that she couldn't be in charge of her training in case it smacked of favouritism, which was how Beatrice had been paired with Miss Brewster, worse luck.

Beatrice made her way to Miss Brewster's office. The other people who worked in Welfare occupied shared offices but Miss Brewster had a room of her own. It wasn't large but it evidently afforded her the privacy she preferred. Apparently, she had appropriated the room at the beginning of the war when a number of offices were to be reassigned. At first no one had noticed, and then no one had dared challenge her.

Beatrice paused outside the closed door. Other office doors were generally left open unless a meeting was in progress, but Miss Brewster kept hers shut. Beatrice drew in a long breath through her nose and blew it out steadily between her lips as if that would magically straighten her appearance. Then she tapped on the door.

'Come!'

Beatrice had learned to detest that 'Come!'. 'Come in' would have been friendly. 'Come!' sounded like Miss Brewster was summoning a dog.

She gave Beatrice a narrow-eyed look. 'You have finally deigned to turn up, I see, Miss Inkerman.'

Finally? Yes, she was late, but 'finally' made it sound far worse than it was.

'Only by ten—'

'—fifteen—'

'—fifteen minutes.' Beatrice took a moment, then started

again. 'I apologise for being late, Miss Brewster, but I did leave a message.'

'So you say, yet I did not receive it.'

'It must have gone to Miss Brewer in error.'

Miss Brewster gave her a look that said she didn't believe a word of it and Beatrice felt a stab of annoyance. But even though she didn't much like Miss Brewster, she had learned a lot from her and there was a great deal to be said for keeping the peace.

There was a knock on the door and Fay Brewer looked in. She smiled when she saw Beatrice.

'Oh, good, you're here. I just popped by to give Miss Brewster your apologies. The message came to my desk by mistake.'

'You took your time about it, Miss Brewer,' said the older lady. 'I should have been informed as soon as you knew of Miss Inkerman's tardiness.'

Fay Brewer's smile didn't slip. 'I was out of the office at a meeting,' she explained cheerfully. 'I've only just got back. I came as soon as I knew.'

Even Miss Brewster couldn't argue with that.

'And I'm afraid I've taken a bit of a liberty,' Fay Brewer went on breezily, 'though I didn't realise it until after I'd done it. There were two messages for you, Miss Brewster, both on the same piece of paper and I'd already responded to the other one before I twigged that it was really for you.'

'Responded to what?' Miss Brewster enquired.

'A request from the Welfare Department in Salford. Somehow or other they've got wind of the club for children with responsibilities and they're keen to know more. I rang back immediately and made an appointment for a Miss Cawsley and a Mrs Young to come here.'

'You've taken a lot on yourself,' said Miss Brewster.

'A harmless error,' replied Fay Brewer, unfazed. 'I've written down the details for you.' She put a slip of paper on the desk. 'You need to make a note of the date as well, Miss Inkerman. I told the Salford ladies that the club is your pet project.'

Miss Brewster's lips tightened for a moment, then she wiped the annoyance off her face. 'Thank you, Miss Brewer,' she said coolly.

'Always a pleasure,' said Fay Brewer. 'Toodle-oo.'

'I must get on with writing my case notes,' said Beatrice.

Miss Brewster nodded graciously as if bestowing permission. After Beatrice had finished, Miss Brewster would read them through like a school ma'am hunting for mistakes. She didn't like the fact that Beatrice was without formal qualifications.

Beatrice made a point of working an extra fifteen minutes at the end of the day just in case Miss Brewster should bring it up again. She put on her coat and felt hat, slung her gas-mask box over her shoulder and took her handbag from her drawer, unable to resist taking a quick peek at the manicure set within. Abbie was going to be thrilled.

Beatrice felt a warm glow inside. Abbie was such a dear girl. From time to time Beatrice boggled at her own good fortune that she should find herself living with a child, even if it was just for the duration of the war. She had always wanted children of her own, but she'd never had the chance. She had been engaged once, years ago, but then it had turned out that Frank, even though he wanted a wife, had no desire to be a father. After much heart-searching, Beatrice had ended the engagement, unable to commit herself to a marriage without children. After that she had never met anyone else, so as well as being childless, she had been doomed to spinsterhood.

When she went downstairs to the chessboard-tiled foyer, Beatrice noticed Fay Brewer chatting with a pair of girls from the typing pool. When Miss Brewer glanced across and saw her, Beatrice acknowledged her with a small wave and carried on walking towards the doors, then realised that Miss Brewer was coming her way and stopped to speak to her.

'I hope you've put the meeting with the Salford bods in your diary,' Miss Brewer said.

'Of course,' Beatrice answered. 'I'm looking forward to it.'

'Lucky for you I intercepted that message.' There was a distinct twinkle in Miss Brewer's eyes.

'Intercepted? D'you mean you didn't receive it by mistake?'

Fay Brewer shook her head and the feather in her hat shimmered. 'I bumped into the messenger boy in the corridor. He was on his way to Miss Brewster's office so I offered to deliver the message for him. Had it been just your apologies, I'd have done so, but as soon as I saw the other message, I decided to do something about it. If it had gone directly to Miss Brewster, you may be sure she wouldn't have included you in the meeting. In all likelihood, she wouldn't have given the Time Off Club the recognition it deserves. She'd have wanted to put the Salford ladies off the idea.'

'But it's of such benefit to the children,' Beatrice protested. 'It gives them the chance to be ordinary children for a while.'

'As you know better than anybody,' Fay Brewer replied, a sympathetic look coming into her hazel eyes, 'having been a child with responsibilities yourself.'

'We were just called looker-afters in my day,' Beatrice said drily.

A looker-after back then, a child with responsibilities now, was a youngster, usually a girl, who had the job of taking care of a mother with a long-term illness. On top of this, she had to look after the house, which meant shopping, cooking and cleaning, not to mention keeping an eye on any brothers and younger sisters. It involved placing a huge responsibility on young shoulders and often caused the invalid mother no end of guilt, but what other choice was there? For the girl herself – and it was almost always a girl – all this was done at the expense of a proper education.

Beatrice, remembering her own childhood experiences, had, with Fay Brewer's help, set up a club at Dunbar's for children like this, so that for a few hours each week they could meet other children who fully understood what their lives were like and enjoy games and other activities. The Time Off Club had started last summer with a dozen children, a number that had almost at once increased to fourteen, and was now on its way to thirty.

'I can't understand why Miss Brewster doesn't approve,' Beatrice said.

'It's very simple,' Fay Brewer told her. 'She doesn't think children should be lumbered with these responsibilities – and she's right, of course, but things have been this way for a long time. That doesn't make it right, but it's the situation we find ourselves in. Miss Brewster sees the Time Off Club as something that enables this profoundly undesirable state of affairs to continue.'

A cold feeling struck Beatrice deep inside. 'I didn't create the Time Off Club to perpetuate this way of life. I did it to help the children and give them a regular break from it.'

'Exactly,' said Miss Brewer, 'and that's why I've supported you every step of the way. I don't like children caring for their parents and looking after their homes any more than you do or Miss Brewster does – but I also know that this is how they live and I want them to have whatever assistance is available. Miss Brewster takes the view that we shouldn't allow children to have these responsibilities, which is all very fine and moral, but I live in the real world, where undesirable things happen and we have to do our best to make them less undesirable if we can.' She grinned. 'I shall now climb off my soapbox.'

'Thank you for saying all that,' Beatrice replied. 'You've made me feel better.'

The smile melted from Fay Brewer's face and she looked serious. 'You did a splendid thing when you set up your Time Off Club, Miss Inkerman – and your Gentlemen's Club as well – and don't let anybody tell you otherwise.'

4

It was the last weekend in March and Bill was coming home on leave. Abbie couldn't have been more thrilled. Whenever in years past Kitty had privately seethed over Bill's unstoppable extravagance, she only had to see the bond between father and daughter and something inside her melted every time. It wouldn't make her forgive Bill but it certainly served as a reminder that there was a lot more to him than just the reckless spendthrift who could leave her not knowing whether to be frightened silly or hopping mad when the debts mounted up.

Ivy was looking forward to Bill's leave too. Well, of course she was. She was his mother. Kitty didn't call her Ivy to her face, because that would have been plain rude, but last year she had started thinking of her as Ivy at a time when she had badly needed to take her mother-in-law down a peg or two, even though she'd only done so in her head.

'And how do you feel about Bill coming home on leave?' Naomi asked her when the two of them were sitting together at the table in Dunbar's large basement kitchen. Naomi tilted back her head a little to blow a stream of cigarette smoke into the air. 'After the way you got him sent away, I mean.'

'Hush!' Kitty couldn't prevent herself from glancing around swiftly as if listeners might spring out from the corners. 'Not so loud.'

Naomi laughed. 'Abbie's at school, Miss Inkerman is at work and Lily is out on WVS duty. There's only us here. No need to panic.' She looked expectantly at Kitty.

'Abbie can hardly wait,' said Kitty.

'That's not what I asked.'

'I feel... torn, I suppose. There's part of me that wants to bash him over the head with the frying pan because of the spending that brought the bailiffs down on Dunbar's like a plague of locusts; and there's another part that's dying to show off the storage company I've built up.' Kitty huffed out a sigh. 'The main thing is to make sure that everything goes smoothly for Abbie. Her daddy won't be here for very long and I want it to be perfect for her.'

'Of course you do,' said Naomi.

Kitty leaned forward. 'I'll tell you something I'm going to do before he comes. I'm going to move the alcohol out of the cellar and lock it away in one of the rooms.'

'You've still got the hotel's booze?' Naomi asked. 'That must be worth a fortune now, with all the shortages.'

'Exactly. I can't risk letting Bill get his paws on it.'

'Locking it away does sound rather extreme,' Naomi remarked.

A little chill passed through Kitty. 'It was the alcohol that was the final straw.'

Naomi's blue eyes widened. 'You're not telling me he's a drinker as well?'

Kitty shook her head. 'It was after Uncle Jeremiah died and

Bill inherited Dunbar's, shortly before we moved into the family flat. We came here to have a look at it. The former residents' sitting room was full of guests and Bill wanted to celebrate, so he poured sherry and whisky all round with a generous hand, and all on the house, if you please. He obviously saw himself as the gracious host, but all I could think was that, if he stayed, we'd end up in the bankruptcy court.' Kitty looked at her sister. 'That was when I knew I had to get rid of him. Soon after that, I sneaked his name onto the call-up list in Congreve's.'

'Heavens,' Naomi murmured. 'But it's not as though there are any guests now for him to impress.'

'No, but he has friends and old colleagues from the shipping warehouse,' said Kitty. 'And there's Mr Barnes from the Grove, the hotel over the road. Bill wanted to sell Dunbar's to him after the bailiffs' visit. A couple of our old resident guests are residents at the Grove now and I wouldn't put it past Bill to pay a visit, armed with a bottle or three. It would be just like him to play the big man.'

'What if he asks where the drink has gone?' Naomi asked.

'I'll tell him the bailiffs took it,' Kitty answered without hesitation, 'just like they took everything else.'

Naomi gave her a sympathetic look. 'Kitty, my sweet, what a lot you've had to contend with – still have to contend with,' she added wryly.

'Oh, it doesn't bother me. I'm used to it,' Kitty said, not entirely truthfully. 'The main thing is that Abbie never finds out. Protecting her is the most important thing.'

* * *

The door to the family flat banged open and Abbie raced in,

flushed and breathless, her blonde hair having worked loose from its ponytail in her rush to get home from school.

'Is he here yet?' she asked, bouncing on her toes in anticipation.

Kitty smiled to see her so excited. 'Not yet. It's a long way from the south coast. He has to get to London first, then across London to catch the train to Manchester.'

'In that case, can we go to the station to meet him?' Abbie begged, not for the first time.

'The station will probably be heaving with people and there's no knowing how late the train could be.' Kitty hated pouring cold water on Abbie's wish, but it needed saying. 'It's better to wait here, I promise.'

For a second, Abbie looked mutinous, but then her sunny nature reasserted itself and she nodded.

'Change out of your gymslip and put a dress on,' said Kitty. 'I'll tidy your hair for you.' She smiled. 'You look like you've been dragged through a hedge backwards, as my mam would have said.'

'May I wear my hair loose?'

'Since it's a special occasion.'

'I'm never going to wear a ponytail again after I leave school,' Abbie announced before she darted away.

A moment later Ivy walked in.

'Is he here yet?'

Kitty laughed. 'You sound like Abbie.'

She understood that Ivy was anxious to see her son, of course she did, but in her heart of hearts Kitty couldn't suppress a stab of disappointment. For years Bill had lied to Ivy, telling her that it was Kitty who was responsible for all the spending, that she'd put pressure on him to give in and let her have everything she wanted. Kitty had been appalled when she'd found out – just as

Ivy had been appalled in her turn when she'd eventually been obliged to confront the truth. That being the case, there was a part of Kitty that wanted Ivy at the very least to be reserved towards Bill, if not to punish him outright, so he would know without doubt that he wasn't in favour, but apparently this wasn't going to happen.

Was it mean of her to want that? Possibly. On the other hand, she didn't really want anything to spoil this short visit. She couldn't bear Abbie to be disappointed – or Ivy, for that matter, which in itself was something of a revelation after the years of coolness between them, thanks to Bill and his rotten lies.

Abbie reappeared, wearing a knee-length flared skirt and a polka-dot cotton blouse with short sleeves. Her hair tumbled around her shoulders and down her back.

'Doesn't that skirt have a matching bolero jacket?' Ivy asked.

'I don't want to wear it,' said Abbie. 'It makes me look like a little girl dressing up for a party.'

'I think you look very nice as you are,' said Kitty, 'but you need hair clips or an Alice band to keep your hair tidy.'

Abbie hurried out again, returning with her hair brush and a cloth band, both of which she handed over to Kitty, who brushed her hair until it gleamed before putting the band in position. When she stood back and looked at her daughter, she pulled in a deep satisfying breath of pure pride.

'There. Your father will be chuffed to bits.'

'D'you think so?' There was no doubting how pleased Abbie was to hear it. 'May I go and wait in the old dining room and watch from the window?'

At a nod from Kitty, off she went. Kitty and Ivy looked at one another and laughed.

'We might as well go with her,' said Kitty.

A squeal from downstairs had them hurrying downstairs into

the foyer, where the front doors were standing open and Bill was swinging Abbie around in a circle, his kitbag by his feet. When he set her down and looked towards the staircase, the breath caught in Kitty's throat. Bill had always been handsome and his army uniform made him even more so. He was a well-built man with blue eyes beneath a broad forehead.

Without letting go of his daughter, he held out his other hand towards Kitty and Ivy. Kitty had to remind herself that he had no notion he had her to thank for his having been called up. She let Ivy go first down the final stairs.

Bill slung an arm around his mother's thin shoulders and planted a hearty kiss on her temple. 'It's good to see you, Mum.'

'You too, son.' Ivy – sharp-eyed, sharp-tongued Ivy Dunbar – actually sounded tearful.

Three pairs of blue eyes turned to Kitty. She walked forward to join the family cluster. Oh, if only Bill hadn't let her down repeatedly over the years, how happy they might all have been together – well, the others were already happy. How happy *she* might have been.

* * *

Kitty prepared a special meal of devilled fish jazzed up with Worcester sauce, served with cauliflower and mash, followed by Florida pudding made with gingerbread and tinned peaches, though the desiccated coconut soon had all of them sucking their teeth to get the bits out.

Bill was affability itself to Beatrice and Lily, and no one watching would ever have imagined that he was responsible for the downfall of Dunbar's Hotel.

He described his job in stores, accounting for all manner of supplies and sending them off to wherever they needed to go.

'I imagine I was given the job because of my experience at Congreve's,' he said.

'Even though you never actually worked in the warehouse,' Abbie chimed in.

Bill, at his most charming, directed a smile at Lily and Beatrice. 'My daughter wants you to appreciate that I was a clerk in one of the shipping offices, not a warehouseman handling the goods.'

'What sort of goods do you deal with?' Beatrice asked.

'Army blankets, kitbags, canned foods, medical equipment, gun turrets, tanks, spare engines... you name it.'

Lily smiled at Abbie. 'It's lucky tomorrow is Saturday and you can spend all day with your dad.'

'I wish he didn't have to go back on Monday,' Abbie said, gazing at Bill.

He was clearly enjoying being the centre of attention and Abbie hung on his every word. Kitty found herself wishing, as she so often had, that Bill was sensible with money. Then their lives could have been perfect.

Abbie was allowed to stay up later than normal. When she was sent off to bed, she kissed her parents goodnight, hugging her father's neck before she disappeared.

Bill turned to Kitty. 'She's grown.'

'Only an inch,' said Kitty. 'Two at the most. I haven't had to let down the hem of her gymslip like some mothers have.'

'Maybe she's not bigger,' said Bill, 'but she's more grown-up.' His forehead creased in a frown in which pain was easily discernible. 'I hate missing out on seeing her every day.'

'Do you remember how we missed her when she was evacuated?' Kitty asked.

'We couldn't wait to bring her back again when the bombings didn't happen immediately.' Bill smiled reminiscently.

'We have to hope this war doesn't drag on as long as the last one,' said Kitty. 'What you should concentrate on while you're away is that Abbie has a secure home here with me.' She fixed him with a look.

'Don't go giving me the evil eye,' he replied. 'It wasn't my fault the bailiffs came.'

'Not your—?' Kitty stopped herself. She moderated her tone, aware of the proximity of Abbie's bedroom. 'Not your fault? Then whose fault was it? Who else spent all that money?'

'Sheer bad luck,' said Bill. 'That's what it was.' And that evidently was the end of that topic because he continued, 'But you're not doing badly with this new venture, are you?'

'Not doing badly?' Kitty could have crowned him. 'If by that you mean I'm keeping a roof over our daughter's head, then yes, I am, and successfully too.'

'I didn't appreciate being prevented from selling the hotel, my own building,' said Bill, 'but you're bringing the money in, I'll grant you that.'

'I need to talk to you about that,' Kitty answered quickly.

'It'll keep until tomorrow,' Bill said in a tone of finality. 'I'm bushed. It's been a long day.'

'You'd best go to bed, then,' she told him. 'I'll do the rounds of the building and make sure everything is locked up.'

Aye, and she'd take her time about it, and hope he was out for the count when she'd finished. If not, well, she would do her wifely duty if she had to, but only out of duty, only because, as her husband, Bill was entitled. She hadn't been in love with him for a long time, although she had continued to have steady, warm feelings for him, feelings she had clung to, anxious for her marriage to be successful in spite of the deep divide caused by their completely opposite attitudes towards money, and wanting above all else to provide Abbie with a solid background. Abbie meant the world to both her and Bill. But last year, a crack had appeared in Kitty's feelings for Bill after she had found out about the lies he had been telling Ivy about her for years.

It was a crack that could never be mended.

* * *

Master key in hand, Kitty was all set to take Bill on a tour of the building and show him some of the rooms full of bombed-out belongings. She could see how intrigued he was. He knew about the storage business, of course, but this chance to see it for himself had awakened his curiosity. Kitty was pleased. Years ago, when Abbie was a baby and she had first discovered the extent of his spending, she had wanted to get a job to pay off what he owed, but he wouldn't let her. Now it was going to afford her a great deal of satisfaction to show him precisely what she was made of.

Abbie, of course, had no intention of being left out. Plenty of fathers would have said, 'No, this is grown-up business,' but not Bill. Abbie was his pet and this weekend meant everything to the pair of them.

Kitty handed Abbie the master key. 'Why don't you take Daddy on the grand tour? You don't need to show him every room, just two or three so he gets the idea.'

'I can do that,' Abbie said happily. 'We need to start in the old dining room, Daddy, because that's where people's things used to be put when they first arrived so they could be cleaned properly before they went into storage in the old guest bedrooms. Now that the storage rooms are full up, we've been able to turn the old dining room into a parlour, though, to be honest, it's not the best parlour you've ever seen...'

Abbie bore her father away, leaving Kitty with an amused smile on her face. Perhaps it was a good idea to let Abbie do the honours. She would get Bill into a better mood than Kitty would. Today she needed him in a receptive mood.

When Bill's tour was over, Kitty sent Abbie to the tobacconist's to buy him a packet of cigarettes.

'What did you think?' she asked Bill.

'Impressive,' he said. 'Not as impressive as the hotel used to be, of course, but it'll do for now.'

Kitty refused to let herself respond to that. 'There's something important we have to discuss about the business. It's the Dunbar's bank account. I get paid in a mixture of cheques and cash. I deposit all the cheques in the account along with most of the cash. The rest I keep for expenses. The trouble is, I can put money in, but I can't take it out because the account is in your name.'

'What of it?' Bill asked. 'You get money from my army wages. You don't need access to the Dunbar's account.'

'Yes, I do,' Kitty replied firmly. 'Before you catch the train on Monday, I want you to go to the bank with me and arrange for me to be a joint signatory.'

'No,' Bill said flatly.

'*No?*' she repeated. 'I'm not going to run away with the proceeds. I need access to the money for business reasons. It's ridiculous to prevent me.'

His eyes narrowed. 'Oh, so I'm ridiculous now, am I?'

'Bill, be reasonable. You can't expect me to run this business and maintain the building without proper access to funds.'

'I never wanted you to set up a business in the first place,' Bill retorted. 'I wanted to sell to Barnes over the road and he was happy to pay – until you got all cosy with the Corporation and stopped me.'

Kitty opened her mouth to reply but he held up his hand.

'No, Kitty, and that's final.'

That wouldn't have stopped her, but that was the moment Abbie came back. Kitty had to turn away so she could smooth her expression before Abbie cottoned on that something was amiss. Leaving her husband and daughter together, she went into the bedroom to give herself a minute.

She had already made the bed, but Bill had left some things lying around and she automatically tidied them up, wishing she could tidy her feelings as easily.

A letter had fallen out of Bill's kitbag. She stooped to pick it up, seeing at once that it was a business letter – no, not a letter. The envelope was open and a bank statement was clearly visible. Well, that answered one question. Now she knew why a bank statement had never arrived here at Dunbar's. Bill had arranged for them to be sent to him.

Without hesitation, Kitty removed it from the envelope, unfolded it and quickly scanned the figures. For a moment her head swam as the past rushed to engulf her... Those times when she had scoured the house in search of statements of account from Flittick & Green's and Westall's, the department stores... The times she had gone stone cold inside when she'd seen the extent of what Bill owed...

She was forced to wait all day before she could say a word. It was either that or else run the risk of embroiling Abbie in the inevitable uproar. Instead she fumed silently.

At last, when Abbie was in bed, Kitty flung the bank statement at Bill. He let it fall to the floor between them.

'No wonder you don't want to give me access to the Dunbar's account,' Kitty accused him. She had to speak in an undertone but it was surprising how angry and forceful an undertone could be. 'You didn't want me to know, did you?' She shook her head. 'I don't know why I'm surprised. This is typical of you. You've been helping yourself to the money I've made.' Frustration and fury mingled. 'You've just... *taken* it.'

To her vexation, Bill was unperturbed.

'You can be as outraged as you like, Kitty, but it won't get you anywhere.' His tone was filled with condescension, the informed, worldly-wise man speaking to his needy, ignorant little wife. 'Ask any bank manager. You're so indignant that I've *taken* that money when the fact is that it's mine to take. You'd do well to remember that in future.'

Kitty's lips parted on a soft gasp of shock – and that was the moment when it happened. When the crack in her heart that had appeared last year turned into a vast gap. When the residual warmth and affection for Bill that she had done her best to cling to and cultivate all these years simply vanished.

Bill was looking at her, his expression complacent. He must think he had finally browbeaten her into submission, into accepting his way of doing things. But that wasn't the case at all. The shock she felt was nothing to do with that. It was because all feeling for her husband was now gone.

5

Usually it was Kitty who did the daily shopping, but on this Saturday Beatrice had insisted on doing it. With Kitty's husband at home, Beatrice wanted the three Dunbars to have time together as a family. She believed in family time in much the same way some people believed in the power of prayer. If she'd had any family time as a child, she couldn't remember it. What she remembered was her mother largely incapacitated by a stroke at a horrifyingly young age, and then her dad clearing off, leaving her to cope. There hadn't been anybody to help out because her parents had defied their families and run away to get married.

As an adult Beatrice had imagined the family time that lay ahead for her and Frank... until he'd announced he didn't want children.

Now, living in Dunbar's after more years than she cared to remember of being one of several lodgers in Mrs Thornton's boarding house, Beatrice felt that family time had come her way at last. She, Kitty and Lily were three very different women, but circumstances had brought them together and moulded them into a tight-knit group of people who cared about and supported one another... and if that wasn't the best possible definition of a family, then Beatrice didn't know what was. And having young Abbie as one of them was the cherry on the cake.

Beatrice spent Saturday morning at work, as she always did. As soon as she could, she headed off to the shops, running through a selection of meals in her head. That was what you had to do these days. You couldn't depend on anything definitely being available. So: sardine pancakes if there were tins of sardines to be had, though what she really hoped for was corned beef to make rissoles. Either of those would be a treat for tea. Something more substantial than usual was called for with a man in the house.

First, though, she had to get to the butcher's. Pork chops were most unlikely to be available at this time of day but sausage meat could be fashioned into fillet shapes with a little help from bread-crumbs. Or a cheap cut of beef plus a dollop of vegetables would make a hearty stew for tomorrow.

With a smile of greeting for the other shoppers, Beatrice joined the queue. There had been a time last year, after she had been accused of theft, when she'd avoided shopping because of the sideways glances and challenging remarks, but all that was behind her now and she enjoyed the opportunity to chat.

A couple of women whom she knew slightly from the world of queuing nodded to her. They were Mrs Winters and Mrs Stanley.

'...this French thing I read about in a magazine called a *bouquet garni*,' Mrs Winters was saying.

'Ooh, very posh,' said Mrs Stanley.

'That's what I thought,' Mrs Winters replied. 'Then it turned out to be a load of herbs.'

Mrs Stanley laughed. 'Fancy! I've had the makings of a

bouquet whatsit on my windowsill all these years and I never knew. How are you, love?' she asked Beatrice.

'Fine, thanks. All the better for not having had an air raid for some weeks.'

'Long may it last – touch wood.' Mrs Winters raised her fingertips to her temple.

'Did you see in the paper that Cadbury's have stopped production of their milk chocolate so the milk can be given to children?' Mrs Stanley asked.

'Trust you to latch onto that,' said Mrs Winters. 'You've always had a sweet tooth, ever since we were kids. Me, I'm more bothered about the points value of tinned meat and tinned fish going up.'

'It's a way of controlling demand,' said Beatrice. 'They must be in short supply.'

Mrs Winters made a 'huh' sound. 'Everything's in short supply.'

'The number of clothing coupons has been reduced an' all,' said Mrs Stanley. '*And* you have to make them last for longer.'

'I don't mind that so much,' said Beatrice. 'It's having soap on ration that gets me.'

'Three ounces a month!' said Mrs Winters. 'I thought things would get better after the Yanks joined the war, but if anything, they're worse.'

'Oh, I don't know,' Mrs Stanley said with a twinkle in her eye. 'I for one don't mind seeing those handsome Yanks striding about.'

'Oy, you,' her friend answered. 'Don't go getting any fancy ideas, not at your age.'

'A girl can look, can't she?' said Mrs Stanley.

Mrs Winters snorted. 'Girl? Who are you trying to kid?'

Beatrice joined in their chuckles. Queuing for ages might

make your feet ache, but there was no denying that there were times when it did your heart good.

* * *

After the clever way Fay Brewer had ensured that Miss Brewster would have to include Beatrice in the meeting with their welfare colleagues from Salford, there was something appropriate about holding the meeting on April Fool's Day, though Beatrice kept that thought and the resulting smile very much to herself.

The two Salford ladies were Mrs Young and Miss Cawsley. Beatrice had not exactly expected Mrs Young to be the older one because of being married, but even so she found herself quickly rearranging her thoughts. Mrs Young was in her mid-twenties, with shingled hair and an earnest expression, while Miss Cawsley was around Beatrice's age. Another spinster, thought Beatrice. Her next thought was an acknowledgement that while nobody would ever wonder at her, ordinary old Beatrice Inkerman, being on the shelf, there was no obvious reason for Miss Cawsley, with her graceful carriage and her laughter lines, to be there. Maybe she was one of those surplus girls everyone had talked about after the last war, that unfortunate generation of young women whose potential husbands had copped it on the fields of Flanders.

'We're very interested in this friendship club we've heard about for children with responsibilities,' said Miss Cawsley.

'Don't read too much into it,' Miss Brewster said. 'In my opinion, it's a scheme you should not wish to emulate.'

'Oh, but—' Mrs Young began.

'It is a scheme that panders to the highly undesirable practice of keeping girls off school and denying them an education so they can fulfil the family's domestic obligations.'

'It doesn't pander to it at all,' Beatrice put in. By nature she was a polite person, respectful of authority, but Fay Brewer had given her this chance to speak up and she owed it to herself as well as to Miss Brewer to grasp it with both hands. 'Girls have been kept off school this way for decades, ever since school attendance became compulsory. Organising a friendship club is a way of helping them shed their responsibilities for a while.'

'If you want them to shed their responsibilities,' Miss Brewster said in a clipped tone, 'then evacuate them.' She looked at the visitors. 'That is my considered recommendation.'

The Salford ladies exchanged a glance, then Miss Cawsley said, 'If that's your view, why have the club at all?'

'Because it isn't actually a Corporation club,' Beatrice put in quickly before Miss Brewster could bang another nail in the coffin. 'I set it up myself before I worked in Welfare.'

'Ah, yes,' Miss Brewster murmured, 'when you were an inco woman.'

The jibe was clearly intended to reduce her in the visitors' eyes. Beatrice lifted her chin.

'As a girl, I took care of my mother and our home, so I know what it's like. I loved my mother and I'd have done anything for her, but at the same time I resented her telling me what to do. I didn't see why I should be bossed about when I was the one doing all the work. Being resentful made me feel guilty. I never hated my mother, but I sometimes hated myself.'

'Another reason why these children should be evacuated,' said Miss Brewster.

'One of the things that made it difficult for me,' Beatrice ploughed on, 'was that all the other children in our road had ordinary lives. I didn't know another family that lived the way we did. That's one of the reasons the Time Off Club is good for these youngsters. It reassures them they're not alone.'

'As you can see, Miss Inkerman is devoted to this crusade of hers,' said Miss Brewster, causing Beatrice to look at her in surprise. A compliment? But then Miss Brewster went in for the kill. 'But she is so full of pity for the child she herself used to be that she can't see beyond providing immediate help to this new generation of children. She views them in the same way she thought of herself when she was a child. What she would do well to concentrate on is supporting their removal. Send them off to foster parents in the countryside and let them benefit from the childhood she is the first to admit they are currently lacking.'

Full of pity for the child she used to be? Beatrice most certainly was not – or was she? If she was, it wasn't in a maudlin way. She wanted to turn it into something positive.

The visitors looked at one another again, then they came to their feet.

'Thank you very much for your time, ladies,' said Mrs Young. 'You've given us a lot to think about.'

Beatrice quickly rose too. 'Let me see you out of the building.' If she could just get them on their own...

But Miss Brewster wasn't having that. 'I need you here, Miss Inkerman.' She looked at the Salford women. 'Would you like a clerk to escort you out?'

'There's no need, thank you. We can find our way.'

The door shut quietly behind them.

* * *

That evening there was a meeting of the Gentlemen's Club. This was another of Beatrice's ideas. After the Time Off Club had started, word had got round and some local lads – local tearaways, more like – had turned up on Dunbar's doorstep, wanting to be allowed to join. Instead, Beatrice had dreamed up the Gentlemen's Club, which, broadly speaking, required them to show good manners in return for an evening of games and activities.

The doorbell rang while Beatrice and the others were still downstairs in the kitchen.

'Someone's early,' Lily remarked. 'They must be keen.'

'I'll go and tell them they'll have to wait until the club room is ready,' said Beatrice.

'I'll come and help you get the room ready,' said Kitty, though it took her a moment to say it. She had been preoccupied ever since her husband had left on Monday.

They went upstairs, leaving Lily and Abbie to finish clearing away. Beatrice opened the door, ready to speak firmly to the boys, only to find Fay Brewer at the top of the steps with Miss Cawsley and Mrs Young in tow.

'Evening, Miss Inkerman,' Fay Brewer said genially. 'I'm sorry to barge in unannounced but I have visitors who are most interested to see the Gentlemen's Club in action.' Her eyes sparkled. 'Isn't it fortunate that I bumped into them just as they were about to leave the Town Hall? May we impose on you?'

Beatrice opened her mouth, but it was a moment before anything came out. 'Of course. Come in. Welcome.'

Fay Brewer introduced the Salford ladies to Kitty.

'We're intrigued by this idea,' said Miss Cawsley. 'Children these days, boys in particular, are missing the influence of a father.'

'I don't discipline them,' Beatrice said quickly.

'No, but Miss Brewer has explained the requirement for good behaviour,' said Mrs Young. She and her colleague seemed far more relaxed and comfortable this evening than they had been in Miss Brewster's presence.

They watched while Beatrice, helped by Fay Brewer and Kitty, set up the club room, taking some of the board games from the cupboard, attaching the ping-pong net to the big table and putting out a selection of comics and a couple of packs of cards.

A few minutes later the doorbell rang again. When Beatrice opened the door, she stood a little to one side so her visitors could see the line of boys down the steps. She stood on the top step to address them.

'Good evening, boys. We have visitors this evening so when you come in, you may simply say, "Good evening, ladies" rather than greeting us one by one. You may now come in.'

Miss Cawsley and Mrs Young watched, entranced. As each boy entered the building, he wiped his feet and put on one of the ties that Kitty held out, then he raised his cap and wished the ladies good evening before hanging up his cap and heading into the club room.

Soon all the boys were engrossed in the various activities. The adults stood in the foyer, looking into the room from a short distance.

'Miss Brewer tells us this was your own idea, Miss Inkerman,' said Mrs Young, tearing her gaze away from the club room for a moment.

'As was the Time Off Club,' Fay Brewer said. 'Miss Inkerman set up both clubs before she came to work in our Welfare Department, so you can see how fortunate we are to have secured her services. She also had that other idea I mentioned to you about children with responsibilities attending school half-time.' She looked at Beatrice. 'Perhaps you would care to expand on that.'

'It's to do with the amount of education the children miss out on,' said Beatrice. 'When I was growing up, there was a system whereby the children in the top class, once they'd had their twelfth birthdays, were allowed to take a paid job in the after-noons and come to school just in the mornings.'

'I remember that,' said Miss Cawsley. 'My mother got me a job plucking chickens. I hated it, but we needed the money.'

'My idea was for children with responsibilities to go to school in the morning when the three Rs are taught,' said Beatrice, 'and use the afternoons for their domestic responsibilities.'

'Unfortunately, not all the families concerned see it in the same way,' said Fay Brewer, 'but we're making headway.'

Miss Cawsley looked thoughtful. 'Your colleague Miss Brewster sees all this as a means to enable the current system to continue. While she is correct to wish this system could vanish, there is nothing suitable at present to replace it, and therefore we have to make the best of what we've got.'

'Your ideas, Miss Inkerman,' said Mrs Young, 'are well worth considering. I think I can safely say that we'll recommend them, or something very like them, for Salford.'

'Oh,' breathed Beatrice. She didn't know whether to reel in surprise or swell up with pride.

Fay Brewer gave her a highly unprofessional nudge in the ribs as she said to their visitors, 'There. I told you she's a marvel, didn't I?'

* * *

Lily smiled to herself when she saw the admiration in the expressions of Mrs Young and Miss Cawsley when, at the end of the evening, the lads of the Gentlemen's Club tidied up the club room.

'Thank you for doing that quietly, boys,' said Beatrice. Lily had noticed how she always praised them for their good behaviour. 'I'll just remind you of our visitors' names so you can thank them when we say goodnight.'

The boys lined up to shake hands with the adults and say

thank you. After that, they took off their ties and put on their caps. The admiration of the Salford ladies was laced with a healthy dollop of surprise – astonishment, really – and pleasure. Lily's smile broke free in what felt like a huge beam. After the boys had disappeared, Miss Brewer bore Mrs Young and Miss Cawsley away. Lily, Kitty and Beatrice put everything away in the club room and trooped downstairs for cocoa and a final cigarette.

'Well!' said Kitty. 'I think we can call that an unqualified success. Congratulations, Beatrice.'

'Especially as you weren't expecting visitors,' Lily added.

'The boys did you proud,' said Kitty.

'Thank heaven,' said Beatrice. 'Imagine if they'd chosen this week to run amok.'

'They'd never do that,' Lily said confidently. 'They know the club rules and they're not going to spoil things for themselves. They're not stupid.'

'I know you aren't one to blow your own trumpet, Beatrice,' Kitty said with a smile, 'so I'll blow it for you. Fay Brewer thinks well of you and she brought those women here so that your ideas, *your* ideas, Beatrice, can spread further.'

A flush crept into Beatrice's cheeks, making her brown eyes look darker. 'It's kind of you to say so.'

'It's not kind at all,' Kitty said matter-of-factly. 'It's the plain truth. Being taken on by the Welfare Department was a massive opportunity for you and you're making the most of it.'

'Yes.' Beatrice laughed. 'I am. I feel lucky every single day when I walk in through the Town Hall doors – even if I do have Miss Brewster to contend with.'

'Only until you're fully trained,' said Lily. 'You can cope with her until then.'

'Especially with Fay Brewer keeping an eye on you from the sidelines,' Kitty added with a chuckle that brightened her face and made her eyes crinkle. 'I'm glad your new venture is working out well for you.'

Beatrice looked at Kitty and Lily, making Lily's heart pitter-patter, but Kitty was the one Beatrice addressed.

'I'm not the only one with a new venture. You've been rather preoccupied since your husband went back, Kitty. Tell me to mind my own business if it's something between husband and wife, but I'm concerned it's to do with Dunbar's.'

Kitty drew a deep breath and sighed it out. 'You're right. I need access to the Dunbar's bank account and Bill said no.'

'But how can you run the business properly without it?' Lily asked.

'Obviously I've managed this far,' Kitty said drily, 'and that apparently shows I don't need it.'

The words 'Easy for him to say' hovered on Lily's tongue. She pressed her lips together to hold them in. As a chambermaid, she had glimpsed many a tiff between married couples and, having seen relatives attempt to intervene, she knew it was best to keep out. More recently, her mother-in-law's interference in her own marriage had been nothing if not deeply unhelpful.

In any case, Kitty didn't wait for comments. 'I'm sorry if I've been preoccupied.'

'Don't apologise,' Beatrice exclaimed. 'I ought to apologise for bringing it up.'

'Nonsense,' said Kitty. 'You wanted to show your concern and I appreciate that. Don't ever feel you can't speak freely. It's having that sort of confidence in one another that makes us a good team.'

Lily nodded. She liked the idea of them being a team. It summed up the way they stuck together. They weren't just three women sharing a billet. They were loyal to one another. She felt safe here, watched over but not criticised or pushed into sharing information.

Her heart pitter-pattered again, but she wanted to say this.

'You never pin me down with personal questions, but I know you must wonder about Daniel and me.'

'We do.' Kitty's voice was both frank and kind. 'But you've got a lot of thinking to do and we understand that.'

'I told you last summer that our marriage is over,' said Lily. 'Nothing has changed since then – or maybe it has. Maybe I've changed a bit, or if I haven't, maybe I need to. Toby's anniversary is coming up this month.'

'Oh, sweetheart,' Kitty murmured, reaching for her hand.

'I'm sorry,' said Beatrice. 'I can't begin to imagine how hard this is for you.'

'It is hard,' Lily agreed, fighting against a lump that was swelling in her throat. She tried to shrug. 'But it happened and I have to live with it. I'm trying to see the anniversary as a milestone.' Now her throat really did close. The constriction went all the way up to the backs of her eyes and her vision blurred.

'A milestone on the way to what?' Kitty asked gently.

'My future, my new life, I suppose. On my own.'

'Oh, Lily,' Beatrice exclaimed, her voice loaded with distress.

'Don't be upset for me,' said Lily. 'Be glad that I'm determined to move on. They're already talking about the number of divorces there are bound to be after the war. It's sobering to think that Daniel and I are going to be on that list, but that's the way it has to be.'

6

Early in April, cereal and tinned milk were both added to the points system and white bread wasn't going to be available any longer. Because of a serious shortage of imported wheat, the nation's millers had been ordered to make only the national wheatmeal that the Ministry of Food had been trying to convert the general public to for months. Most folk, though, had a strong preference for good old white bread – and now they weren't going to be able to get hold of it for the duration.

Kitty was annoyed. She had so much to cope with on a day-to-day basis – rationing, shortages, the blackout, her WVS duties, the Dunbar's storage business – and now, on top of all that, the white bread she and Abbie both loved was vanishing for the rest of the war.

It sounded silly to suggest that this made something inside her snap, but it did.

'If I have to live without white bread,' she declared with some heat, 'I'm jolly well going to open my own Dunbar's bank account, and let Bill put that in his pipe and smoke it.'

She went to the bank to make an appointment.

'Of course, madam, and when would it be convenient for your husband to come here?'

Kitty stared. 'The appointment isn't for him. It's for me.'

The clerk looked first surprised, then dismayed. 'Oh, I beg your pardon. I assumed... Never mind. Let me see what appointments are available.'

'Thank you,' Kitty said in a bright, smiley voice as if she hadn't just been put firmly in her place. How dare this clerk treat her as if she was her husband's secretary? Weren't women allowed to have a say in financial matters now there was a war on?

Once the appointment was in her diary, she made a point of telling Ivy what she was up to. No, not what she was *up to*. That sounded like she was playing games or taking advantage, both of which were very far from the case.

Kitty caught the bus to Withington to call on her mother-in-law, only to find she had gone out.

'I didn't think today was one of her WVS days,' she said to a couple of Ivy's neighbours who were passing the time of day in the street.

'It isn't, love, but last night someone happened across an unexploded bomb in a garden on Parrs Wood Road.'

'But we haven't had an air raid since the beginning of the year,' said Kitty.

'Exactly.' Mrs Headley stuck her chin out and nodded. 'Lord alone knows how long it must have been there.'

'Anyroad,' Mrs Townsend continued, 'loads of folk had to leave their homes with nowt but their nightclothes and dressing gowns. The WVS had to provide them all with somewhere to kip and, of course, they all needed suitable clothes to go to work in this morning.'

Kitty felt a little surge of pride. She loved belonging to the WVS. Its members could be relied on to rise to every single challenge, be it plugging the gaps in Corporation services or responding to whatever demands wartime threw their way.

'Mrs Dunbar was one of those who were sent for in the middle of the night,' said Mrs Headley. 'I daresay she'll fetch up back here soon enough.'

She was right. Ivy appeared a few minutes later. She looked tired, but the moment she spotted Kitty, she put a smile on her face. Kitty understood. She did the same thing herself. Everybody did these days. No matter how exhausted you were, the moment you saw someone you knew, especially if it was someone who mattered to you, you immediately hitched a cheerful expression into place.

Ivy exchanged a few words with her neighbours, then she led Kitty into her neat little house. The front room was furnished with Victorian items she and her late husband had inherited, though the room was nowhere near as cluttered as Kitty remembered it having been when she'd first known Bill. In common with many others, Ivy had followed the 1930s trend of 'de-crowding'. She had also, after holding out for years, given in and made the wireless, instead of the fireplace, the room's focal point.

While Ivy took off her things, Kitty went through to the kitchen. She filled the kettle at the deep Belfast sink beside the wooden draining board, and put a flame to the gas.

Soon they were sitting at the Morrison. Ivy didn't have her own Anderson shelter because of having a backyard, not a garden. Instead, in her kitchen she had a Morrison shelter, which was big enough to accommodate two adults and two children within the wire mesh. Ivy used it as her kitchen table during the day.

She took a sip of tea and shut her eyes. 'It's good to take the weight off my feet.'

'Slip your shoes off,' Kitty suggested. 'I don't mind.'

'I might not get them back on again,' Ivy said drily. 'My feet feel as if they'd swell up like balloons.'

'I gather it was a busy night,' said Kitty.

'Aye, it was, but never mind that. What brings you here?' Ivy delivered one of her trademark sharp looks.

Kitty explained the situation with the bank account.

'So I've made an appointment with Mr Loftus – he's the bank manager – and I'm going to ask for Dunbar's to have a second account, with me as the named person. I wanted you to know because, after all the tales Bill told you about me and money, I want everything above board.'

Ivy nodded. 'Thank you, Kitty. I appreciate that.'

'And if Bill should write to you in due course, complaining that I'm trying to diddle him—'

'I'll tell him to stick his complaints where the sun doesn't shine,' Ivy answered.

Kitty laughed. It was odd now to recall how thoroughly she used to dislike Ivy, a feeling that had been entirely mutual. It felt good to have her mother-in-law on her side.

* * *

Mr Loftus was a distinguished-looking gentleman with a neat moustache and lean cheeks. His three-piece suit complete with watch chain made Kitty glad she had worn her Sunday best of dark-blue suit, felt hat, gloves and navy slingbacks for their meeting. She had brought a full set of accounts with her and she waited quietly, hoping she was projecting an air of confidence, while the bank manager went through them carefully.

At last he looked up. 'Yes, everything appears to be in order, Mrs Dunbar. I will write to Mr Dunbar and tell him so.'

'There's no call for that,' said Kitty.

'On the contrary, I'm sure he'll be gratified to know that, under his long-distance guidance, you have dragged Dunbar's back from the brink.'

Kitty caught her breath. 'Do you imagine the storage business was his idea? I can assure you it wasn't. It was mine.'

'Well, well,' Mr Loftus said in a neutral tone. 'Then why are you here, Mrs Dunbar, if not to provide information for me to pass on to Mr Dunbar?'

Kitty sat up straighter. 'I wish to open a new bank account, please. For the business. My husband has refused to let me have access to the existing account.'

'I see. Have you Mr Dunbar's permission to take such a step?'

'No, but as the person who runs the business, I need to have a bank account. You can understand that, surely?'

Mr Loftus regarded her steadily. 'I'm afraid what you suggest isn't possible, Mrs Dunbar. Firstly, you haven't the authority to open a new account for Dunbar's. Secondly, even if you did, there might be a question as to whether you were doing it for fraudulent purposes.'

Kitty stared at him. 'Fraud? That's preposterous. I'm doing this because I wish to be an honest businesswoman.'

'Your accounts certainly show that everything is as it should be,' said Mr Loftus and Kitty felt a flicker of hope, but his next words dashed it. 'I cannot, however, permit Dunbar's to have two separate bank accounts.'

Kitty's shoulders dropped, but then she pushed them back.

'Very well.' She employed her most reasonable tone. 'If a new business account is out of the question, then I'd like to open a personal account for myself, if you please.'

A complacent expression settled on Mr Loftus's features and his tone took on an avuncular note. 'Of course, Mrs Dunbar. That will be quite in order. All I require is a letter of consent from your husband, giving his permission.'

* * *

Kitty was with her sister in Naomi's parlour. Naomi called it her parlour but it was posher than that – larger. She and Derek had a modern house, built a few years after the last war. There was a stained-glass panel in the front door and instead of a narrow hallway, there was a proper hall, wide enough for a hall stand complete with cupboards below and shelves above and an umbrella stand attached to the side. If you'd tried to wedge one of those into the house Kitty and Naomi had grown up in, you'd have needed to build a bridge over it to get to the kitchen.

Naomi and Derek had moved here shortly before Kitty's wedding and Naomi had offered to host the reception, but of course Bill had insisted they hold it at Dunbar's, courtesy of Uncle Jeremiah. It had been his wedding present to them.

'So there you have it.' Kitty didn't know whether to be glum or outraged. 'Bill won't let me have access to the bank account for the business, and if I want an account in my own name, I need to get his permission. Can you credit it?'

'Yes, I can, actually.' Naomi took a sip of her tea. 'It's the way of the world. The husband is responsible for the wife's debts, so obviously she needs his consent, not to mention the fact that it's his duty to provide for her, so plenty would say she shouldn't need an account anyway.' She laughed. 'Don't look at me like that. I don't make the rules.'

'Well, I think it's disgraceful,' Kitty retorted. 'Here we are in the middle of a war, with women being expected to take on all the jobs that were left when the men were called up, and I still need my husband's consent before the bank manager will let me have my own account.' A small huff of outrage escaped her.

Naomi put down her tea and leaned forward. 'You've worked so hard to get the storage business up and running,' she said soothingly. 'You don't deserve this setback.'

'Thanks.' Kitty blinked away unwelcome tears. Naomi's sympathetic support meant everything to her, as always.

'I know how vexing this is, and how unfair it feels, but you have to accept it,' Naomi went on. 'You'll just have to carry on the way you've been managing.'

She was right and Kitty knew she ought to agree. After all, she had got by this far, paying in the cheques and some of the cash while keeping most of the cash. It hadn't been easy but she had made it work. She'd been proud of herself too. Proud of establishing and running her own business. Proud of keeping a roof over her daughter's head.

And for what? So that Bill could help himself to the profits?

'You can't change this,' Naomi said in a kind voice.

We'll see about that, thought Kitty.

* * *

Mrs Williams opened the door to Beatrice. She was the middle-aged daughter of old Mr Trent, who lived in the downstairs rooms of this house. Back when she was with the inco service, Mr Trent had been on Beatrice's list and she had come trundling along every week on her old boneshaker of a bicycle, hauling her covered trolley behind her, to deliver the latest consignment of adult nappies. As she often had on her stops, Beatrice used to put the kettle on or change a damp bed or hang out freshly washed sheets on the line. It hadn't been part of her job to perform such tasks, but she'd wanted to provide practical help to the women – it was always women – who, on top of their other domestic and family responsibilities, and very likely also on top of their war work, had to care round the clock for an incontinent adult with restricted mobility.

Unfortunately, by helping out in these ways, Beatrice had caused trouble for her successor, Miss Murray, who was probably quite pleasant-faced as a rule but on the occasion when Beatrice had bumped into her, her mouth had turned into a bitter line.

'So you're the famous Miss Inkerman,' she'd said sourly in reply to Beatrice's friendly overture. 'I'm sick to death of the sound of your name. "Miss Inkerman used to help me change the bed... Miss Inkerman helped me put the sheets through the mangle." They all think you're a ruddy saint.'

'I was just lending a hand,' Beatrice had started to say.

'Being a busybody, more like,' Miss Murray retorted. 'Setting me up to look bad. I do my job exactly as I'm meant to. I deliver the nappies and get them signed for, and everyone looks at me as if I'm bone idle because I don't heave soiled sheets into the copper. Thanks very much!'

'I'm sorry,' Beatrice said but it was too late. Miss Murray practically threw herself onto her bicycle and pedalled away, leaving Beatrice gazing helplessly after her.

The encounter had provided her with a lot of food for thought, much of it uncomfortable. She had never thought of her good-hearted help leading to difficulties for her successor – but then, she'd never expected to have a successor, had she? She had imagined herself being an inco lady until the day she unhooked her trolley for the final time and retired.

It wasn't only Miss Murray who was vexed with her. Mrs Williams was too. When Beatrice had seen other looker-afters, they said they missed her assistance but they said it in a friendly or rueful way. Not so Mrs Williams. She had yet to forgive Beatrice for, as she saw it, leaving her in the lurch. The first few times she'd answered the door to Beatrice, she'd greeted her with, 'Oh, it's you,' uttered in a disgruntled tone until the day Beatrice had answered brightly, 'Good morning, you. That is what we're calling one another now, isn't it? You?'

Mrs Williams had looked sullen, but she'd replied, 'Morning, Miss Inkerman,' backing down in the face of Beatrice's cheerful challenge, just as Beatrice had thought, or at least hoped, she would. Mrs Williams was the sort who pushed her luck to see how much she could get away with.

Now Beatrice smiled as Mrs Williams opened the door to her.

'Good afternoon, Mrs Williams.'

'Afternoon, Miss Inkerman. Come to see her upstairs, have you?' Then, evidently catching the slight raising of Beatrice's eyebrow, she added, 'Mrs Chapman.'

'Yes, I have – and Dora, of course.'

'You'll be lucky,' Mrs Williams muttered, turning away.

Beatrice's heart dipped. Oh no.

Little Dora Chapman was indirectly the reason why Beatrice now had her beloved job in the Welfare Department. Mrs Chapman rented this house from the landlord and sublet the downstairs to Mr Trent. A bedridden invalid, Mrs Chapman always sent Dora downstairs for the rent, which Mrs Williams hadn't exactly been prompt in paying, not least because her father insisted on keeping his money under the floorboards. Beatrice had stepped in and made sure the rent got paid on time, and that was how she'd met the Chapmans.

In young Dora she had seen herself as a child, kept off school, doing all the household tasks as well as fetching tonics for her mother and giving her bed baths.

Fired up with determination to help Dora and other children like her, Beatrice had set up the Time Off Club. She'd also come up with the idea of asking for these children to attend school every morning and be at home just in the afternoons. Mrs Chapman would far rather have had it the other way around but eventually, after much persuasion, she'd given in. Beatrice had also arranged for Dora to have a school dinner every day, and the skinny little waif of last year had shot up a full three inches as a result.

Beatrice knocked and entered the room Mrs Chapman lived in. As well as being her bedroom, it was also a parlour as well as the room where mother and daughter ate their meals, and the storeroom where bedding, medicine and other supplies were kept. The air contained a heady mixture of the eucalyptus that helped keep Mrs Chapman's airways open, disinfectant and the contents of the commode.

Beatrice refused to let herself pull a face. She would willingly have emptied the commode into the privy at the end of the over-grown garden, but Fay Brewer had made it clear she wasn't allowed to do anything beyond her remit; and if ever she felt tempted, she only had to remember Miss Murray.

'Hello, Mrs Chapman,' Beatrice said. 'How are you keeping?'

Mrs Chapman drew several quick, short breaths to prepare herself to speak. 'Doing well, thanks for asking.'

'Where's your Dora? Out shopping?'

Mrs Chapman looked away. 'At school.' After a pause she added, 'I kept her home this morning. I needed her here.'

'We've talked about this,' Beatrice said gently. 'Dora needs to go to school.'

'And I've sent her, haven't I? That's where she is right now.'

'But she's meant to be there in the mornings. You know that – and you know why.'

'You don't understand,' Mrs Chapman complained.

'You know that I do,' Beatrice said gently. 'I was like Dora when I was a child. She really does need to go to school, you know – in the mornings, when they do the three Rs.'

'You don't have to keep telling me.' Mrs Chapman was starting to get agitated. 'But if I need her here, I need her here and that's all there is to it.'

Beatrice sighed. Honestly, there were times when it was like banging her head against a brick wall – but no, that wasn't being fair to Mrs Chapman. Like the other invalid mothers, she needed support; and in the absence of adult relatives, that meant relying on the children. Beatrice urgently wanted to help the Dora Chapmans of this world, and she thought that by encouraging morning attendance at school she had achieved it, but evidently not. What else could she do?

* * *

Never mind April showers. This was nothing less than a downpour, with sheets of rain soaking everything and clumps of grey cloud blocking out the light. Clasping her handbag against her coat with one arm while her other hand hung on to her hat, Beatrice hurried in the direction of the Town Hall, dodging puddles and then having to perform a swift double-dodge to avoid other pedestrians who were skirting the same puddles.

When a crowded bus trundled by and sent a spray of water over her shoes, Beatrice uttered an exclamation of dismay and decided to take shelter in a doorway at the same time as a man with his trilby pulled down to keep the rain out of his eyes hurried into the same doorway from the other direction. Beyond a brief nod, Beatrice didn't so much as glance at him. She gazed out at the sheets of rain, wondering how long it would last and doing mental calculations regarding today's work timetable.

Then, with a sigh, she made herself relax. There was no point in getting het up. That made her feel a bit better. She looked at her companion, ready to commiserate – only for her eyes to spring wide open and her jaw to drop. Her skin tingled all over – no, not tingled. Prickled. An almost painful sensation. Bombarded by shock and disbelief, she went cold inside and, for a moment, felt dizzy.

It couldn't be. It couldn't.

But it was.

'Frank...?' It came out as little more than a breath. It felt like the most important word she'd ever spoken, yet she could barely make a sound.

He looked at her. It was him. It was. Those light-blue eyes. He was older and his body had filled out, but she would know those eyes anywhere. He had the same moustache too.

'Frank?' she said again, louder this time.

He was still looking at her, eyebrows drawn together in a frown. After a moment he said, '*Beatrice?*'

She felt a twist of disappointment or maybe it was humiliation. She'd known him the moment she'd looked at him, but he had seemed to hesitate and wonder before he could place her. Had she really aged so badly?

A smile flickered across his lips. 'Beatrice?' he asked again. There was more certainty in his voice this time.

She nodded, very aware of how wet her hat and hair were. Was she bedraggled? Had the rain ruined the neat roll of hair at the back of her neck?

Frank let out a laugh. 'By the stars, what a surprise! Fancy the two of us diving for cover in the same doorway.'

Beatrice gave a half-hearted smile. Ought she to curse herself for taking shelter? Was seeing Frank a good thing or a bad one? She couldn't tell, but Frank appeared friendly and pleased.

'How the devil are you?' he asked her.

'Fine, thanks. And yourself?'

'Likewise.' There was real warmth in his smile now. 'I hope – well, if you'll allow me to say so, I hope life has dealt kindly with you. What I mean to say is, I hope you ended up with what you wanted.'

Beatrice's inner turmoil froze. She knew exactly what he meant and couldn't pretend otherwise.

'I never married, if that's what you mean, but I have an interesting job. More than just a job. A proper career.'

'Doing what?'

'I work for the Corporation in their Welfare Department. I specialise in working with children.'

Specialise. That was a good word. It made her sound professional, committed. It was a kind of armour.

Frank nodded understandingly. 'I hope it gives you the chance to be a mother in spirit to the children under your care.'

Beatrice was stumped. What was she meant to say to that? And he had remembered how much she'd wanted a family of her own.

Into the silence he said, 'And your mother? Is she still with us?'

'No. She died years ago.'

How strange. There had been a time when Frank knew everything about her, and now he knew nothing.

'What about you?' Beatrice asked. 'Are you still an engineer?'

'That's me,' he said cheerfully.

'In the toy factory?' she asked.

Frank, the man who had never wanted his own children, had worked in a toy factory, servicing the production equipment and tinkering with the intricate workings of mechanical toys for the children of the wealthy.

'I don't suppose there are any toy factories left now,' Beatrice added. Everything had been turned over to war work long since.

'I left as soon as war was declared,' Frank told her. 'I wanted to put my knowledge and skills to good use in the war effort, in common with many others.' He glanced up and down the pavement. 'The rain is easing off.'

'Good,' said Beatrice. 'I mustn't be late.'

'Work?' he asked.

She nodded. 'You?'

'Day off.' He looked along the pavement again.

'Are you meeting somebody?' Beatrice asked.

'We split up just before the heavens opened. I wanted to go to the tobacconist's. We're due to meet up again over there on that corner.'

'You'd best get going, then,' said Beatrice, wanting him to go, wanting him to stay.

Frank started to peel back his gloves. 'Sopping wet. I had to rescue my hat from a puddle.'

Beatrice couldn't help looking. A wedding ring. Did that matter? Did it matter that she'd had to admit to being a spinster?

She was about to say 'You married someone else?' but that might sound pushy so she changed it to – she didn't know quite what to change it to, but it didn't matter because he caught her looking.

'Yes, I got married,' he said.

Before he could say anything more, a boy and a girl came running up to him, calling, 'Dad!'

The breath froze in Beatrice's throat. 'You have two children...?' she said, stunned. The man she had left because he didn't want a family now had two children.

Frank laughed and his face lit up, making him startlingly handsome.

'No, I don't have two children – I have five.'

7

Kitty sat at the table in the family flat, her head bent over the accounts, but for once her mind wasn't on the task and she sat back with a sigh. Handling the money and keeping records was something she had always been proud to do, but now that Bill had refused to let her have access to the Dunbar's bank account, it felt different, and not just because he'd been helping himself to the money she had made. Although Naomi wanted to make her feel better about things continuing as they were, Kitty was determined to make changes – but how?

One reason for her frustration was Abbie. How proud she'd been to think of herself setting the best possible example of female capability to her daughter. She'd even – heaven help her – she'd even daydreamed about things doing so well that Abbie would be able to join the business when she left school at the end of the summer term. What a joke! Kitty could hear her dear mam's voice in her imagination saying, 'Pride goes before a fall.' Had she let her success in setting up the storage business go to her head?

A quiet tap on the door made her look round.

'Come in,' she called, closing her accounts ledger.

Beatrice walked in, looking pale and drained. Kitty immediately jumped up and went to her.

'Are you all right?' she asked, all sorts of images pouring into her mind. An unexploded bomb suddenly detonating – bodies, injuries – a ruptured gas main. 'Has something happened? Come and sit down.' She guided her friend to a seat, looking at her anxiously. She wasn't just pale. Her skin was positively grey. 'Are you ill?'

Beatrice raised her brown eyes. 'I've never done this before.'

'Done what?'

'Bunked off work.'

'You don't look well to me,' Kitty said. 'Shall I telephone the Town Hall and say you've taken bad ways?'

Beatrice rose to her feet. 'No. I must get back.'

Kitty gently pushed her back onto the chair. 'You'll do no such thing, certainly not before you've had a cup of tea and got your colour back. I'll go and put the kettle on. You stay put.'

Before she could move away, Beatrice caught hold of her hand. As her friend's eyes filled with tears, Kitty crouched in front of her.

'Tell me,' she said simply.

Beatrice scrabbled for a hanky and dashed away the tears. Kitty sat back on her heels and waited.

'Do you remember when I told you about Frank?'

'Your old fiancé who didn't want children, so you broke it off.' Kitty angled her head so she could see Beatrice's face. 'What about him?'

Beatrice breathed in and out slowly, then she swallowed. 'I've just seen him. A few minutes ago. We sheltered from the rain in the same doorway, and it was him.'

'That must have come as a shock,' Kitty said, feeling her way.

Beatrice nodded. There was a faraway look in her eyes. 'It was. In all these years, I've never seen him – and then, there he was.' She made a tutting sound with her tongue and began to look more like herself. 'The years have been kinder to him than they have to me, that's for certain.'

'Don't put yourself down, Beatrice Inkerman,' Kitty replied firmly. 'You're a good-looking woman and your work in Welfare has put a fresh light in your eyes.' In a gentle voice, she added, 'It must have brought it home to you that he was your one chance of marriage and you sent him on his way. Oh, Beatrice, I know that can't have been an easy decision for you, but you made it for the best of reasons.'

'Reasons that came to nothing,' Beatrice said. 'I was young enough and stupid enough to think I'd meet someone else. Do you know what he said to me? I told him I work with children and he said he hoped it had given me the chance to be a spiritual mother to them.'

'Oh, Beatrice,' Kitty murmured.

'He's got five of his own.'

Kitty frowned, knowing what Beatrice meant but at the same time sure she must have misunderstood. 'Pardon?'

'Five children. I saw two of them. They came running up to him. He's a father of five.'

'*What?*'

Beatrice's voice was stronger now. 'He's married with five children, and not just that but he looked *happy*. When they ran up to him, it was obvious how pleased they all were to be together.' She had to stop speaking for a moment, but then started again before Kitty could say a word. 'The man who swore blind to me that he didn't want to be a father, and so I broke off our engagement, now has five children. *Five*, Kitty! If I could have known all those years ago—'

'Don't,' Kitty said. 'Don't torture yourself.'

'How can I not?' Beatrice asked. 'Those children could have been *mine*.'

* * *

Beatrice returned to work. Kitty didn't feel comfortable letting her go but knew there was no alternative.

'It'll be good for you to have other things to concentrate on,' she told her friend as they walked downstairs together. Kitty stayed by Beatrice's side all the way to the pavement and watched her walk along Lily Street, the same way she used to watch Abbie walk along their old road on the way to school.

Kitty felt a twinge of annoyance. Honestly, how could she have been so unfeeling, so downright stupid, as to suggest that Beatrice would be able to lose herself in her work? Not to mention how hypocritical it was of her. Wasn't she the one who'd had to set aside Dunbar's accounts not half an hour ago because her mind was full of other things?

Her heart ached for her friend. What a blow. As if bumping into Frank wasn't enough of a shock in itself, how was she going to come to terms with knowing about those five children? *Five!*

Realising that Beatrice was in a situation she could do nothing to rectify increased Kitty's resolve to improve her own circumstances. It was time to stop railing silently against it and get on with doing something about it.

As she was about to turn to go back up the steps, a familiar figure on the other side of the road caught her eye and she waited for Ivy to cross over and come to her.

'Was that Miss Inkerman I saw walking off looking like she has the cares of the world on her shoulders?' Ivy asked without preamble.

'She's fine,' Kitty answered.

'If you say so.'

'What brings you here?' Kitty asked. Then she realised that she'd been infected by Ivy's crisp tone. 'Sorry. That didn't exactly sound welcoming. Would you like some tea? And you must have one of Abbie's oatmeal biscuits. Lily helped her make them. Let's sit in the old dining room, shall we?'

They often still called it 'the old dining room', though they had turned it into the best parlour they could with their limited resources. When they were still taking in consignments of furniture for storage, the polished oak floor had been covered for protection by a thick oilcloth. This had subsequently been removed, but the luxurious dark-blue carpet that used to cover most of the floor had been one of the many things the bailiffs had walked off with. The white marble chimneypiece was still there, of course, and the mantelpiece now had a few ornaments, the original ones having gone the same way as the carpet, as had the grandfather clock, the mahogany tables, the dining chairs with their bronze-coloured leather seats, the oak cabinet with glass doors and the enormous sideboard in which the tablecloths and napkins had been kept along with the finest glass dishes and the cutlery.

Instead, the room now had a couple of worn rugs Kitty had picked up at the market. They didn't cover that much of the large floor, but they broke it up a little. A card table stood in front of one of the bay windows, with a pair of wooden chairs. A couple of armchairs that were past their best had been positioned in front of the fireplace, with a low table between them. Beside the hearth was a pouffe that Abbie generally sat on. Not that any of them spent much time in here. It was too big a space to be cosy and they all preferred the basement kitchen.

Ivy glanced around. 'Being posh today, are we?'

Kitty smiled. 'In honour of Abbie's oatmeal biscuits.'

She nipped down to the basement to prepare a tray and returned to find Ivy standing at one of the windows, looking out at Lily Street. Ivy turned as she entered and helped her unload the tray.

Kitty offered the plate of biscuits and Ivy took one.

'Not bad at all.' Coming from Ivy, this was high praise.

'I'll tell Abbie you said so. She'll be pleased.'

Actually, Abbie would pull a face and they would both laugh at Ivy's mealy-mouthed admiration, but Abbie wouldn't be upset, which was the main thing.

'I've come to find out how you got on at the bank,' said Ivy. 'Have you opened the new account?'

'Ah,' said Kitty. 'It wasn't that simple.' As briefly as she could, she explained what had happened. 'Naomi says I've managed as I am for this long and I should just carry on.'

Ivy shot her a look. 'Oh aye? Well, maybe, maybe not, but something tells me that you want more than that.' Ivy took out her cigarettes. 'Are you going to ask Bill if you can have a bank account?'

'I'd rather stick pins in my eyes.'

'Thought so,' said Ivy. 'It's all well and good being proud, Kitty, but you're in a fix.'

Kitty swallowed the last of her biscuit. Suddenly it didn't taste of anything. 'I know. Some clients pay cash. I could ask more of them if they could do that.'

'They won't like it if they prefer writing cheques,' said Ivy. 'What about a post office account?' she suggested after a few moments' thought. 'Anyone can have one of those, even children.'

'Now there's a thought,' said Kitty. 'I'll set up one of those in my own name and use it for the business. I'll pay all the cash into it. When someone wants to pay by cheque, most of the time I'll ask for it to be made out to Dunbar's, but sometimes I'll ask for it to be made out to me – just enough to enable me to keep the business running. Most of it will go into the Dunbar's account as usual... for Bill to dip into and squander, no doubt,' she added tartly.

'Will a post office account be all you need?' Ivy asked.

'I don't know,' Kitty said honestly, 'but it's a start.'

* * *

Kitty made an appointment to call on Mr Tulip. He owned three warehouses stuffed full of bombed-out furniture and household goods, and he had been a great help to her last year when she'd been looking into how to set up a similar business on a much smaller scale. He had continued to assist her with advice. Moreover, at times when she had needed brawn to shift collections of belongings from the ground floor upstairs into the old guest rooms, Mr Tulip had made his men available – at a price, of course. That was the first lesson Kitty had learned from him. Don't do anything for nothing. That's no way to run a business.

She liked Mr Tulip. As she entered his office, he stood up, tubby and well-dressed, and came round from behind his desk to greet her. He shook her hand warmly while calling over her shoulder to his secretary to fetch tea and biscuits.

'Sit down and tell me why you're here, dear Mrs Dunbar.'

Kitty gave herself a moment by putting her handbag and gas-mask box beside her seat, then she looked at him.

'I've come for your advice – as usual.'

'Then you shall have it. I don't charge for advice.' His eyes twinkled.

'It's rather delicate,' said Kitty.

'Is it to do with Dunbar's Storage? There's no such thing as delicacy. Tell me everything and don't let embarrassment hold you back.'

'I get paid both in cash and by cheque. Most of it has been deposited in the Dunbar's account at the bank, but I've kept back some of the cash for various bills and expenses.'

'Go on,' Mr Tulip said when she stopped.

'My husband has refused to give me access to the bank account.'

'So the funds in there are out of your reach.'

'The bank manager says I can't set up a new account for Dunbar's. I haven't the authority and also it might suggest I'm...'

'Involved in dodgy dealings?' Mr Tulip suggested.

Kitty winced. Damn Bill for placing her in this wretched position. 'I can't even open a new account in my own name without a letter of permission from my husband.'

'And I take it you're not prepared to ask him for such a thing?'

'No, I'm not,' Kitty declared. Lifting her chin, she said, 'I've opened a post office account. It's in my name but I'll use it exclusively for the business.'

'Do you intend to divert all payments into it?' Mr Tulip asked.

'Definitely not,' said Kitty. 'That's what I'd like to ask you about. I'll keep depositing into the Dunbar's bank account because I'm running the Dunbar's business and that's the right thing to do; but I also need this other account in my own name, partly for the business but, to be honest, also for living expenses for me and my daughter. The allotment I receive from my husband's wages is the smallest amount he was allowed to send me.'

'I see.'

'But when the bank manager made that remark about—'

'—dodgy dealings—'

'Yes, well, it left me feeling scared. I don't want to end up being accused of something.' Kitty hurried on, wanting to show Mr Tulip she'd come here with ideas and wasn't simply throwing herself on his mercy. 'I wondered about putting half of Dunbar's income into the bank and half into the post office.'

The edges of Mr Tulip's mouth turned downwards as he considered. 'I would suggest two-thirds to one-third might be better. It would show beyond doubt your continuing commitment to the business.'

'The fact that I built it up from scratch and I keep it going on a day-to-day basis shows that,' Kitty declared with spirit. 'I'm sorry. I don't mean to sound as if I'm taking it out on you, Mr Tulip.'

'That's perfectly all right, dear lady. Tell me, are you paying yourself a salary from the business income?'

Kitty blinked. 'Of course not. Should I be? Am I allowed to?'

He chuckled. 'You most certainly are – unless you propose to work for Mr Dunbar for nothing.'

Kitty could all but feel the steam coming out of her ears. How *stupid* she'd been – how ignorant. It had never occurred to her for one moment that she was entitled to be paid for working for Dunbar's. Not only had Bill helped himself from the profits she'd made, but he had let her work for nothing.

'What salary should I take?' she asked.

Mr Tulip spread his hands. 'I cannot answer that.'

'Well—' She couldn't bring herself to ask what his own salary was. 'May I ask what you pay your men?'

'It isn't really comparable. They're removal men and ware-housemen. They don't have your responsibilities. And they're men. Not that women do the job they do, but if they did, they'd earn less.'

Kitty smiled. 'You mean I have to earn less than you.'

'Most certainly. I own three warehouses and you run one

former hotel turned storage house. The size of my business is much greater than yours.'

'And you're a man.'

'And you, my dear Mrs Dunbar, are not only a lady but inexperienced.'

'But women are earning more than they used to before the war,' Kitty pointed out.

'Yes – for doing men's jobs, but they're not earning as much as the men used to.'

'I'm sorry,' said Kitty. 'I shouldn't be arguing the toss with you like this.'

'I quite understand,' said Mr Tulip. 'It's a fraught time for you.'

An idea popped into Kitty's mind. 'Thank you, Mr Tulip. You've been of enormous help, as always. I've just thought of a woman who works for the Corporation.'

'You don't mean your friend Miss Inkerman?'

'No, this is a Miss Brewer. She is senior to Miss Inkerman, though by no means at the top of the tree herself, but she has various responsibilities and she makes decisions. I'll ask her if she would mind telling me what she earns. That could be my salary too.'

She smiled at her mentor, feeling better than she had for some time – and she knew why. Bill's actions had threatened her independence but now she could feel it coming back to her.

8

Last year Lily's sorrow had dragged her down into the depths. Her bereavement continued to be fierce and painful, but she couldn't afford to let it swamp her life. A whole year had gone by and it was important to her to keep her feet on the ground from now on. She vowed to pay more attention to news of the war – no, that wasn't what she meant. She'd always followed the news. No, what she needed to do, for her own sanity, was to concentrate on developing a real connection to what was happening, an emotional connection, the same one that everybody else experienced. It was starting to happen. She was as moved and as proud as anyone when the King awarded the George Cross to what he called 'the Island Fortress of Malta' in order to recognise 'a heroism and devotion that will long be famous in history'.

Toby continued to be the most important part of her life. She had paid a visit to the cemetery in Sale where he had been laid to rest. She went on his birthday, not the anniversary of his death. In spite of the memories that had washed over her, she'd shed no tears. Part of her mind frankly boggled at the knowledge that her son had been gone for a whole year and that she had somehow lived through that much time without him.

There was a headstone now, which Daniel had arranged. He had tried to consult her, had wanted her to choose the stone with him, but the very idea had proved overwhelming and she'd refused.

'What about the wording?' he had asked, clearly anxious for her to be involved.

She had forced herself to stay put, though she'd felt like taking to her heels. 'His name, his dates.'

'What about *Beloved son of...* or something of the kind?'

But he wasn't your beloved son, was he? You didn't even know if the baby was a boy or a girl.

Lily froze. Her breathing stopped. She held the words in. She hated herself for thinking them.

'Do what you think best,' she'd said, desperate to leave this topic behind.

And Daniel had simply had Toby's name, TOBIAS IRWIN CHADWICK, and his dates engraved on the stone. Had he sensed her response to *Beloved son of*? Had he read her mind?

When she visited Toby's grave, she left a posy of lily of the valley and made a silent vow that, whatever happened to her and wherever her life took her, she would bring him lily of the valley every single year on his birthday for as long as she lived.

* * *

Lily smiled indulgently as Abbie opened her birthday presents. It was a Saturday so there was plenty of time and Kitty wanted to make an occasion of it. Abbie had opened her gift from Beatrice at the breakfast table because of Beatrice having to set off for work, and the adults had glanced at one another with pleasure when the girl had exclaimed in delight over the manicure set.

'Oh, Auntie Beatrice, thank you.'

'Auntie Beatrice made the case for it herself,' Kitty murmured.

'That makes it even better,' said Abbie. 'I love it. It's a proper grown-up present.'

Kitty laughed. 'Don't say that.'

'But I am grown-up now, Mummy, or very nearly. I leave school this summer.'

But the way she pushed back her chair and got up to hug Beatrice's neck and give her a kiss made her look like an eager child.

Beatrice slid an arm around Abbie's waist and kissed her cheek. 'Happy birthday, chick.'

Lily laughed. 'My Auntie Nettie has five children as well as me and we all get called "chick" or "my lamb". She says it saves tripping up over names.'

Beatrice stood up. 'I must get my skates on.'

'I'll clear away.' Lily rose too. 'The birthday girl and the birthday girl's mother aren't on washing-up duty today.'

A while later she joined Kitty and Abbie in the family flat for more present-giving. She had bought Abbie a couple of film magazines, which, even though Abbie didn't say so aloud, were evidently considered to be another grown-up gift.

From her mother, Abbie received a clutch purse and, from her father, a pretty necklace with a sparkly stone surrounded by enamel petals.

Abbie was thrilled with the gifts, though she did remark, 'Normally I get something from both of you.'

'Wouldn't you rather have two presents than one?' Kitty asked lightly. 'Besides, Daddy sent me a postal order to get you something. I suppose he thought I'd add it to what I spent, but I thought I'd get you something specially from him.'

'I'm glad you did.' Abbie held the necklace to her throat with the ends of the chain sticking out behind her head. 'Will you fasten it for me, please?'

Lily couldn't help wondering about the necklace. Separate parental presents to double Abbie's pleasure or, after the bank account fiasco, a way for Kitty to distance herself from her husband? It wasn't the sort of question you could ask.

Lily spent much of the morning in shopping queues to save the birthday girl's mother. When she returned to Dunbar's, Kitty's sister was there. She had brought a jar of rose-scented bath salts for Abbie's birthday.

'I wish I could stay for your birthday lunch,' she said, 'but I've got to get back for WVS duty this afternoon. Have a lovely day celebrating, Abbie, darling.'

'Thank you for coming, Auntie Naomi,' Abbie replied, hugging her.

Lily helped Kitty make lentil cutlets and carrot croquettes for the birthday lunch. Mrs Ivy Dunbar was bringing Martha, Abbie's chum from the school she used to go to before the family moved into Dunbar's. As well as Abbie's birthday, the two friends were going to celebrate having got jobs ready for when they left school at the end of the summer term. Abbie had passed the exam to be taken on by the Town Hall as a trainee clerk and Martha was going to work at Ingleby's. Lily didn't say so, but she thought that she personally would have much preferred shop work to office work – but then, she would never have had the chance of the latter, because she'd never have passed the exam. She was proud of Abbie for doing so.

That afternoon, the two girls were to be allowed to go around the shops together. Then, along with Kitty and Mrs Dunbar, they would catch the bus to Withington, where the girls were to go to the early evening showing of the musical comedy, *Moon Over Miami*.

'As long as Abbie doesn't come home wanting to style her hair like Betty Grable,' Kitty had murmured to Lily earlier on.

When the film ended, Kitty was going to meet them outside to walk Martha home, then she and Abbie would go to Mrs Dunbar's for a while before coming home to Dunbar's later in the evening.

Lily had her own midday meal early on her own, because she had to go on WVS duty. She had volunteered to have extra hours tacked onto her shift so that Kitty could have this evening free for Abbie.

She spent most of the afternoon cleaning in the home of a lady who was convalescing after, as she informed Lily, 'having her boiler removed', which turned out to mean she'd undergone a hysterectomy. The WVS were mucking in to help her sister look after her.

After that, Lily did the teatime shift at the British Restaurant and then she went to the Foreign Servicemen's Club, where men from overseas could get a snack and some company. The other WVS ladies sat and chatted with the men, but Lily had made it clear from the outset that while she was happy to work in the kitchen, she would do nothing front of house. She might be separated, but she had no intention of looking available, especially now the Yanks were here. They'd only started arriving in January, but they already had a reputation.

At the end of her shift, Lily handed over to her replacement and got ready to walk back to Dunbar's. With May coming into view, the days were warm but the evenings and nights were still chilly. There was a real nip in the air this evening, possibly because of the lack of cloud cover. She stopped for a moment to look up at the stars. One of her WVS colleagues had lost her son at Dunkirk and she'd said that she had chosen a particular star to be his star. Lily wondered if she should choose one to be Toby's, but she was a year too late and it would feel like cheating.

She continued on her way, directing her little torch at the pavement in front of her. It didn't give out much light because you had to cover the lens with layers of tissue so the beam couldn't be seen by Jerry if he flew over. Not that they'd had any raids for weeks now, but the rule mustn't be broken or you risked a hefty fine.

'Help! *Help!*'

A child's voice, pitched high with terror – racing footsteps – a hand clutching Lily's arm.

'Please, miss, please! They've all fell in! They're going to drown!'

'Where?' Lily demanded. 'What's happened?'

'Please, mister.' Another voice, some yards away. 'They're in the water tank.'

'Good grief.' A man's voice. 'Which building?'

'What were you doing in there anyway, you young tyke?' asked another male voice.

'Never mind that now,' the first man said urgently. 'Find a telephone box or an ARP post and ask for an ambulance.'

A small hand slipped inside Lily's and she found herself being tugged up the steps that fronted a large building. The next moment she almost went flat on her face as someone ploughed into her. She gave an exclamation as she barked her shins on the edge of one of the steps.

'What the— sorry, sorry.'

It was the man who had sent his companion to find help. He made a grab and hauled her upright without stopping to see if she was all right. At the top of the steps, one stride took him to the door. Lily heard the protesting squeal as he turned the handle, then some thuds as he tried to force the door open. She was beside him by that time.

'Nah, mister, the door's locked,' said one of the kids. 'This way.' And he vanished through a window.

'C'mon, miss, come *on*.' The girl pulled Lily's arm. 'Mind where you put your hands, miss. Just hold the wooden frame.'

Before Lily could stop her, the girl had hauled herself through the window. Lily was all set to follow but the man stepped in front of her.

'I'll go. You wait here for the ambulance. Ow! Damn!'

'What is it?' Lily asked.

'Shards of glass protruding from the window frame. Those little blighters must have broken in.'

Taking hold, he pulled himself through the window. Jamming her torch in her pocket, Lily followed without hesitation, stumbling awkwardly as she landed inside.

'I told you to wait outside—'

Sounds could be heard – echoey cries, splashes.

'This way,' said the boy just before he disappeared around a corner.

Lily and the man quickly followed, but the boy had vanished. The girl darted past them and went through a doorway. They followed her and found an enclosed staircase. As they descended, the sounds became louder.

Lily went hot and cold. She knew that some large buildings had huge water tanks in their cellars to provide water for the fire brigade, especially if the mains should be ruptured in a bombing. These weren't the first children to get into difficulties. You heard of children drowning.

Following the lead of the man, she tore the tissue from her torch and played the beam over the scene. Three children were thrashing about in the middle of the tank, arms waving frantically.

'We were playing at running across,' the boy who accompanied them said desperately, 'but the tarpaulin split down the middle and the others fell in.'

'The tarpaulin didn't split,' the man said firmly, shrugging out of his jacket. 'It's two separate tarps, each covering half the tank. Here, boy, take this torch. Your job will be to light up the tank.'

There wasn't a ladder attached to the side of the tank, but the children had dragged some crates across the floor to create an uneven staircase of sorts. The man undid his shoes and kicked them off before tugging off his coat, jacket, tie and shirt, and tossing his hat aside. He made short work of the makeshift staircase. The boy climbed up after him, torch at the ready. Lily automatically followed. Sitting on the edge, the man swung his legs over the side of the tank and lowered himself in, holding on to the side so he could look up at Lily.

'Stay out there. Don't come into the water. It's dangerously cold.'

With that he started to haul himself through the water, pulling himself hand over hand along the edge of one of the tarpaulins.

Lily scrambled back down to the floor and spoke urgently to the girl. 'Go outside and be ready to flag down the ambulance. Go – *now!*'

The girl ran. Lily pulled off her jacket and jumper and, yes, dammit, her skirt and blouse. The less she had on to weigh her down the better. She climbed back up the crate-stairs. The boy was busy directing the torch beam at the struggling children. The man had already heaved one of the children, a girl, onto one of the tarpaulins. Sobbing loudly, she crawled unsteadily to safety, the tarp lurching up and down with each movement she made.

Lily let herself into the water, forcing herself into the gap between the two tarpaulins, her breath forming a deep gasp as the bitter cold enveloped her. It was a struggle to move with the tarpaulins' tough edges pressing against her. No wonder the children were trapped beneath. Hanging on to one of the tarpaulins, Lily hauled herself towards the middle of the tank. How long had the children been in the water? They must be frozen. Imagining it was her young cousins who needed rescuing gave her all the determination she required.

By the time Lily had got as far as the man, he had dragged a boy through the narrow gap between the edges, shoving him unceremoniously onto the tarp. Lily was in time to help him lift a third child the same way.

The lad with the torch was practically jumping up and down.

'Under the water!' he yelled.

The man swore under his breath, then shouted back, 'How many?'

'Three! Another three!'

The man blew out a couple of short breaths, then sucked in one massive one and submerged. Lily did the same. Beneath the water, everything changed. It was pitch-black. She cast about with her hands, stretching as far as she could. She couldn't feel anybody. She couldn't even sense movement. It was as if she were all alone in the inky water. For one horrible moment, she didn't even know which way was up. Was she going to drown because she couldn't find the surface? As her lungs started to flag, she pushed instinctively in the right direction, only to hit the underneath of the tarp. New fear cascaded through her. She'd found the surface but it was covered over, trapping her underwater.

Then she glimpsed a dart of light and thrashed her way towards it, finding the gap just as her lungs were on the verge of exploding. She gulped in some air, then got knocked aside by a disturbance beside her as the man burst through the narrow gap, bringing a small body with him. Lily helped heave the child out of the water and onto the tarpaulin, where he lay spluttering.

'Alive – good,' the man muttered before he sank beneath the surface again.

Lily heard voices then and relief flowed through her. Beams of light cut through the cellar's darkness. It would have been easy to leave the remaining rescues to the newcomers, but Lily refused to do any such thing. There were still two children trapped down here and she wouldn't leave them. She couldn't let another mother suffer as she had done.

Filling her lungs once more, she slid back beneath the surface. She was so cold that it was hard to move, but she forced herself. She had always blamed herself for Toby's death, believing that she must have failed to nourish him and provide him with what he needed for proper growth when he was inside her. She would *not* be responsible for the death of another child.

That spurred her on. She kicked out as strongly as she was able – and bumped into something. Thrusting out her hands, she grabbed the child, but there was no answering grab. Terrified, Lily pulled the child upwards. It was easy to see the gap now because there were more torches.

Strong hands plucked the child from her and then she herself was lifted out onto the wobbling tarpaulin. She was too cold and weak to crawl to safety and had to be helped.

'The children?' she asked just before her teeth commenced a violent chattering.

'All accounted for,' said a man's voice.

Lily wasn't quite sure how she had got there, but she found herself sitting on the floor, where a WVS woman wrapped her in a blanket and produced a thermos of tea.

A man hunkered down beside her.

'I'm Dr Barry,' he said and Lily recognised his voice: he was the man who had run off to summon help. Well, he'd certainly done that. The place was swarming.

'Are the children...?'

'Alive, yes. All of them. Two of them had to be resuscitated and they're already on their way to hospital. You and Dr Shawston – well, jolly good show is all I can say, Miss...?'

'Mrs,' said Lily. 'Mrs Lily Chadwick.'

'Well, Mrs Lily Chadwick, you're a heroine.'

'No, I'm not.'

'I'll tell you what you are,' said a new voice.

Lily looked up to see the man who had dived under the water to rescue the children. Like her, he had a blanket around him. A flash of torchlight caught his profile, showing Lily a strong jawline and an aquiline nose, which gave him a stern appearance. His hair was mussed; he had evidently used the edge of his blanket to dry it.

He towered over her. 'You're unbiddable,' he said. 'First I told you to stay outside and wait for the ambulance – and you didn't. Then I told you to stay out of the water – and again you didn't.'

Lily wasn't having that. She scrambled to her feet, shocked by how weak her chilled limbs felt. Were her legs about to give way, leaving her slumping to the floor? Only willpower kept her upright. She clung grimly to her blanket, remembering the clothes she had taken off.

She glared at the man, Dr Shaw-something, aware that her chattering teeth were taking the edge off her hard look.

'I'm a surgeon and I'm not accustomed to being disobeyed,' he said.

'Now see here—' she began.

To her surprise, he smiled and his austere features softened. 'But thank the stars you did disobey. I couldn't have fished out all three of those kids in time, so – and here's something I never expected to hear myself say – good for you for following your instincts instead of listening to me.'

'Oh.' That wasn't what Lily had braced herself for. 'Thank you, Dr Shaw...'

'Shawston,' he replied. He smiled again. 'Now you'll get it right next time.'

Lily gawped. She started to say, 'Next time?' but a policeman appeared, wanting statements, and the moment vanished.

Next time?

* * *

A couple of WVS ladies took Lily into a corner and held up blankets to provide the privacy she needed to put her clothes back on. She removed her soaked petticoat, folded it and squeezed it into her handbag, then peeled off her stockings, balled them up and crammed them into her pockets.

Emerging from behind the blankets, she asked, 'What can I do to help?'

'Nothing, thanks. Have you got far to go to get home?'

'No. Only to Lily Street, off Oxford Road.'

'Then get home and put the kettle on. A hot strip-wash and a cup of tea is what you need.'

Lily wasn't sorry to obey. Her dip in the tank had chilled her to the bone.

'Do you need one of us to go with you?' asked one of the WVS ladies.

'I'll be fine, thanks.'

Lily made her way upstairs. Her legs were still wobbly. Maybe she would forego the strip-wash and take a hot water bottle to bed instead. The rescue party had broken down the front door so at least she didn't have to brave the window again. She wasn't sure she would have had the strength left to pull herself through without getting slashed to ribbons.

After the noisy echoes in the cellar, it felt unnaturally still and quiet in the street in spite of a handful of pedestrians going by. Lily shivered, but not because she felt cold. Everything was normal out here, but inside the building behind her a terrible tragedy had only narrowly been averted. It was all too easy to imagine the children – only now it was her young cousins she was picturing – running around on the tarpaulin, laughing and squealing as it shifted beneath their feet – then the gasp, the shock, the moment of utter terror as they vanished down the middle.

She heard running footsteps behind her.

'Mrs Chadwick! Hold on a minute.'

A man's voice. Lily turned. Dr Shaw – the other bit escaped her again – ran up to her.

'Yours, I believe.' He held out a gas-mask box.

'No, mine's here.' Lily moved her shoulder, bringing the box swinging forward. 'But thanks for trying, Dr Shaw... ton.'

'Shaw*ston*, with an S in the middle, but you were nearly right. You just need a bit more practice.'

Lily blinked. 'Excuse me. I must get along.'

'It was only a gentle tease,' he said.

'I'm not interested in teasing, gentle or otherwise.'

'I apologise. Permit me to escort you home.'

And find out where I live? Not on your nelly!

'No, thanks. I'm fine by myself.'

Just as she was about to march off, the mournful sound of the air raid siren lifted into the air. It had always sent shivers through Lily, but now, after an absence of weeks, her fear was sharp.

Dr Shawston took her arm. 'This way. Back to the cellar.'

They hadn't even got as far as the corner before a series of long-drawn-out whistling sounds came from above.

'Incendiaries,' said Lily.

The doctor dragged her towards the nearest building, where they both stumbled on the sandbags in front of it before they dived into its dark doorway, and not a moment too soon. One – two – three – four incendiaries landed in a spread-out line along the road. Lily had seen incendiaries before on various occasions. They were roughly the size and shape of a rounders bat and it was essential to disable them quickly.

'Stay here,' Dr Shawston ordered, but Lily wasn't going to be bossed about when she knew exactly what to do.

As the doctor left the doorway, she was on his heels, shedding her handbag and gas-mask box before bending to grab a sandbag. Either it was heavier than normal or else her cold-water dip had knocked the stuffing out of her. With an effort, she heaved it into her arms and staggered towards the closest incendiary. After dropping the sandbag on top of it, she jumped backwards to get well away, as everyone had been trained to do.

She darted back to fetch another sandbag and collided with Dr Shawston, who quickly put out a hand to steady her. He picked up another sandbag and dumped it in her arms, its weight almost causing her to double over. She made her way to the next incendiary, knowing that with each passing second, the chances of detonation increased. She dropped the heavy bag and sprang away. A moment later there was a loud splutter and the sandbag lifted several inches off the ground, but the explosion was contained.

With all four incendiaries taken care of, Lily grabbed her things, ready to make a final dash for the cellar where the water tank was. The two of them had just reached the corner when an almighty explosion occurred further down the road. The breath was ripped from Lily's lungs as the force plucked her and Dr Shawston up into the air and slammed them against a wall, pinning them there for long moments before letting go and allowing them to slide to the ground. Every bone in Lily's body vibrated, every muscle hummed. The ability to breathe came back to her and she made a series of tiny gasps. It was all she could manage.

Dr Shawston's face appeared in front of hers. His hands held her upper arms.

'In through your nose, out through your mouth, as slowly as you can. Good girl. In through your nose.'

His instructions helped and Lily regained control.

'Come on,' he said.

He pulled her to her feet, a quick glance apparently assuring him she wasn't going to topple over. He still had hold of her hand as they set off at a brisk pace.

There was another explosion and the world shook. All the paving stones on both sides of the road lifted up one after another in rapid succession and dropped down again. Dr Shawston thrust Lily onto the road. They started to run and then—

—the road vanished, simply vanished from beneath Lily's feet. Still clutching Dr Shawston's hand, she plunged straight down into the darkness.

9

When the siren had first sounded, Kitty was at Ivy's house. She'd been on her feet, in fact, about to tell Abbie to get ready to head for the bus stop to go home. As the familiar wail rose in the air, Ivy jumped up and the three of them quickly went through the routine of preparing the house for an air raid – switching off the gas, electricity and water; and opening all the curtains so that a fire indoors would be spotted from outside.

Then, instead of diving into the Morrison shelter in the kitchen, Ivy legged it up the stairs and came back down two minutes later in her WVS rig-out.

'The WVS will be needed tonight,' she said.

'I'll come with you,' said Kitty.

'So will I,' Abbie added at one.

'No, you stay here,' said Ivy. 'You'll be safe inside the Morrison.'

Kitty felt torn in two. She ought to stay with her daughter – but she also had her duty as a war worker. Ivy was right. Already explosions could be heard. The more WVS women who turned out the better.

Abbie was gazing fixedly at her. 'I can work in the rest centre. I can wash up. I can get blankets ready. There are messenger boys who cycle about in air raids and they're younger than I am, some of them. Please, Mummy, I want to do my bit.'

Of course she did. She was fourteen and thought she was grown-up. Unsure if it made her the worst mother in the world, Kitty nodded.

Ivy looked as if she might argue, but then didn't. She flung open a kitchen cupboard and produced a metal colander and an enamel bowl.

'Here – one each. Put them on your heads. They can be your tin hats out in the streets.'

She put her tin box of important documents – birth certificate, insurance papers and so forth – inside the Morrison for safety, then led the way out.

It was a clear, starlit night. Was that what had tempted the Luftwaffe?

'Stay close to me,' Kitty told Abbie as the three of them hurried on their way.

Enemy aircraft streamed overhead, with the ack-ack guns trying to bring them down. The firing was loud for a few seconds, then it faded a little, then grew loud again, as the huge guns were swung this way and that.

At the rest centre, Ivy and another woman soon disappeared into the night pushing an old pram containing an urn to dispense tea to those in need.

'Stay with me,' Kitty said to Abbie. 'Even if someone tries to give you a different job, stick beside me. Understand?'

'Yes, Mum,' said Abbie.

Kitty's heart lurched. Mum? What had become of Mummy? But there was no time to dwell on it now.

They were put on sandwich-making duty first, churning out

fish-paste butties both for the rest centre and for the mobile canteen that would travel to areas that had been badly hit. Kitty kept Abbie in the kitchen for as long as she could, wanting to protect her from other aspects of rest centre work – dealing with pale-faced, wide-eyed folk who had been evacuated from a public shelter that had taken a direct hit; making lists of the names and addresses of the missing; explaining the procedure to people who had been bombed out, then explaining all over again because they'd been too shocked to take it in the first time.

Kitty couldn't help but be impressed by the way Abbie knuckled down to work. She would take pride in telling Bill in her next letter. He would no doubt send a blistering reply, demanding to know what the heck she thought she was up to, letting their daughter work through an air raid, but she still wanted him to know they had a child to be proud of. She might not love him any more; she might be hopping mad with him over the matter of the Dunbar's bank account; but the two of them would always be Abbie's parents and she must never forget that.

The raid, though fierce, was relatively short, the all-clear sounding after forty minutes or so.

'Does that mean we've finished here now?' Abbie asked.

'No,' said Kitty. 'There's a lot of tidying up to do and there are still people who need attention.'

She spared a moment to be thankful that this latest batch of people was here because of a burst water main and not because their houses had been blown to kingdom come.

At last she, Abbie and Ivy headed for Ivy's house. It made sense for Kitty and Abbie to stay there overnight now instead of trying to get home.

'This has been a birthday to remember, hasn't it?' Kitty said lightly to her daughter.

As they entered the road around the corner from Ivy's, Kitty was doubly glad that Ivy had their company. The smells of cordite, rubble and soot filled the air and the road was in ruins, with paving stones, clumps of brickwork and lumps of plaster dumped here and there, and with roof tiles and shards of glass scattered in between.

Ivy's footsteps slowed. 'What a mess. That's Mrs Philpott's house – it's lost its whole front. And the Browns' house is as flat as a pancake.'

'Should we help?' Abbie asked, looking at the rescue teams, the ARP wardens and the firemen.

'No,' said Kitty. 'There are plenty of people working here, including the WVS.' To Ivy she added, 'Abbie's had enough for one night.'

'*Mum*,' Abbie protested.

Ivy solved the problem by turning on her heel. 'Let's go the long way round. I'm not walking past all this damage as if I'm having a nosy.'

She stalked off, leaving Kitty and Abbie to follow. When, after a few minutes, they turned into Ivy's road, an ARP warden spotted them and came hurrying towards them.

'Oh, Mrs Dunbar, there you are.'

And Kitty knew. She just knew. So did Ivy, she could tell. They looked past the warden to where Ivy's house, the place where Bill had grown up, stood halfway along the street. Kitty's heart turned over and her pulse raced. She clutched Ivy's arm with one hand and pulled Abbie to her side with the other.

Ivy's house had taken a direct hit.

* * *

It had happened so fast that Lily hadn't even had time to shriek as she dropped like a stone into the hole that the road had vanished into. She landed on what felt like rubble, all hard edges and sticking-out bits, and the air spurted out of her lungs. She felt Dr Shawston land beside her. The next moment, he moved, covering her body with his, squeezing out whatever tiny bit of breath she still possessed. Not that she had any hope of moving, but she wanted to give him a shove and get rid of him. He pushed himself up on his elbows, one either side of her, and Lily felt rather than heard the whumps as debris from above landed on his back.

It landed around them as well, kicking up clouds of grit and dust, making Lily cough. When stillness descended on the hole, Dr Shawston stayed put.

Eventually Lily half-whispered, half-croaked, 'Get off me.'

'Just making sure nothing else is going to land on us.'

Lily lay utterly still, her heart pounding. Over the doctor's shoulder she could see the sides of the hole – and it was a hole, too, not a saucer-shaped crater – a hole with steep sides. What if they gave way and came pouring down on top of them?

Dr Shawston's face was close to hers. 'Keep still while I move. It'll take me a moment because I've got goodness knows what on top of me.'

Lily nodded. Dr Shawston placed one hand near her head, wriggled it a bit to ensure it was on something solid, then pushed himself up, locking his elbow. Puffs of dust rose as bits and pieces tumbled off his back. Bending his elbow, he then gave a shove that pushed him up once more and something crunched as it rolled from his back onto the floor of the hole.

'If you hadn't thrown yourself on top of me—' Lily began.

'You'd have got that whatever-it-was straight in the solar plexus.'

'Thank you,' Lily whispered.

'You're welcome. I'm going to have a cracker of a bruise on my back. Now keep still. There's stuff on top of my legs and I need to get them free. I also don't want to set off an avalanche.'

Dread slowed Lily's heartbeat. 'D'you think there might be one?'

'Let's not find out, shall we?'

He gradually worked his way out of the nest of debris. To Lily it seemed to take a lifetime. Lying awkwardly on her back, being jabbed and prodded by lumps of rubble, she looked past him up at the stars, which were inside a distressingly small circle high above. The rest of her vision was filled with the deepest blackness she'd ever seen. She couldn't help but picture the hole closing in on itself and burying them alive.

Then – a moving light – a shooting star? No, a beam of torchlight.

'Anyone down there?'

Lily tried to call, 'Here,' but her windpipe still seemed to be coated with grime.

'Two of us,' Dr Shawston called.

'Stay put. Help is on its way.'

Lily had to force herself not to weep with relief. Up above she could make out some heads poking over the edges. The men were obviously lying on the ground. Torchlight played down the rough sides of the hole and voices too quiet to be heard clearly at the bottom discussed what to do.

Then a ladder was fed down. Dr Shawston grabbed it and jammed it against the uneven ground, making it as steady as he could.

Turning to Lily, he held out his hand. 'Up you come.'

He hauled her to her feet, keeping hold as she steadied herself. Automatically she bent to pick up her bag. Whatever else you lost in wartime, you couldn't afford to lose your identity card. As she leaned over, her head swam and when she stood up straight again, it took a few seconds before she stopped feeling seasick.

'I'll hold the ladder for you,' said Dr Shawston.

Lily grasped the sides and placed her foot on the bottom rung. The men at the top offered words of encouragement, but Lily sensed there was more to this than she was aware of. As she approached the top, hands reached down to heave her back onto the road. No sooner had Dr Shawston joined her than the rescuers all suddenly rolled away from the mouth of the hole – just before it toppled in on itself.

'If rescue hadn't come when it did—' Lily whispered.

'But it did,' Dr Shawston said firmly. 'Are you all right? Covered in scrapes and bruises, I imagine. Does anything feel worse than that?'

She shook her head. Dr Shawston turned to speak to one of the rescuers. Lily waited for him.

'Dr Shawston?' she said.

He turned back to her. 'Yes?'

Simply but with great sincerity, she said, 'Thank you.'

He nodded. 'I see you've got the hang of saying Shawston at last. In that case, would you like to have a go at Vivian?'

* * *

Ivy's house still had its downstairs, but the upstairs was gone. Like many people facing such a calamity, Ivy focused on one single detail and became distressed about her bedroom curtains flapping feebly on top of a pile of rubble. Fortunately, one of her neighbours, Mrs Headley, intervened and soon the Dunbars were clustered around her kitchen table, supping tea, the adults smoking and comparing notes about the raid.

Abbie was pale and quiet as she sipped her tea.

'Are you all right?' Kitty murmured, leaving Ivy and Mrs Headley talking to one another.

Abbie nodded. 'Yes, thanks, Mum.'

Perhaps she shouldn't make anything of it, but Kitty couldn't stop herself. 'Mum?' she queried, raising her eyebrows.

'I'm too old for Mummy now.'

'Because you're fourteen?'

'Because I'm old enough to work in air raids.'

Kitty felt as if she'd had cold water dashed all over her. She had *loved* being Mummy, especially after the mothers of Abbie's friends and schoolfellows had one by one become Mum years ago. Being Mummy had made her feel cosy and close to her daughter. It had made her feel Abbie needed her.

Abbie leaned a little way towards her. 'I enjoyed working at the rest centre. I felt busy and useful. I felt grown-up. I *enjoyed* it. But if I'd known...' Her blue eyes were huge.

Kitty put a gentle hand on her arm. 'I know. It was an awful shock to come back here and see what had happened.'

It wasn't until Ivy spoke that Kitty realised the other two women had stopped talking to listen.

'Two things, Abbie,' Ivy said. 'One: it's good that you enjoyed being at the rest centre. It's good that you helped out and there's nothing wrong with feeling that what you're doing is important and worthwhile. And two: if you and your mum had stayed in the house like I wanted you to, you'd have been perfectly safe inside the Morrison shelter. I'm lucky. I only lost the top half of my house, but even if the whole lot had come tumbling down on top of you, you'd have been all right inside the Morrison. You'd just have had to wait to be dug out, that's all.'

'Your nan's right,' said Mrs Headley. 'The most important thing with an air raid is to keep your head during it and count your blessings afterwards.'

Abbie nodded and looked thoughtful. Maybe she was starting to realise there was more to being grown-up than she'd thought.

'Do you all need to be put up for the night?' Mrs Headley asked. 'I take it you aren't going to try to get home,' she said to Kitty.

'No,' said Kitty. 'Even if it was feasible...' She flicked a glance in Ivy's direction.

'You needn't stop here for my benefit,' Ivy declared at once, sounding more like herself.

'Don't be daft,' said Kitty. 'As if I'd leave you when you've been bombed.' She smiled at Mrs Headley. 'I reckon you've got some unexpected guests tonight, if you don't mind.'

'Not me,' Ivy said at once. 'I'm not leaving my house unattended. You hear about looters taking advantage in the blackout. I've already lost my upstairs and presumably all my bedroom furniture along with it. I'm dashed if I'll risk losing my downstairs things as well.'

'You can't go back in the house,' Kitty said, 'not until it's been declared safe.'

'Then I'll sit on the doorstep,' was Ivy's obstinate reply. Earlier on, shock had blurred the edges of her features, but now the sharp lines were back in place and the light of battle was in her blue eyes.

'Here's what we'll do,' said Kitty. 'Mrs Headley, please may Abbie stay here with you?' She gave her daughter a look and Abbie's protest vanished unspoken. To Ivy she said, 'You and I will go and spend the night over the road.'

'But what if the house isn't safe?' Abbie asked anxiously. 'What if it falls in on itself?'

'We'll be inside the Morrison, so we'll be fine,' said Kitty. 'It'll be your job to make sure we get dug out in the morning,' she joked.

'Don't fret, chick,' Ivy said to Abbie. 'The chances are that nowt will happen – no looters and no houses tumbling down. But I've lived at that house ever since I got wed. It's the house your dad was born in and I need to be in it for the rest of the night to make sure all's well.' Not entirely joking, she added, 'We'll take the frying pan and the poker into the Morrison with us, and heaven help anybody who tries to break in, that's all I can say. I'm in just the mood for bashing someone over the head.'

* * *

First thing the next morning, Kitty went to the nearest telephone box and put through a call to Mr Tulip. As she waited for the call to be connected, she crossed her fingers that he would be in his office. She felt sure he would be, because of the air raid last night.

'My dear Mrs Dunbar,' he said, 'please tell me that Dunbar's is unscathed.'

'As far as I know, it is,' she replied, 'but my mother-in-law's house in Withington has been badly damaged. Could you possibly send some of your men to collect her remaining furniture?'

'I'll put her at the top of the list. What's her address?'

Kitty tipped her head back and shut her eyes in pure relief. She gave Ivy's address. 'And everything needs to be taken to Dunbar's, please.'

'Of course.'

Kitty ended the call and returned to give Ivy the news.

'Are you sure about me moving in with you?' Ivy asked her.

A lot more sure than she would have been in the days before they had discovered how Bill had lied for years to Ivy about Kitty's supposed spending habits, that was for certain.

'Of course,' said Kitty. 'You'll be very welcome.' She laughed. 'And so will your furniture in the family flat. What we've got at present is basic, to say the least. It'll be nice for Abbie to have your things around her.'

'It'll be nice for me too,' said Ivy. 'Usually when folk go off to live with family after they've been bombed out, they won't see their belongings again until after the war.'

'You stay here and wait for Mr Tulip's men,' said Kitty, 'and I'll take Abbie home. We'll see you later.'

There were things to be done at Dunbar's, to make ready for the arrival of Ivy's belongings. Kitty wanted to shove the furniture in the family flat to one side so that Ivy's things could have pride of place. They also needed to set up a bedroom for her.

'Mr Tulip's men can bring down one of the spare beds from the third floor,' said Kitty, 'as well as a hanging cupboard and a chest of drawers.'

'All Mrs Dunbar's things will need cleaning when they get here,' said Lily. 'They'll be coated in household dust and probably plaster dust from the ceiling.'

'How did you get that graze on your chin?' Kitty asked, looking at her.

'I fell into a hole in the road,' said Lily.

'How on earth did you manage that?'

'Very easily,' Lily answered lightly. 'The ground opened up beneath my feet. No effort at all required on my part.'

'You're all right?' Kitty pressed, concerned.

'A few bruises, nothing more. I felt a bit stiff earlier, but giving Mrs Dunbar's furniture a good clean will loosen me up nicely.'

Kitty couldn't help thinking there was more to it than Lily was letting on, but she didn't push any further. There was a lot of work to get through today and by the end of it, she wanted Ivy to feel – well, as good as anybody could feel after they'd lost their home.

When Ivy arrived, she looked strained and tired. Kitty greeted her with a kiss on the cheek.

'Welcome to Dunbar's,' she said. 'Go up with Abbie and she'll show you your new home. Mr Tulip's men will be back presently to take your furniture upstairs after it's had a good clean.'

If Ivy was miffed at the suggestion her things needed cleaning, she took it on the chin. By early afternoon, with Lily's and Beatrice's help, the family flat had been transformed.

'It's strange seeing all your things here,' Abbie told her grandmother, 'but good-strange.'

Ivy said nothing. She must have felt overwhelmed.

'Let's all go down to the basement and have a cup of tea,' said Kitty. 'We could all do with a pick-me-up.'

Ivy broke her silence. 'Thank you all for working so hard today.'

'It's important to help one another,' said Beatrice.

On their way downstairs, the doorbell rang. It was a friend of Abbie's from school. Abbie looked at Kitty over her shoulder.

'Off you go,' Kitty said, understanding that Abbie would want to pour out all last night's experiences to an admiring audience.

The four women trooped down to the basement. Soon they were all grouped around the large table.

Kitty took a drink and then sighed. 'There's nothing that revives you like a cup of tea. Sorry,' she added, looking at her mother-in-law. 'It's going to take more than a cuppa to make you feel better.'

Ivy sat up straighter. 'Don't worry about me. I've lost my house and that's a terrible thing, but I've come directly to a new home and all my remaining things have come with me. That's more than a lot of folk can say. Before Mr Tulip's men came, I went down to the rest centre and filled in the forms for compensation, so that's all in hand. And I was given some toiletries and clothes.'

Beatrice said quietly, 'You must have helped plenty of others with all that in the past.'

'Aye, that's true enough,' said Ivy. 'I never imagined I'd be on the receiving end, but you never think of it happening to yourself, do you?'

Kitty decided to take advantage of Abbie's absence. 'Since Abbie isn't here, can we talk about the business? Specifically about money. You all know I've opened a post office account because of not having access to the Dunbar's bank account.' She gave Ivy a smile of acknowledgement for having had the idea in the first place.

'Has that sorted out the problem, then?' Lily asked.

'Up to a point,' said Kitty. 'We still need more income. The business needs more income.'

'I thought all your storage accommodation was full,' said Ivy.

'That's exactly it,' Kitty answered. 'The money the storage business generates isn't enough, not without access to the bank account. Somehow or other, I need to make more money.'

'How?' Beatrice asked.

'You tell me,' said Kitty. 'All ideas gratefully received. I don't see how the storage business can do more than it does already. I charge for the hire of tea chests and dust sheets and regular cleaning. I've been racking my brains but I can't think what other services I can possibly offer.'

They all looked at one another.

'I can think of something,' said Ivy.

The others turned to her immediately.

'What is it?' Kitty asked.

'The family flat,' said Ivy. 'You could rent it out, Kitty. You could be a landlady.'

'But you've only just moved in,' Kitty exclaimed.

'So what? Needs must. There are enough staff bedrooms for you, me and Abbie to move up to the third floor, aren't there? The flat has three bedrooms, and the sitting room looks better now with my furniture in it, though I do say so myself.'

'But... you've lost so much,' said Kitty. 'I don't think you should be making decisions like this just yet. You're still in shock.'

Ivy laughed, a harsh sound. 'I've lost my home and you've taken me in. That's you doing something for me. Now, thanks to my furniture, your family flat is good enough to rent out. That's me doing something for you. That's how it is with families. They help one another out. Don't say no, Kitty. It makes sense and you know it.'

Ivy was right, Kitty knew, but she still felt reluctant to chuck Ivy out of the family flat when she'd hardly moved in. Yet what other choice was there? Kitty was sure Abbie wouldn't mind moving up to the old staff bedrooms, but what would she make of her mother sending her grandmother up there?

The sound of the doorbell gave her the chance to dodge the conversation. She jumped to her feet and hurried up the stairs to the foyer.

She opened the door to find a handsome man outside. He was tall with broad shoulders. He politely raised his trilby to her, showing dark, slicked-back hair with the beginning of a widow's peak. His eyes were dark brown and he had a strong jawline. Kitty reckoned he was about the same age as she was, maybe a little older.

'Can I help you?' she asked.

'I hope so. I'm looking for Mrs Chadwick, Mrs Lily Chadwick.

We took part in a rescue last night and I've come to let her know how the children are.'

Kitty blinked. Lily had rescued children? It was the first she'd heard of it.

When she didn't immediately reply, the man spoke again.

'I'm Dr Vivian Shawston. Is this where Mrs Chadwick lives?'

Kitty pulled herself together. 'Yes, she does live here, but I'm not sure if she's in at present. If you don't mind waiting, I'll go and see.' Should she invite him into the foyer? No, this wasn't a hotel now. She closed the door quietly.

She went through the basement door and down the stairs. At the bottom, she addressed Lily without going into the kitchen.

'Lily, could I borrow you for a moment, please?'

Turning, she headed upstairs again, obliging Lily to follow. Halfway up, she stopped.

'There's a Dr Shawston here to see you, Lily,' she said softly. 'He doesn't know you're here, so I can send him on his way if you like. What do you want me to do?'

* * *

Lily opened one of the double doors a fraction and peeped through. Yes, it was Dr Shawston. Well, of course it was. Kitty had said so. Lily's heart delivered an unexpected thump.

He raised his hat to her and was about to speak but she forestalled him.

'What do you want?' Her voice was low, not much above a whisper, as if the other residents of Dunbar's were hovering in the foyer behind her, dying to listen in.

Dr Shawston's eyebrows lifted. 'To see you, obviously.'

'How did you know where I live?'

'This is the address you gave to the police constable who took our statements.'

'Oh.'

'I didn't creep after you through the darkened streets, if that's what you're thinking. Incidentally, if you'd care to open the door a trifle further, I promise not to come storming in.'

Heat touched Lily's cheeks. Feeling wrong-footed, she opened the door properly. She also took a step closer to the doorway so Dr Shawston didn't get any fancy ideas about nipping inside.

She shifted uncomfortably. 'If you've come to see how I am, I'm fine, thank you. Just one or two bruises.'

'Same here,' he answered, and Lily remembered the debris landing on his back as he used his strong frame to shield her from injury.

'Are you really all right?' she asked, concerned.

His smile made his eyes crinkle. 'I'll do. The bruising has revived memories of my grandmother's sage and vinegar poultices. The vinegar was to bring the bruise to the surface and the sage was to soothe it.'

Lily couldn't help returning his smile. 'It sounds very old-fashioned.'

'There's a lot to be said for these old remedies. My grandmother was one of the first lady-pharmacists. She was obliged to give it up, of course, when she got married.'

'She must have been clever to train for something like that,' said Lily. 'But imagine having to give it all up.'

She stopped speaking. For a few moments she had felt comfortable in his presence, but now she remembered that she was supposed to be feeling awkward.

Awkward? Why?

Dr Shawston said, 'What brings me here – other than to make

sure you're still in one piece – is that I thought you'd like to know how the children from last night are faring.'

Lily brightened. Of course. That made sense. He probably worked at the hospital where the children had been taken. How silly of her to fear there was a personal reason behind this visit.

'How are they?' She could hear the confidence in her voice now that she understood why he had turned up on her doorstep.

'They're all fine. They were kept in overnight and they'll be allowed home later today, along with strict instructions not to use a water tank as a playground again.'

'Let's hope they listen,' said Lily. 'You know what children are like.'

'Two of the ones who were rescued are twins. I'm sure you can appreciate what an emotional upheaval this has been for their mother. She'd very much like to meet you so she can thank you.'

'There's really no need,' said Lily. 'I'm just glad everyone survived.'

'It would mean a lot to Mrs Jenner,' said Dr Shawston. 'It might also help the children realise their larks put adults in danger too. Mrs Jenner has already said, "What if Mrs Chadwick had died saving you? What about her family if that had happened?"'

'I don't have a family,' Lily said, her voice suddenly tight.

'I'm sorry to hear that,' he said softly.

Annoyance bubbled up inside Lily, making her heat up inside. 'Are you? Sorry? Sorry I'm on my own?' A breathy laugh burst from her in a scornful sound. 'As I recall, you were the one who invited me to use your first name after we were rescued. You like trying it on with girls, do you? Even though you knew I'm a Mrs?'

'I apologise if I sounded flirtatious. Put it down to the adrenaline that was sloshing around in my system. That, and my admiration for your courage. Forgive me, Mrs Chadwick, but if you don't have a family, does that mean you're a war widow?'

She could have said, she *should* have said, 'I'm happily married,' but the words that came out were, 'I'm separated.' She quickly added, 'As for going to see Mrs Jenner, I don't know.'

'There's no time to mull it over, I'm afraid,' said Dr Shawston. 'The children will be discharged shortly, so it's now or never. What d'you say, Mrs Chadwick? Will you let me take you to the hospital?'

10

Kitty had pressed her linen jacket the previous evening. Now, she put it on over a blouse and skirt and looked in the mirror to put on her blue felt hat. It had a pleat at the front of the brim, which she thought very elegant. It had been what had sold the hat to her in the first place, back before the war. She'd felt guilty buying it because, even though it was moderately priced, it looked costly, and she'd *never* wanted to appear extravagant in front of Bill in case he threw it in her face when she complained about his own spending.

She wanted to wear the hat today because she was going to see Fay Brewer at the Town Hall. When Miss Brewer was out and about, she wore a hat with a jaunty feather, and Kitty wanted to show that she could be stylish too. Not out of competition or jealousy, but simply because Fay Brewer was the sort of person who made you feel good about yourself.

Kitty picked up her leather handbag, slung her gas-mask box over her shoulder and headed downstairs. Just as she was about to open the front door, the bell rang.

She swung open the door to find Naomi on the step. For once, she wasn't in her WVS uniform, but was wearing a becoming suit with a long jacket that was trimmed with a bow of wide ribbon on each of the hip-level pockets and also on the breast pocket. Trust Naomi to turn make-do-and-end into something eye-catching.

She took one look at Kitty and burst out laughing, her blue eyes twinkling. 'If I didn't already know May was here, I'd know now. Look at you in your linen!'

Kitty laughed too. It had been one of Mam's rules. You could wear linen from the beginning of May until the middle of September – which, for Mam, had meant never, because she'd never possessed the money to have clothes that could only be worn at certain times of the year. Kitty's laughter subsided into a shaky sigh. She never stopped missing Mam.

'What brings you here?' she asked Naomi.

'Charming!' Naomi answered lightly. 'You might at least have said, "What a wonderful surprise, sister, dear", but apparently that's too much to ask for.'

'Idiot,' Kitty retorted affectionately. 'It *is* a lovely surprise.'

'And you obviously read my mind and dressed for the occasion,' said Naomi. 'That hat suits you. You should wear it more often.'

'Thanks,' Kitty said, pleased with the compliment. 'What occasion?'

'I knew you didn't have WVS today, so I thought we could amble around the shops and lament the lack of stock, then have a cup of tea and a slice of carrot cake at the Claremont. My treat.'

'That sounds perfect, but—'

'You've already got plans,' Naomi finished.

Kitty set everything aside. 'Nothing that can't wait. I'd love us to spend the morning together.'

She locked up behind her and they set off for Market Street, where they wandered around Ingleby's, Affleck & Brown's and Flittick & Green's. Kitty could never pass through the doors of the latter department store without recalling the day back when Abbie was a new baby, when she'd found out the shocking truth about the extent of Bill's extravagance.

Afterwards, they made their way to the Claremont, where the doorman in his braided uniform opened the door to admit them to the gracious foyer.

'I love this,' said Naomi. 'Never mind all the sandbags lining the front of the building and the anti-blast tape on the windows. The moment you set foot in here, it's like stepping back in time.'

'This is what their guests pay for,' Kitty replied, quashing a pang for dear old Dunbar's Hotel. 'The handsome furniture, the plants, the sweet little alcoves where couples can be private.'

'The quietly spoken staff,' Naomi added, 'even if they are all as old as the hills because the young ones have been called up.'

Soon they were seated comfortably in one of the alcoves on the far side of the foyer, with tea and cake in front of them.

'Shall I be mother?' Naomi lifted the teapot.

'This feels very decadent,' Kitty told her appreciatively. 'Thank you.'

'Pleasure,' her sister replied. 'Actually, I thought you might have popped round to see me before this. I had to hear on the WVS grapevine about Mrs Dunbar's house taking a hit, and her moving in with you.' Naomi's finely arched eyebrows lifted enquiringly.

'Steady on!' Kitty exclaimed, replacing her slice of cake on the plate. 'It only happened two or three days ago – the night of Abbie's birthday – and what with getting Mrs Dunbar moved in—'

'I know, I know,' Naomi said in a conciliatory tone. Leaning across, she dropped her voice to a confidential note. 'But honestly,

Kitty – Mrs Dunbar! Living with you! I know there isn't any love lost.'

'Things are a lot better between us than they once were.'

'They'd need to be,' Naomi answered drily.

'And it's fortunate that they are,' Kitty said stoutly, 'because what else could I have done aside from invite her?'

'True,' Naomi agreed. 'I just hope you don't live to rue the day.'

'I'm sure I shan't,' said Kitty.

'So, is she living with you and Abbie in the family flat or have you stuck her up in the attic?'

'The third floor isn't an attic,' Kitty replied. 'It's the old staff accommodation. Since you ask, all of us are up there now. I'm going to rent out the flat to bring in more income – or at least I hope I am. I need to speak to someone at the Town Hall first.'

All at once, Naomi stopped needling her and looked concerned. 'Kitty, you can't! You can't possibly take on any more work.'

'I need the money,' Kitty repeated.

'Doesn't the storage business make enough?' Naomi asked.

'I need something where people will pay the bill directly to me, not to Dunbar's,' Kitty explained. 'The storage business brings in an ample amount but, as you know, I can't touch most of it.'

Naomi frowned thoughtfully. 'Even so, you've managed this far.'

'I've kept things ticking over,' Kitty replied.

'Ticking over is as much as you need to do,' Naomi said firmly. 'Honestly, Kitty, you don't have to do anything more than that – and why would you, after the way Bill has behaved? Listen to me. You're my little sister and I don't want you wearing yourself to a frazzle.'

Kitty's heart melted. 'You're always thinking of what's best for me.'

'Yes, I am,' said Naomi. 'Besides, who's to say what sort of lodgers you'd end up with? Once the billeting officer gets his hooks into you, you won't have a choice. You could end up with *any*one.'

That made Kitty laugh. 'If we're all murdered in our beds by the lodgers, you can have "I told you so" engraved on my headstone.'

'I'm serious, Kitty,' Naomi insisted. 'What you're contemplating is a lot more work. Please reconsider. You said yourself that I'm only thinking of what's best for you.'

* * *

Later, on her way to the Town Hall to see Fay Brewer, Kitty thought about Naomi's advice. She appreciated her sister's love and concern, but Naomi could be overprotective, and this was one of those times. Naomi's mother-hen instincts had come racing to the fore ever since Kitty had set up the storage business. Kitty smiled to herself. If she'd listened to her sister's advice, she'd never have set up in business at all.

At the Town Hall, she went to see Fay Brewer. She spoke to one of the ladies on reception, who picked up the internal telephone and made a quick call.

'If you don't mind waiting,' she said to Kitty, 'Miss Brewer will be down to collect you shortly.'

Miss Brewer took Kitty upstairs into a large office with a number of desks and cupboards. The other desks were arranged such that when someone sat behind them, their back was to the wall, but Fay Brewer headed for a desk the other way round, with its chair backing the room. She picked up an empty chair from another desk for Kitty and turned her own chair around to face it, without the barrier of a desk in between them.

'What can I do for you?' she asked pleasantly.

'Two things,' said Kitty, 'and one of them – well, you may find it rather cheeky.' She broke off, chewing her lip.

'Let's get that one out of the way first, then, shall we?' Miss Brewer suggested, sounding not at all fazed.

Kitty explained about wanting to pay herself a salary. 'I thought that if you would kindly give me an indication of what you earn, then I could knock a bit off and award myself that.'

'Why knock any off?'

'You have so much more experience in the workplace than I have.'

'Don't put yourself down,' Miss Brewer advised with some spirit. 'I'm all in favour of women earning every penny they're worth.'

Realising she hadn't given offence, Kitty relaxed. 'Are you talking about equal pay?'

Fay Brewer leaned forward, her hazel eyes, which were normally either soft with kindness or twinkly with wit, now serious. 'I certainly am. Did you know that men in general earn a third more than women for doing the same job? And some men earn double.' She sat back, saying drily, 'You may have noticed that it's a pet hate of mine.' With a chuckle, she added, 'I think it comes of having a twin brother. I've never been able to see why boys are given so many advantages.' Smiling at Kitty, she told her, 'I don't mind you knowing that I'm paid three pounds twelve shillings a week, minus tax.'

'Three pounds twelve,' Kitty repeated, committing it to memory. 'Thank you.'

'You're welcome,' Fay Brewer replied. 'Have you heard of this new tax system that's being brought in later this year? Your employer will have to work out your tax for you and deduct it from your wages before you get paid.'

'How weird,' Kitty commented, not sure what to make of it.

'Still, it won't apply to you,' Miss Brewer said with a smile, 'because you're your own employer. Anyway, I digress. You said there were two things you wanted to talk about?'

'That's right,' said Kitty. 'My daughter and I, and now my mother-in-law as well, all live in a flat inside Dunbar's. We've decided to move upstairs into the old staff accommodation and rent out the family flat – assuming the Corporation doesn't mind.'

'Why would the Corporation mind?'

'Because of the permission to change the use of the building,' said Kitty.

'That was when Dunbar's changed from being a hotel to becoming a storage house. If you wish to rent out the flat, that's none of the Corporation's business.' Miss Brewer smiled. 'It's the billeting officer you need to speak to, not me. Although...' she added, then stopped.

'Yes?' Kitty prompted.

'How many bedrooms does the flat have?'

'Three. Well, to be honest, one of them is really the box room, so it's not very big. The flat has its own bathroom, but not a kitchen. My mother-in-law is going to do the catering for the lodgers. That will be included in the rent.'

'I'd rather not go into detail just now in case it comes to nothing,' said Fay Brewer, 'but would you mind awfully if I ask you to postpone seeing the billeting officer just for today?'

It was clear that she had something in mind and Kitty was more than happy to trust her. Miss Brewer had never let her down.

Kitty went home and settled down to write some bills for her clients. Mr Fordyce, Mr Michaels, Mr Arbuthnot and others wrote cheques to Dunbar's regular as clockwork and a rebellious part of her was briefly tempted not to bother billing them. Why fill the coffers at the bank just so Bill could dip his fingers in? But if she ever failed in her duty, he would bring Mr Loftus's authority down on her like a ton of bricks, making her name mud in the business world. She couldn't afford to let that happen.

Abbie arrived home from school and started her homework. Ivy was busy ironing. Kitty smiled to herself: that was one advantage to having her mother-in-law living here. She watched as Ivy stood the iron on a newspaper for twenty seconds. A scorched newspaper would mean the iron was too hot for rayon.

Shortly after six, there was a tap on the door and Beatrice walked in.

'Evening,' she said. 'Kitty, Fay Brewer walked home with me. She'd like to see you.'

Kitty closed her ledger and stood up, trying to see past Beatrice. 'Don't stand in the way,' she said, smiling. 'Send her in.'

'She's waiting in the foyer,' said Beatrice. 'I took the liberty of inviting her up, but she said she'd rather wait downstairs.'

'For a word in private, I suppose,' said Ivy, without looking up from her ironing.

Kitty went down. Would this be to do with what Miss Brewer had talked about – or rather, what she had *not* talked about – in her office that morning?

Fay Brewer tilted her face upwards as Kitty descended the stairs. She was smiling and Kitty smiled back. She liked and admired Miss Fay Brewer.

'Good news,' Miss Brewer said. 'Your first lodgers, if you want them.'

'I must admit I did suspect when you dropped hints earlier,' said Kitty.

She ushered her visitor into the former dining room and they sat down.

'It's three girls from the Town Hall,' said Fay Brewer. 'They're here on secondment from London. Their stay has just been extended by a few weeks, but their landlady has already got new people lined up to have their rooms.'

'And you're going to send them to Dunbar's.'

'If you're happy to have them. You'd be doing them a huge favour.'

'It sounds ideal,' said Kitty.

'It's not permanent. They'd be here until the end of July or early August. I'd understand if you'd prefer to have proper lodgers.'

'By "proper", you mean long-term?' Kitty asked. 'In wartime we do what's needed. These girls need a billet and I can provide it. We'll need a day or two to get the flat ready because we're still living in it, but after that they can come as soon as they like.'

* * *

Lily changed her library books and walked home to Dunbar's. It was her turn to do the cooking. She had chopped up the vegetables earlier and left them in a pan of water. Now she needed to slice up the cabbage for the coleslaw and prepare the fish. It wouldn't take long. Fish stew wasn't like meat stew, where you had to cook the meat for ages.

Kitty, Abbie and Mrs Dunbar were all upstairs in the family flat and Beatrice would be home from the office presently. Lily took her books up to her little bedroom, made sure her hair was tidy and came back downstairs. How different Dunbar's was now, how quiet compared to when it had been a thriving hotel. But at least she was still here. Dunbar's had been, and continued to be, her refuge in troubled times.

She was halfway down the basement stairs when the doorbell sounded. She turned and went back up, smiling to herself. As a Dunbar's chambermaid, she had never been allowed anywhere near the front door.

She opened the door and her heart seemed to stutter. Dr Shawston was outside, with another man.

'Mrs Chadwick.' The doctor raised his trilby. 'I hope this isn't an inconvenient moment.'

Lily stared up at him. More than stared – positively gawped. She shut her mouth with a snap.

Dr Shawston cleared his throat. 'This is Mr Marsden. He is the father of the third child we saved from under the tarpaulins, and he would like to thank you.'

Mr Marsden lifted his hat politely, but his light-blue eyes showed his discomfort.

'I'm sorry to intrude,' he said. 'I can see you're busy. I shouldn't have allowed myself to be persuaded—'

Lily recalled her manners. 'Not at all, Mr Marsden. It's just a surprise, that's all.'

'May we come in?' Dr Shawston asked. 'Just for a minute. This isn't the kind of thing that can be said on the doorstep.'

'Of course. Please do – just for a minute,' Lily added, repeating the doctor's words. 'I've got the meal to prepare.'

The men walked in, carrying their hats. Lily showed them into the old dining room, her eyes quickly scanning it. It was always clean and tidy. They hardly used it. Not that that was any reason to let the dust gather if you'd been trained in the Dunbar way.

'Permit me to perform proper introductions,' said Dr Shawston. Lily thought him very suave. 'Mrs Chadwick, may I present

Mr Marsden, who would very much like to thank you for your part in the rescue of his daughter. Mr Marsden – Mrs Chadwick.'

They both said, 'How do you do,' and Lily waved her visitors towards chairs. She didn't want them to sit down and get comfy, but she had to be polite.

Mr Marsden didn't waste any time. 'Mrs Chadwick, thank you for seeing me like this. I was told by the mother of a couple of Rowena's friends that one of the rescuers was a doctor, so I went to the hospital in the hope of finding him in order to thank him for his part in saving my daughter's life. He told me about you and – well, here I am. I apologise for the intrusion, but that was a remarkable thing you did – both of you. The thought of my little girl—' He had to clear his throat. 'She wouldn't thank me for calling her a little girl. She's my eldest.'

'Rowena's a pretty name,' said Lily.

That made him smile. His discomfort at having barged in fell away and Lily realised he was good-looking, though nothing like as handsome as Dr Shawston. She felt a little jolt inside. When had she noticed Dr Shawston's looks?

'Thank you, yes,' said Mr Marsden. 'It was her mother's choice.'

'Mrs Marsden must be relieved to have her back safe and sound,' said Lily. 'Please tell her there's no need for her to come here and thank me.'

'Would that she could,' said Mr Marsden. 'I'm afraid I'm a widower.'

'Then Rowena must be all the more precious to you,' said Dr Shawston, and Lily looked at him admiringly. It was exactly the right thing to say. As a doctor, he must often be in the position of having to speak words of comfort, but something told her this wasn't just professional finesse. Dr Shawston was a man of real kindness and compassion, maybe even charm. Now where had that thought sprung from?

Hearing the front door open, Lily jumped up and hurried across to the door to see Beatrice in the foyer.

'Come in and let me introduce you.'

The two men rose to their feet as Beatrice appeared in the doorway. Lily expected Beatrice's eyes to settle on Dr Shawston because he was the handsome one, but instead she stared straight at Mr Marsden.

'Frank!' she exclaimed.

* * *

It wasn't long to wait until the evening meal. Kitty had decided to tell the others all together at the table. Lily had made a stew of white fish, vegetables and chunks of potato, seasoned with herbs, which she served with coleslaw, containing chopped chives instead of onion. Onions were precious these days.

As the five of them ate, Kitty explained about having tenants for the flat.

'Just for now, until they go back to London in the summer, but it'll get us started.'

She had deliberately chosen to have this conversation in front of Abbie. Not only was Abbie directly affected, but it was high time Kitty started treating her in a more grown-up way.

'That's excellent news,' said Beatrice.

'We'll have to move upstairs as soon as we can,' said Abbie.

Kitty looked at Ivy. 'Are you still sure about using your things to furnish the flat?'

Ivy nodded. 'I'd be a pretty poor sort if I chopped and changed my mind.'

Kitty realised Abbie was regarding her closely.

'Shouldn't you look more pleased about this, Mum?'

'Whatever d'you mean?' Kitty asked breezily. 'Of course I'm pleased.' Then, with all eyes on her, she opted to tell the truth. 'Well, I'm pleased up to a point.' She released a sigh. 'To be honest, the thought of becoming a landlady doesn't exactly thrill me.'

'But you wanted another way of bringing in money,' said Lily.

'I did. I do,' said Kitty, 'but I'd imagined more of a business opportunity.'

'Taking in lodgers is a business opportunity, as you call it,' Ivy said crisply. 'A job is what I'd call it.'

'I don't mean any disrespect to landladies,' said Kitty, 'but I don't see myself as one. What I loved about setting up the storage business was that it was new and different, a real challenge. It made me see what I'm capable of.'

Ivy snorted. 'Hark at you! Don't you fancy yourself all of a sudden! Is making beds and cooking meals too good for you now?'

'Of course not.' Kitty had to quell the urge to say 'Not in front of Abbie'. She had decided to include her daughter and now she had to stand by that choice. Speaking to Abbie, she went on, 'There's nothing wrong with being a landlady. It's hard work if it's done properly, and a good landlady is loved and appreciated by her lodgers. To them, she's worth her weight in gold. But the war has opened my eyes to what women are capable of, and I don't want to do something that is traditionally what women do. I'd like the chance to try something more.'

'Like you've already done with the storage business,' said Abbie.

'Exactly,' said Kitty. 'I'm glad you understand.' She looked at Ivy, willing her to understand too.

'It's a good job you've got me here, then, isn't it?' said Ivy. 'I'm not at all stuffy about being a landlady. In fact, I'd enjoy it. So you can go looking for whatever it is you're looking for, Kitty, and I'll look after the lodgers.'

'Are you sure?' Beatrice asked.

'It'll suit me fine,' said Ivy. 'It'll be a way for me to earn my keep here.'

'You don't need to earn your keep,' Kitty said at once.

Ivy ignored that. 'I'll like working in Dunbar's. Jeremiah Dunbar was my brother-in-law, don't forget. My husband was his younger brother and so Jeremiah inherited the hotel. It wasn't always easy having to watch from afar, I can tell you, especially as me and Miriam, Jeremiah's wife, never saw eye to eye. She liked nowt better than being Lady Dunbar.'

Abbie frowned. 'She wasn't really Lady Dunbar, was she?'

'No, she was plain Mrs,' said Ivy, 'but you'd never have known it. So for me to work here in the old Dunbar's Hotel, looking after guests, being their landlady – I reckon that'll suit me down to the ground.'

* * *

It was all change at Dunbar's. Beatrice had been very happy with things the way they were previously and she'd have liked them to continue in the same vein, but that was selfish and probably unpatriotic. The new lodgers had moved in and the Dunbar family now slept on the third floor. The lodgers were Miss Tennant, Miss O'Brien and Miss Gregson, all girls in their twenties, and they couldn't have been more delighted with their billet.

'Our previous landlady crammed the three of us into one bedroom. There wasn't room to swing the proverbial cat,' said Miss O'Brien, a good-looking girl with merry eyes. 'This is a palace by comparison.'

'We've even got our own bathroom,' said tall, willowy Miss Tennant. 'That beats having to queue along the landing.'

'And we've got a sitting room,' Miss Gregson added. 'We'll refuse to go back to London at this rate.'

Mrs Ivy Dunbar was in her element, which included laying the law down left, right and centre.

'The girls' – the lodgers had immediately become 'the girls' – 'will have their meals with us downstairs in the kitchen. We'll all eat together at the big table.'

Beatrice wasn't sure how she felt about that. She had enjoyed being one of a 'family' of four – herself, Kitty, Lily and Abbie. Then Mrs Ivy Dunbar had moved in and before Beatrice had had time to get used to that, now there were three more around the table. Yes, it was lively and the girls were pleasant and easy to get on with, but the atmosphere of confidentiality had gone.

But the new girls made a fuss of Abbie and talked to her about film stars and hair styles. Abbie lapped it all up, which was lovely to see and, as far as Beatrice was concerned, more than made up for anything that had been lost.

If she, Kitty and Lily were to continue to be close to one another, then it was up to them to make sure it happened. They had been able to talk to one another about anything – such as Frank. Oh, glory. Beatrice wasn't at all sure she wanted to talk about him at the moment. She simply didn't know what she could say. Seeing him here in Dunbar's had come as a huge shock. Here – in Dunbar's, in her home. She had felt all fluttery, what her mother used to call all of a doo-dah, for days afterwards.

Which just went to show how stupid she was. Frank had left her behind long ago, him with his five children. But one thing Beatrice had picked up from Lily was that he was a widower. She wasn't sure if that made things better or worse. Worse for him, obviously – but for herself? It was irrelevant to her because –

because she was never going to see him again. His coming here that time had been a fluke. He'd been brought here so he could thank Lily – and why did that made Beatrice's ribs tighten? Was she envious? If she'd been out on WVS duty on that fateful evening, she might have been the one—

No. Thinking like that made her worse than stupid. Imagining herself rescuing Rowena – honestly!

It was high time she put Frank out of her mind. She was glad his daughter had been rescued and that was all there was to it.

She vowed to focus on her work. That was her real life. The rest was just a silly dream. Not even that. Just... a disturbance. The sooner she smoothed it over, the better.

Besides, she felt sure Miss Brewster was up to something. She had vanished from the office several times recently without telling Beatrice where she was going. Not that she was obliged to say anything, but she always had before. And last week Beatrice had found her looking through Beatrice's early case notes from when she'd been new in the Welfare Department.

'Can I help you with anything?' Beatrice had asked.

To which the answer had been a brisk, 'No, thank you,' that had rendered it impossible to ask further questions.

Now, heading up the stairs in the Town Hall first thing in the morning, Beatrice half-listened to other people talking to one another about British troops invading Madagascar so as to forestall the Japanese. It was important, of course. All war news was important, but Beatrice couldn't help feeling more interested in Princess Elizabeth having signed up to do war work.

Soon she was at her desk. Miss Brewster had left her a stack of files to put into alphabetical order and Beatrice took the opportunity to skim through the contents while she was at it.

Miss Brewster walked in halfway through the morning. She held up her chin in a way that radiated superiority.

'There you are, Miss Inkerman.' She made it sound as if Beatrice had just come racing in, horribly late and out of breath. 'Good. I need a list from you, please.'

'Of course,' said Beatrice.

'I require the names, addresses and schools of all the children who attend that ridiculous club of yours for children with responsibilities.'

'But – why?'

Miss Brewster's thin eyebrows climbed up her forehead. 'I'm not required to explain myself to you, Miss Inkerman. Kindly furnish me with the information I have requested.'

Beatrice's heart beat hard. Struggling for a steady voice, she said, 'I'm not sure you're entitled to it, Miss Brewster. The Time Off Club doesn't belong to the Corporation. It's something I personally set up before I worked here.'

'Indeed you did – with Miss Fay Brewer's assistance. She's the one who made use of Corporation information to identify the children, which I think means you'll find I am entitled to those names and addresses. It's no good pressing your lips together like that, as if nothing will prise them apart. If you decline to assist me, I will come to Dunbar's myself and get the information from the children, and after that I will report you for insubordination.'

Beatrice gave in. She had no option. Not for her own sake but because if Miss Brewster came to Dunbar's and hectored the children, she might frighten them off from coming back again, and Beatrice couldn't allow that to happen.

'Thank you,' Miss Brewster said. 'Have the list typed out in full for me by dinnertime. I need to check it against my own list. I wouldn't want to miss anyone out.'

She looked at Beatrice and waited. Beatrice knew what she wanted and didn't want to provide it, but on the other hand she really needed to know.

'Miss anyone out of what, Miss Brewster, if I might ask?'

Miss Brewster didn't reply at once. She made a show of straightening her already tidy desk. Then she stood up with a tight smile.

'I'm tired of standing by while you, Miss Brewer and others with bleeding hearts allow a disgraceful system to continue, Miss Inkerman. Therefore I am making arrangements for the children with responsibilities to be evacuated.'

11

When Lily opened the front door and found Dr Shawston on the step, it ought to have come as a surprise, but for some reason it didn't. Deep down, she had known he would turn up again to see her. To see *her*. She didn't want to think about that too closely and she definitely didn't want to acknowledge the tiny feeling of pleasure that dared to unfurl inside her.

'Dr Shawston.' She made sure to inject a note of surprise into her tone.

'Mrs Chadwick.' He raised his hat. 'I'm afraid I haven't brought anyone with me today to oblige you to let us in.'

Now she really was surprised. 'Do you mean you brought Mr Marsden here simply to get over the threshold?'

He gave her a half-smile. 'Can you blame me? I wanted to see you again.'

Lily restrained herself from folding her arms as annoyance flared up. 'Yes, I do blame you, since you mention it. How could you drag that poor man here under false pretences?'

'Not entirely false. It's true he was keen to thank you.'

'To thank me, maybe,' Lily conceded, 'but to be brought out of his way to do it? I don't think so.'

Dr Shawston looked straight at her. 'It was a choice between enlisting Marsden's unwitting help and turning up here alone and inviting you to have dinner with me.'

Heat flooded Lily's face. It was all she could do not to turn away. She was determined not to do that. It was bad enough that her cheeks felt beetroot-red without her looking like a coward as well.

'I think you should go,' she said.

'I think you should tell me the meaning of that blush,' he replied, his eyes never leaving hers. 'A blush of embarrassment because I'm an insufferable clod who's making a nuisance of himself – or a blush of delight because you're as intrigued as I am and you'd like to know what might transpire between us?'

'I can assure you I'm not in the slightest bit intrigued,' Lily retorted.

'And yet you don't claim not to be embarrassed.' He tilted his head to one side as if assessing her reaction. 'There's hope for me yet,' he added, his tone mocking himself, not her.

'Hope for what?' As soon as the words were out, Lily wished she hadn't asked.

It was a moment before he answered.

'Clearly there's no hope of being invited inside, so I'll pin my hopes on your willingness to come for a walk with me.'

'I'm not interested in being taken out, thank you,' Lily said primly.

'It's just a walk, Mrs Chadwick. Not dinner and dancing at the Midland Hotel, not even beans on toast at the Worker Bee café. Just a stroll in the May sunshine.'

Another refusal was on Lily's lips. It wasn't so much that she wanted to say no as that she knew she ought to. But just then she spied Abbie coming along the street on her way home from school. She didn't want the girl overhearing anything as she mounted the steps and entered the foyer. She definitely didn't want Abbie dragging her feet while her ears flapped frantically.

'I'll meet you on the corner,' Lily said quickly.

She stepped back and closed the door. Feeling unbearably foolish, she ran all the way up to her bedroom, leaving her door slightly ajar so she could listen for Abbie's arrival. One of the rooms up here had been turned into a sitting room for Kitty, Abbie and Mrs Ivy Dunbar. Beatrice had one as well. Lily was the only member of the household not to want one for herself.

She waited for Abbie to disappear into the family sitting room, then she grabbed her outdoor things and made a dash for it.

Outside, Dr Shawston was waiting at the corner. He didn't walk towards her. Should she be pleased or disappointed?

Without any words being spoken, they set off side by side. He didn't offer his arm, which saved her from refusing it. She didn't want anybody who saw them to imagine there was anything going on.

It wasn't until they'd left Lily Street and turned right onto Oxford Road that Dr Shawston spoke, having first changed sides so he was walking between her and the road like a proper gentleman.

'I like you, Mrs Chadwick,' he said in a conversational tone, 'and you've said you're separated, so I feel there's no harm in it.'

'I don't know what you expect me to say to that,' Lily answered.

'Well, it didn't make you storm off in a huff, so presumably you aren't offended.'

Drat. She'd missed her chance to leave him standing.

'I still don't know what I'm supposed to say.'

'That's all right,' he replied. 'If you're separated, naturally you feel wary.'

'There's nothing to be wary about,' Lily answered. 'Wariness would suggest... well, that something was going on.'

'Or that something could be about to start,' he said.

Lily didn't reply to that. What on earth did she think she was doing? She ought to turn on her heel and march back to Dunbar's, having first told him in no uncertain terms to leave her alone in future. That was what she ought to do, but somehow she didn't do it. She wanted to see what was going to happen.

'Let me tell you how I see it,' said Dr Shawston. 'You're beautiful and courageous.'

'I'm not!' Lily said at once.

'You can't deny you're brave after what you did when the children ended up in the drink, so maybe you think you're not beautiful. Have you looked in a mirror recently? Your eyes are the blue of forget-me-nots and you're as dainty as a pixie.'

'Stop,' said Lily, aware of speaking far too late. She ought to have stopped him before he was halfway through the first sentence.

A bus went past. Lily suddenly had the feeling she was in full view. She turned right at the next corner. Down here was the bomb site where Abbie had hurt her ankle and ended up being brought home by Beatrice. That was how Beatrice had met the Dunbars.

'Mrs Chadwick,' said Dr Shawston, 'I would very dearly like the chance to get to know you. Will you please say yes to that? Or... is your separation still too raw?'

Lily hesitated, then found to her surprise that she wanted to say this. 'It isn't the separation. It's my son.'

'The last thing I would want is to make things awkward between you and your child.'

'He died,' Lily said flatly. 'Just over a year ago.'

Was she really saying this? She *never* told strangers. She didn't even speak of it to people she knew.

'I'm very sorry to hear it,' Dr Shawston said quietly. 'You have my deepest sympathy.'

'I'm making more of an effort to live my life,' Lily said as steadily as she could. 'It's blossom time. I could torture myself with thoughts of Toby being enchanted by stray blossom petals landing on his head, but instead I choose to enjoy the signs of springtime. I don't know if it's possible to make yourself happy simply by choosing to be, but I know for certain that you can thrust yourself deep into unhappiness. That's something I am trying to train myself out of. It feels trite to say that I have to live my life to the fullest to honour my son's memory, but I know I absolutely must not wallow in the depths of grief.'

'I'm sure that it isn't a question of wallowing,' Dr Shawston said gently. 'Losing a child has to be the worst bereavement there is.'

Lily shook her head. She might sound as if she had the answers, but she didn't really.

Silence fell between them, then Dr Shawston said, 'Mrs Chadwick, will you allow me to be a part of the full life you hope to lead?'

* * *

Beatrice stood just outside the club room's open door, looking in at the Time Off Club children. Almost all of them were girls but she had a couple of boys too. They were a mixture of ages. Some would shortly leave school, while the youngest were only seven or eight – heartbreakingly young to carry so much responsibility, but for them, as indeed for all these youngsters, this was their ordinary everyday life.

Kitty came and stood by her shoulder.

'You look thoughtful,' she said quietly. She looked not at Beatrice but into the room at the children. 'Are you remembering your own childhood?'

'It's partly that,' said Beatrice. 'I remember what it was like knowing that the other children in our road had normal lives, with mums who looked after them. Being a looker-after makes you grow up quickly and other children the same age as you can seem immature.'

'You must have felt isolated,' Kitty commented.

'Sometimes, I suppose,' said Beatrice, thinking about it, 'but I wouldn't want you to imagine I was completely friendless. I just didn't know any other child who had the same kind of life as I did.'

'That's something you've done for these children,' Kitty said, and even though they weren't looking at one another, Beatrice could hear the smile in her voice. 'They all have the company of children in the same situation, and shall I tell you what I really like about it?'

'What?' Beatrice asked, turning to face her.

'They don't sit around comparing notes and sharing their experiences. They just get on with being children. It's good to see. It's heartening to know they have this opportunity – and it's thanks to you.' Kitty slid her arm through Beatrice's. 'What else is on your mind?'

'Who says I've got something on my mind?'

'You did, sort of. You said you were partly thinking of your childhood, so that means you're partly thinking of something else too, and unless I'm mistaken, it's something that's troubling you.'

'You're right,' Beatrice admitted. With a small jerk of her chin, she indicated that they should move back from the doorway. She couldn't afford to let the children hear any of this.

'What is it?' Kitty asked quietly.

Beatrice explained about Miss Brewster's plan to have the children with responsibilities evacuated.

'I can see why you're upset,' said Kitty.

'I feel guilty,' said Beatrice. 'If I hadn't stuck my oar in and decided to do something to help these children, they would have remained largely unseen.'

'Stop right there,' Kitty said firmly. 'You have nothing to reproach yourself for. You've made a real difference to these children. You've given them the chance to step away from their responsibilities and just be kids for a while.'

'But at what price?' Beatrice asked, her heart aching.

'Oh, Beatrice,' Kitty murmured, her hazel eyes filled with sorrow.

Beatrice made up her mind. 'I can't let this evacuation just happen. I'm going to do something about it.'

'Good for you,' said Kitty. 'Just be careful, that's all.'

'What d'you mean?'

'I mean, don't put your job in jeopardy. That wouldn't help anyone.'

The warning gave Beatrice a little jolt. This was important, but she mustn't lose her position over it. Quite apart from the fact that she relied on her wages, this Welfare post was the best thing that had happened to her in years. Even so, she had to do something to scupper Miss Brewster's plan.

But what?

* * *

Beatrice left the Town Hall behind a trio of girls. They were all young and pretty, their chatter lively and filled with laughter. She didn't know them to speak to, but she knew them by sight. One was that girl from the Food Office, with her dark-brown hair and bright-blue eyes in a heart-shaped face. Another was a short, full-figured, bubbly girl from Housing, and the third, something of a beauty with masses of reddish-gold hair, worked in Transport.

How lucky they were, Beatrice thought. They were good-looking with interesting jobs and they probably all went to the pictures together in the evenings or maybe they went dancing. To Beatrice, their lives seemed to be filled with promise in a way her own life had never been at that age. She hoped they made the most of every single day.

While other Town Hall employees headed for the bus stops or to the station, Beatrice was one of the very few who could actually walk home. All around her was heartbreaking evidence of Hitler's evil ambitions, but also proof of Manchester's determination to carry on. Up above, the face of the Town Hall clock had had to be boarded up last summer while it waited for the glass to be replaced and the minute hand to be straightened, repairs that would have to wait until after the war was over. The Free Trade Hall was gone, a victim of the terrible Christmas Blitz of 1940, but its former resident orchestra, the famous Hallé Orchestra, after first taking up residence in the Odeon cinema, was now ensconced in the Opera House.

Timpson's shoe shop, which had also been destroyed in the Christmas Blitz, had subsequently reopened on the opposite side of the road; and Goulburn's the grocer's was now located in the basement of the Grosvenor Hotel.

Beatrice walked along the top part of Oxford Road and turned right into Lily Street. It was a pleasant spring evening. Along Lily Street, window-boxes showed off lettuce leaves and dark-green spinach. Beside doors, along with buckets of sand, were tubs showing the large leaves of potatoes and the feathery tops of carrots.

Beatrice breathed in the aroma of rich earth and green growth. She closed her eyes, enjoying the moment. When she opened them again, there was Frank walking along Lily Street towards her.

Her heart seemed to stutter inside her chest. Frank! What was he doing here? He raised his hand in a wave of greeting. Beatrice realised her face had gone slack with shock and she quickly pulled the muscles back under control. What should she do with her expression? Look pleased? But if she looked pleased now from a distance, would she have to carry on looking pleased all the way until they met up? She plumped for a faint smile that brought a slight life to her face and, she hoped, gave her an affable expression. Then again, how could it possibly matter if she looked agreeable? This was Frank. They'd split up donkey's years ago.

But it did matter. She didn't know why – she didn't want to know. But it did.

'Beatrice!' He came striding towards her. At first glance, he was all bonhomie, but was that a suggestion of uncertainty in his eyes? 'What a surprise. A delightful one, of course. How are you?'

'I'm well, thank you,' said Beatrice. Her mind was working furiously on that word *delightful*. Could he really be that pleased to see her or was it an exaggeration to hide a feeling that was the very opposite of delighted? Well, it couldn't be the former, so it must be the latter. And her insides had no business shrinking in disappointment. 'What brings you here to Lily Street, Mr Marsden?'

'Oh.' He looked taken aback. 'I apologise for using your first name. I lost the right to do that a long time ago.'

Beatrice immediately felt mean. She shouldn't have slapped him down like that. Yes, she should. She was entitled to slap him down after the way he'd left her high and dry – no, wait. He hadn't left her. She'd left him because he didn't want to have children, and now he had five of them. *Five.* And she was a forlorn old spinster. Please don't let him see the pain in her eyes.

'I'm here because I'm going to Dunbar's,' said Frank.

'What?'

'You asked why I was in Lily Street. I'm going to Dunbar's. I have a letter to deliver to Mrs Chadwick.' Frank produced it from his jacket pocket. 'It's from my daughter, the one whose life she saved.'

Beatrice's fingers clenched briefly as annoyance spurted up inside her at the memory of that little heart-stutter when she'd set eyes on Frank. What a traitor her heart was. Of course he wasn't here to see her. Of course it was to do with his daughter. Another memory smote her, that of the smiles on the faces of the boy and girl who'd come running along the road to him that rainy day. Frank wasn't a stern Victorian papa. He was a loving, involved daddy. Oh, how was she to bear it?

She had to get rid of him. 'I'd be happy to take the letter for you. Then you can be on your way.'

Frank frowned and glanced away for a moment. Then he laughed, a forced sound. 'Are you trying to get rid of me?'

'Of course not,' she lied gamely.

'Good. For a moment there, I wondered.' He smiled. 'Thanks for the offer, but I'd like to hand it over myself. This is my daughter thanking the person who saved her life.'

Beatrice softened. 'I understand.'

Frank took a step to the side as if waving her forward towards Dunbar's. 'May I accompany you?'

Good grief, was he about to offer his arm? She couldn't think what she'd do if he did. But he didn't. Beatrice refused to examine her feelings.

They walked down the road side by side and went up the steps. Beatrice delved inside her handbag for her key.

'Beatrice – Miss Inkerman.'

She ought to carry on feeling for her key ring. Instead she stopped, her hand still in the depths of her bag, and looked at him.

Frank shook his head. 'I can't think of you as Miss Inkerman, but of course if that's how you wish to be known...'

'It doesn't matter,' Beatrice said. 'It isn't as though we'll see one another again.'

'Do you think not?' After a pause, Frank asked, 'Do you *want* not?'

For a moment Beatrice couldn't breathe. Her cheeks felt tingly, though whether they had turned deep red or deathly white she had no idea.

'Because I would very much like to see you again... Beatrice.' Frank looked at her, his eyes holding hers. 'You want the truth? It was my idea that Rowena should write this letter. Under any other circumstances, I would simply have addressed it to Dunbar's, stuck a stamp on it and put it in the pillar box. But I knew that if I delivered it by hand shortly after six o'clock, there was a chance I might see you again. I've lost count of how many times I've walked up and down Lily Street in the past half hour, waiting for you to come home. And now you have, and here I am, and I would very much like, I would be honoured, if you would allow me to take you out one evening.'

12

Lily could barely believe it. She was seeing Dr Shawston – Vivian. It was easy to dodge the truth because she didn't let him collect her from Dunbar's or walk her home at the end of the evening. That way, she didn't have to let on to anyone in Dunbar's. In a strange sort of way, she didn't have to let on to herself either. She didn't have to look too closely at what was happening. Nothing was happening, not really. Nothing important. Just an evening out now and again. She wouldn't even agree to have a meal with him because she didn't want an evening of conversation. Besides, it would have felt too public. Much safer to go to the flicks and sit in the tobacco-scented darkness.

Not that she seemed able to lose herself in a good film. Oh, she went through the motions. She chuckled at Laurel and Hardy's antics in *Great Guns* and Abbott and Costello's in *In the Navy*; and she hummed along to the songs in *Lady Be Good* and *Babes on Broadway*; but at the same time she was constantly aware of herself and Vivian and how close they were sitting. When he casually rested a hand on the armrest in between them in a discreet invitation to place her hand in his, Lily stuck her fingers inside her handbag so she couldn't do anything foolish by mistake.

At the end of the film, they stood for the national anthem, then joined everyone else in the slow, steady shuffle along the crowded aisles to the door and out into the foyer. Outside, the blackout was as deep and dark as ever.

'Young children think that evenings and nights as black as ink are normal,' Vivian said. 'They don't remember the streetlamps and the headlights on motorcars. Oh, I beg your pardon,' he added as he bumped into someone. A moment later, he burst out laughing.

'What is it?' Lily asked.

'I've just apologised to a pillar box,' he told her.

Lily laughed too and once she started she couldn't stop. When finally her laughter eased off, Vivian was still laughing and that set her off again. Then, when it seemed he might stop, she infected him all over again.

Lily groaned. 'I have to stop. My ribs are aching.'

'So are mine,' said Vivian, his laughter finally winding down. 'But it's worth it,' he added seriously. 'The sound of your laughter is worth any price.'

Lily drew back. 'Don't be silly.'

'It's true,' he insisted. 'You carry such deep unhappiness around with you and I can understand that, but just now, the pair of us laughing at something as daft as saying sorry to a pillar box, was a moment of lightness. Hearing you laugh lifted my spirits in the same way that hearing the church bells ringing again will at the end of the war.'

Lily did her best to brush it off. 'Now that really is an exaggeration.'

But he stood in front of her, not touching, just standing close.

There was a stillness about him. When he spoke, his voice was serious and deep.

'It isn't an exaggeration. I care for you. Each time you allow me to see you, I care for you more. I know that seeing me is a big decision for you, so big that my ego would be profoundly wounded if I thought about it too much.'

Lily felt shaky as fear speared her. 'Then maybe this isn't a good idea,' she said desperately.

'On the contrary,' he replied firmly, 'it's the best possible idea. I know I have to take things slowly and carefully. I know you need time. Before meeting you, I would never have described myself as a patient man, but now I know I will wait for as long as it takes, as long as you need. You're more than worth it to me, Lily Chadwick.'

* * *

Beatrice looked at her face in the hinged mirror on top of her chest of drawers. She had never had the kind of looks to set a pond on fire and now she was twenty years older than when she'd known Frank first time around. He had told her he would be honoured to take her out, but it was hard to believe, especially when she looked at her reflection.

There was a knock on her bedroom door and Kitty came in. 'Are you ready? How are you feeling?'

'Ordinary,' Beatrice answered, trying not to sound glum.

Kitty smiled. 'I thought you were going to say "excited" or something of the kind.' She gave her friend a hug. 'You aren't ordinary at all, Beatrice Inkerman. You're kind and generous, and just look at your job. You were *offered* that job, Beatrice. That's how highly thought of you are.'

'Being offered a job by the Corporation doesn't exactly make me feel beautiful and charming,' said Beatrice and immediately wished the words unspoken because they made her sound shallow and needy.

'That's the nerves talking,' said Kitty. 'Don't forget. This is the man who walked up and down Lily Street hoping to bump into you accidentally on purpose.'

'I'm too old to have nerves on this scale,' said Beatrice.

'Is it like being a young girl again?'

'I wasn't a girl when I first knew Frank. I was in my mid-twenties.'

'You know what I mean,' said Kitty. 'Beatrice, listen. If you honestly don't want to go out this evening, then don't go. Tell Frank you've changed your mind.'

'I can't do that. It would be so rude.'

Kitty shrugged. 'Fine. I'll tell him if you want me to. Do you want me to?' She looked challengingly at Beatrice, and was that a twinkle of amusement in her hazel eyes as well?

Beatrice could have crowned Kitty for putting her on the spot, but she couldn't deny it was a fair question. 'The truth is, I don't know if I want to go or not.'

'You must have wanted to in the first place or you wouldn't have agreed to it,' Kitty said reasonably.

'I'm not so sure about that,' said Beatrice. 'From the moment Frank admitted he'd been walking up and down Lily Street, I've been in such a flap I can hardly think straight.'

'Then I'll do the thinking for you,' said Kitty. 'Go out. Enjoy yourself, or at least don't screw yourself up into a ball of anxiety. I'm serious, Beatrice. You work hard. You deserve a night out. Let Frank treat you. You don't have to see him again if you don't feel like it. Just... see what happens.'

'You make it sound so easy,' said Beatrice.

'That's because it is,' Kitty replied. After a moment she added, 'I think you're lucky.'

'To be taken out by Frank?'

'To feel all fluttery,' Kitty answered. 'The last time I felt fluttery was when Bill wouldn't give me access to the Dunbar's bank account and my blood pressure started to bubble up.'

'I'm being daft, aren't I?' said Beatrice.

Kitty smiled. 'Maybe a little. But isn't it better to feel flustered because an old flame has invited you out for an evening than not to have the chance to feel anything at all because he didn't want to know?'

* * *

The evening out with Frank went well – surprisingly well, given the state of Beatrice's nerves. He was the perfect gentleman. Not that that came as any surprise. He had always had good manners and had shown consideration. Beatrice's mother had been impressed. She'd felt she would be leaving Beatrice in safe hands.

Beatrice couldn't help wondering if he would take her somewhere posh like the Midland Hotel or the Claremont Hotel, but he took her to an unassuming little place in one of the streets off Deansgate, where there was a vase with a single peony in the centre of each table.

'How pretty.' Beatrice leaned forward to inhale the scent before realising her mistake. 'Artificial.' Had she made a twit of herself?

'It makes sense,' said Frank. 'The cost of flowers has rocketed since the war began.'

'The cost of *every*thing has rocketed,' said Beatrice, then could have kicked herself for sounding glum. She didn't want to scare Frank off by being a misery-guts. *Oh.* She didn't want to scare him off. A streak of panic raced through her before she tucked the revelation away to think about later.

'Starter and main course, or main course and pudding?' Frank asked, lifting his gaze from the menu to pose the question.

Drat. She should have asked him before he asked her. She didn't want to give the wrong answer.

'I don't mind,' she said. 'You choose.'

'Very well then. Let's have the pud. I remember you had a sweet tooth.' Frank smiled. 'Do you still?'

Beatrice didn't know whether to be flattered or appalled. Did a sweet tooth from twenty years ago make her seem greedy? And why was she reacting to every tiny detail in this ridiculous way? Talk about over-thinking! If she carried on like this, he'd get fed up of her pretty quickly and that would be the end of that, which would probably come as a great relief to her.

Except that it wouldn't.

Beatrice drew in a breath. She might feel all fluttery but that was no reason not to keep control of her tongue.

'Yes, I still like sweet things. I expect that plenty of people are discovering a greater fondness for sweetness ever since sugar went on the ration.'

'Probably so,' Frank agreed. 'What would you like?'

They studied their menus.

'I'd like the cheese-and-vegetable cutlets, please,' said Beatrice.

The waiter came over to ask if they'd made their selection.

'The lady would like the cutlets,' said Frank, 'and I'll have the meat pudding with mint stuffing, please.'

'Thank you, sir,' said the waiter, taking their menus.

Beatrice enjoyed the moment. Frank had given her order for her as if they were a real couple. Then the enjoyment melted, replaced by a pang of loss. If only she'd known twenty years ago –

but he'd been so *certain* he didn't want children. Never mind 'if only she'd known'. If only *he'd* known. Or if only she'd met someone else after him. That was her life in a nutshell. A string of big fat if onlys.

Was coming out with Frank this evening nothing more than an unwelcome opportunity to have her nose rubbed in all those if onlys?

Frank produced a packet of cigarettes from his pocket and offered her one. She shook her head. It might choke her.

'You don't mind if I do?' He was already lighting up. 'We have a lot of catching up to do.'

Beatrice's pulse quickened. He was going to tell her about his children.

But he said, 'I know you have a job with the Corporation, but what war work do you do?'

'I'm with the WVS.'

'The voluntary ladies,' Frank said in a tone of respect, uttering the name many people used. 'What are your duties?'

Beatrice was about to launch into a description, but something made her say, 'I notice you smoke Player's. One of my WVS jobs last year was working in the troops' tuck shop. There were always three of us behind the counter and I always had the longest cigarette queue. Well, it could have been my charming smile, but then one of the soldiers let slip that I'd been selling Player's at Woodbine prices.'

Frank threw back his head and roared with laughter. Suddenly, just like that, it was twenty years ago – except that she'd never made him laugh like that back then. She'd never made anyone laugh, not really. She was altogether too earnest to inspire levity in others. Her heart lifted from its moorings at the sight of Frank's amusement.

You did that, she thought. *You made him laugh.*

It made her want to do it again. It also made her relax. She found herself talking more easily. They chatted for a while about the work of the WVS, but Beatrice didn't want to talk about herself. She would much prefer to find out about him, by which she meant his children, but she couldn't ask for fear of giving herself away.

But it was safe to say, 'You gave up your job in the toy factory.'

'For the war effort, yes. I work in a munitions factory now.'

'Keeping the machines running smoothly,' said Beatrice.

'That's what mechanical engineers do,' he replied. 'And my voluntary work is with a heavy rescue squad.'

'Dangerous work,' said Beatrice.

The heavy rescue and light rescue men were the ones who saved people from collapsed buildings. Light rescue meant shifting rubble with your gloved hands and heavy rescue involved machinery.

'That's why men with proper training and experience are needed,' said Frank.

'At least the air raids have stopped now. Touch wood.' Beatrice tapped her temple. 'Apart from that bad one at the end of April, of course.'

'Yes. I shan't forget that one in a hurry,' said Frank, 'and neither will my daughter.'

A bubble of surprise seemed to pop inside Beatrice's chest. Instead of her having to manoeuvre the conversation, it had ended up with his children quite naturally.

'I hope she's none the worse for her experience,' she said.

'She's fine,' said Frank. 'It terrified her at the time, but children have the capacity to bounce back quickly. I've made it very clear she's never to go anywhere near a water tank again.'

'She must have a lot of spirit to have wanted to play a game like that,' said Beatrice.

'She's nothing if not brave, my Rowena.' After a moment Frank added, 'Thank you for recognising that. The reaction of most people has been to blame her – and me, as her father.'

'Well, she was out rather late,' Beatrice said gently, determined not to sound like 'most people'.

'True. She was out with her chums and they lost track of time. I've never been one of those parents who make the oldest take responsibility for the younger ones.'

'Most people do,' said Beatrice. 'Most people' again!

'Not me. I've never forgotten what you told me about your childhood and how much responsibility you had.'

Warmth brushed Beatrice's cheeks. 'That's not the same thing.'

'Yes, it is,' Frank stated. 'It's putting extra responsibility on a child's shoulders. A different responsibility, I grant you, but the principle is the same. I'm not saying I never put Rowena in charge of the others, because obviously I've had to since we lost her mother, but I don't want her ever to look back on her childhood and think that the younger ones had all the fun. Mind you, if I'd known that her idea of fun would lead to that stupid game of running across the water tank...'

'Children's high spirits,' said Beatrice, 'and everyone lived to tell the tale.'

'Thanks to Dr Shawston and Mrs Chadwick,' said Frank. 'A true hero and heroine.'

'Mrs Chadwick was delighted to receive Rowena's thank-you letter,' said Beatrice. That was something of an exaggeration. Lily had thought it sweet of Rowena, nothing more. What had delighted her was the tale of Frank walking up and down Lily Street in the hope that Beatrice would appear.

'I truly did want her to write the letter,' Frank said, looking a little sheepish. 'It wasn't just a ploy to see you again. It was more a case of two birds with one stone.'

For Beatrice, that was the high point of the evening. She had been so nervous to start with, and now Frank had for the second time admitted to being keen to see her again.

But at the end of the evening, when he escorted her back to Dunbar's, he simply thanked her and wished her goodnight, with no suggestion of seeing her again. Had she disappointed him? And did she want to see him again anyway? Beatrice hesitated at the foot of the steps just in case he wanted to invite her out a second time. He didn't do so, and her neck and ears suddenly felt impossibly hot. What a fool she was. A foolish old spinster.

Yet when she came home from work the following evening, it was to find a bouquet of glorious peonies waiting for her.

* * *

It was a good thing Lily had never let Vivian collect her from Dunbar's when he took her out, because if she had, he'd have been with her when she bumped into Daniel.

It was a warm evening at the end of May and the light was gentle as it headed towards twilight. Only yesterday Lily had parted with a whole eleven of her precious clothing points in order to purchase a new jacket. It had a wrap-over front that felt very stylish, with a wide collar and revers, while the padded shoulders gave it a smart shape even though it fastened with a casual tie-belt of the same fabric. Lily had never had anything so swish in her life. Well, why shouldn't she treat herself? She wasn't stupid little Lily from the back streets any longer.

The others had admired Lily's appearance before she left Dunbar's. No one asked her where she was going, still less who with, and Lily had ignored the unspoken questions. She wasn't ready to talk about Vivian. If she did, that would make the situation more real, more of a commitment. She wasn't ready to think about that because it would involve thinking about the future. For over a year now, her future had been a vast bleak landscape with no Toby in it and it had been too overwhelming to contemplate.

She was going to meet Vivian at the cinema. They always met in the foyer. Even though he had made a point of arriving first each time and had never kept her waiting, she didn't want to meet outside, because if on the off-chance she did get there first, she would feel conspicuous.

Lily paused at the kerb, waiting to cross the road.

'Lily!'

Daniel! She didn't need to look; she knew his voice instantly. She couldn't have said which side of her his voice had come from, but somehow her feet turned her to face in the right direction. Here he was, coming towards her, threading his way between the other pedestrians. He looked – well, if it wasn't a stupid thing to think, he looked so *familiar*. Those warm hazel eyes and the touch of vulnerability about his mouth when he smiled at her – only when he smiled at *her*, never when he smiled at someone else.

For half a second, Lily was pleased to see him – but only for half a second. Then she remembered they were separated, and all the reasons why. She had been utterly alone when Toby died. Daniel hadn't even known he was the father of a boy, let alone that Toby hadn't lived. Lily had battled her way through the early weeks of her loss, and then, when Daniel had come home, his own loss had been brand new and far more than she could cope with. It had all been too much then, and it was still too much now.

Something inside her shut down. Again.

She stepped back from the kerb to wait for him, letting people flow around her, one or two of them clicking their tongues in annoyance.

He came to a stop in front of her. He wasn't as tall as Vivian nor as broad in the shoulder, but his slim frame was strong and purposeful. He moved with the grace of an athlete.

'Lily. It's good to see you.'

There it was again, that slight uncertainty in his smile. She couldn't afford to respond to it.

'Daniel. I'm glad to see you're safe.'

His gaze held hers, or tried to. She glanced away.

'How are you?' he asked.

Seeing another man.

'I'm fine, thank you. Still at Dunbar's, still with the WVS.'

'And you're... managing? I mean, if you need more money—'

'No... thank you.'

He nodded. 'Look, if you have a few minutes, perhaps we could...' His voice trailed off, leaving a trace of hope in the air.

Oh, she couldn't have that. This needed to be squashed flat right now.

'I'm sorry, Daniel. I can't stop. I'm on my way somewhere.'

'Oh. Yes. Right. Of course.' He took a step backwards.

Even though she was eager to escape, Lily felt bad. She wanted to say something kind, something friendly, but that would be a mistake.

'I'd better let you go, then,' said Daniel.

'Yes,' she breathed. 'Take care, Daniel.'

'And you.' Just before she could move, he added, 'That jacket suits you. You're dainty and graceful and... it suits you. Goodbye, Lily.'

13

Beatrice stood over the road from the church, unable to tear her eyes away from the bride and groom posing for wedding photographs with their smiling guests. The bride was a pretty girl and she was all in white. There were more traditional brides around these days. In the early part of the war, it had been seen as patriotic to have a simple wedding with the bride and her attendants in their Sunday best, but now there was a certain pride in having a white wedding that, in spite of all the shortages, looked as close as possible to pre-war.

The early June sun shed golden rays on the happy couple. Beatrice had to swallow a lump in her throat. She had once had dreams of being a June bride. June had always seemed the most romantic month for a wedding.

When the photographer had finished outside the church, the newly-weds posed on the pavement beside a handsome, open-topped motorcar. Then the groom handed his new wife in and she settled her skirts before he followed her. A girl in uniform got behind the steering-wheel. Beatrice was puzzled when six uniformed young men and women formed two lines of three in front of the vehicle. The six of them bent down and when they stood up again, each line of three was carrying a hefty rope. At the rear of the motor, two more soldiers placed their hands on the boot and bent forwards to push.

Oh, how perfect! In these days of petrol shortages, the newly-weds had got both a special motor and the means for it to travel along. Beatrice watched, entranced, as, with huge smiles, the pullers took up the slack, the pushers gave a heave and the vehicle started off at a stately pace, accompanied by cheers from the other guests.

Beatrice sighed. She did love a good wedding. People were ingenious these days when it came to finding ways to make the best of things.

There was sorrow in her sigh too. It was impossible not to think of what she had missed out on, especially now that Frank was back in her life.

'For now, anyway,' she said to Kitty that evening.

'I think it's a bit more than that,' Kitty answered. 'If he'd taken you out just once, that would have been for old times' sake, or out of curiosity. But he's taken you out a second time as well, and there's going to be a third.'

'I don't want to take anything for granted,' said Beatrice.

'Of course you don't. You're much too modest. The question is: what are you hoping for?'

'I don't think of it in those terms,' said Beatrice.

If she'd hoped Kitty would encourage her to do precisely that, she was disappointed. All Kitty said was, 'Fair enough.' Then she asked, 'What do the two of you talk about?'

'All sorts of things,' said Beatrice. 'Work. The news. The war.'

'Hasn't he told you about his children?'

'No. Well, apart from Rowena, the one Lily saved.'

'Beatrice, do you think you're perhaps being a bit... stand-offish?'

'What's that supposed to mean?' Beatrice demanded.

'Don't take offence. It's just that this is the man who traipsed up and down Lily Street because he was anxious to see you again. And then there were the peonies – which incidentally must have cost a king's ransom. Doesn't that suggest to you that romance might be in the air? Or that Frank might want it to be?'

'I honestly don't know what to think,' Beatrice admitted. 'I still can't quite believe it's happening.'

'And if your conversation is sticking rigidly to the RAF bombing Germany and Rommel advancing in Libya,' said Kitty, 'then I imagine Frank doesn't know what to think either.'

Beatrice didn't answer. It all felt too complicated, too fragile.

'May I make a suggestion?' Kitty asked and waited for a nod. 'You're seeing him again tomorrow evening. Stop tying yourself in knots. Treat it as if it's the last time you'll ever see one another and it's your one and only opportunity to say what you want to say and ask what you want to ask.'

'But—' Beatrice began and immediately stopped.

Kitty was right. She had been flummoxed ever since this situation had started up and she'd been frightened of saying the wrong thing. She finally allowed herself to think clearly about what needed to be said. Had the time come to say it?

* * *

Frank took Beatrice back to the restaurant off Deansgate. Beatrice was pleased. She had always liked the familiar. There was safety in it. This time, there was a rose in each vase and she was careful not to comment. She didn't want to seem to be angling for another bouquet.

Frank gave the waiter their order, then he sat back and smiled at her. She was impressed all over again by how well he had aged. It wouldn't be too many more years before people started referring to him as distinguished.

Conscious of her vow to dive in and say what she most wanted to, Beatrice took her courage in both hands and said, 'Tell me about your children. What are their names?'

Frank looked pleased. 'Starting at the top, Rowena, as you know; then Herbie, short for Herbert; Leslie; Georgie – who's a girl, incidentally: Georgina; and Josie-Posy.'

'Is that one name?' Beatrice asked, startled. She hoped she'd hidden how ridiculous she thought it.

Frank smiled indulgently. 'She's Josie, short for Josephine. When she was a tot, the others called her Josie-Posy as a pet-name, and it's still going strong. I'm sure she'll grow out of it; and even if she doesn't, the others will tire of it.'

'Then I suppose, Georgie is lucky not to be Georgie-Porgie,' Beatrice said mildly.

'Children at school have occasionally had a go at calling her that,' Frank said, straight-faced, 'though they have not necessarily lived to tell the tale.'

'I see.' Beatrice rather liked the sound of Georgie Marsden. 'I wish I'd had that sort of spirit when I was a child and was called Beatrice Stinkerman – and not just when I was a child either,' she added with a secret shudder.

'Really?' Frank asked. 'Adults have called you Stinkerman?'

'No, it was some of the boys where I used to live before I came to Dunbar's. As a matter of fact, they were the sons of the men who used to call me Stinkerman when we were children, so you might say it ran in the family.'

'I'm very sorry to hear that,' said Frank. 'I don't like to think of you or anyone being taunted in that way.'

'Thank you for not calling it teasing,' said Beatrice. 'When I was a child, the adults who didn't want to tackle it called it teasing. They turned it round and made it my fault for not being able to take a joke.' Not wanting to sound sorry for herself, she made a point of brightening. 'Anyway, I had the last laugh. The lads who last year were singing the Inky Stinky Stinkerman song are now members of my Gentlemen's Club and their manners are impeccable.'

They talked for a while about the Gentlemen's Club and the Time Off Club. Beatrice lapped up Frank's interest, and was that admiration she could see in his eyes? She felt a glow of pride.

But she was now miles away from saying the things she wanted to say.

Frank said, 'I'm glad you have so much contact with children.'

She could have walloped him. 'So I can be their spiritual mother, you mean?'

'Their what?'

'Their spiritual mother. That's what you said the day we sheltered from the rain.'

'Did I? I don't recall.'

Beatrice's blood came dangerously close to boiling. He had uttered those words that had cut her to the quick and he didn't even remember.

'Yes, you did,' she said sharply. 'You seemed to think you were offering me consolation since I never had children of my own.'

'I apologise if I spoke out of turn.'

'I used to think of you as the injured party,' Beatrice stated clearly. 'More fool me. I broke off our engagement because I wanted a family and you didn't. All you wanted was me, so when I ended things, I thought you were the injured party because you'd lost me.'

'Are you suggesting that I shouldn't have found another woman?'

'No, of course not. But you clearly didn't apply the same rules to her as you did to me.'

'Beatrice, it's water not just under the bridge but miles out to sea. What happened between the two of us took place years ago. I'm very sorry you never met another man. For what it's worth, you deserved to. After looking after your mother for all those years, you deserved a husband and family. The devotion you show to the children in your clubs proves that.'

'Oh, we're back in the realms of spiritual motherhood, are we?'

'When I married Maureen, it was on the understanding that there would be no children. But she secretly wanted a family and she worked on me until I... agreed.'

Agreed? Or gave in?

'When she was expecting Rowena, I wasn't really bothered one way or the other about the baby,' Frank continued, 'but the first time I saw her, my daughter, my first child...' He shook his head, a gleam of wonder in his eyes. 'I fell in love. Those are the only words for it. I fell in love with this tiny, perfect human being. *My* daughter, *my* child. After that I was more than happy to have more. We decided on four but we ended up with five.'

Beatrice's eyes filled with tears. She blinked them back and they seemed to pour down her throat instead.

'And all these years,' she said, 'I thought you were the injured party.'

'Well, I suppose I was – at the time. There must be plenty of men who aren't keen on being fathers until it actually happens to them.'

'It's funny, isn't it?' Beatrice said in her crispest voice. 'I never got what I wanted. *You* got what I wanted.'

* * *

Vivian was delighted when Lily suggested doing something other than go to the pictures.

'Let me take you out for a meal,' he said at once. 'Somewhere nice where we can feel private. Don't worry! I only mean a dining room with tables spaced well apart.'

'Not the Worker Bee, then.' Lily made her voice sound jokey.

'I'd like to take you somewhere rather better than that,' he replied, 'like the Midland Hotel or the Claremont.'

'Not the Claremont!' Not the place where her marriage had officially ended. 'And not the Midland either,' she added in a steadier voice. 'Somewhere smaller.'

'I know just the place,' Vivian answered with a smile.

It turned out to be a restaurant in a road off Market Street. Circular tables were set with shining silverware, and over on one wall was a grand sideboard with a pair of large epergnes on top. Lily knew what they were; she even knew what they were called even though they were old-fashioned, because there had been epergnes at Dunbar's when it was a hotel. She'd thought them very grand, with all their tiers and branches and dishes.

The maître d' showed them to a table that had a pair of cream-coloured candles in cut-glass sticks. He held Lily's chair as she seated herself, then he produced a lighter and touched it to each of the candle-wicks, bringing a pair of flames to life.

Before they looked at the menus, Vivian ordered white wine.

'And could you also ask for our water goblets to be filled, please?'

'Of course, sir.'

As the maître d' withdrew, he signalled to a waiter, who came to their table with a crystal water-jug. The wine waiter followed with the wine. He and Vivian exchanged a few words about it while Vivian tasted it.

When they were alone, Lily leaned forward to say softly, 'Thank you for the water.'

Vivian laughed. 'I thought you were going to say, "Thank you for the wine," but, oh no, it's the water.'

'I only meant I'm not used to wine,' said Lily.

'Then feel free to water it down or leave it altogether, if you like,' Vivian told her. 'I just want you to have what you want – although,' he added quickly, 'even if you don't touch it again this evening, I'd like you to take just a sip so we can have a proper toast.'

He picked up his glass and Lily did the same.

'Thank you for this evening, Lily,' he said. 'Thank you for agreeing to be seen with me in public.' With a small gesture, he waved aside her little gasp of embarrassment. 'I'm not as green as I am cabbage-looking. I'm well aware of your reasons for all those trips to the cinema.'

'I'm sorry,' Lily whispered. 'I didn't know you knew.'

'Sitting in the dark all evening and then walking home through the blackout and leaving you on the corner did give me a pretty broad hint,' he answered wryly. 'But what matters is that we're here now and so...' Lily thought he was about to drink to her, but he said, 'To candlelight.'

'Candlelight,' Lily echoed, lifting her glass before taking a sip. She put the glass down. 'We're the only table with candles.' As soon as she said it, she realised. 'Did you provide them?'

'I most certainly did, for our first meal together.'

'They're in such short supply,' said Lily. No wonder the restaurant couldn't put them on tables as they had done before the war. And how extravagant of Vivian – and also how very kind. He wanted to impress her, and that was a nice feeling.

'Anyway,' he said, 'I much prefer candles to those bizarre vasey-things over there.'

Lily laughed, happy to show off her knowledge. 'They're called epergnes and they're for fruit and nuts and flowers and whatever other decorative things you want to put in them.'

'You learn something new every day.'

'I'm glad to have taught you something,' Lily said. 'Thank you for bringing me here.'

'Do you like it?'

She looked around, absorbing the atmosphere. 'Yes, I do. It's smart but not too grand. It reminds me of when Dunbar's was a hotel. That's a good thing,' she added. 'It makes me feel comfortable.'

Leaning forward, Vivian lowered his voice. 'Our waiter keeps looking in our direction. I think we ought to pick up our menus.'

Lily saw she had been given a lady's menu, with no prices. She read through the list.

'Have you chosen?' Vivian asked, lowering his menu a little so he could look at her over the top. His eyes were very dark in the candlelight.

She was about to embark on the usual starter-or-pudding conversation that everyone went through, but then something told her that Vivian was waiting for her to decide so that he could follow her lead. How polite.

Feeling rather sophisticated, she said, 'I'd like the vegetable ragout, please.'

'Good choice.'

Vivian glanced towards the waiter, who immediately came to their table. Lily allowed herself a private little sigh. There was something about Vivian that declared him to be a man of the world. Daniel's mother had always made her feel that she was little Lily from the back streets, but being with Vivian made her feel that it was who she was now that was important. She'd wanted to move on with her life and now she had. Vivian was giving her that chance. When she was with him, she could be a new person, more confident, more... grown-up, for want of a better word. She had adored Daniel, but his mother had slapped her down every time she got the chance. Daniel had bent over backwards to keep the peace, which had left Lily feeling exposed and vulnerable.

But here, now, with Dr Vivian Shawston, Lily felt admired. He treated her beautifully and he made her feel she was worth it. After more than a year of being dragged down by a sense of guilt and responsibility for Toby's death, feeling special was startling and enticing. If she could have this in her new life, oughtn't she to hang on to it with both hands?

14

When Kitty answered the door, Naomi walked in. Before Kitty could shut the door, Naomi caught her by the arms and looked into her face.

'I'm checking to see if you're exhausted,' she announced, 'now that you've got lodgers to take care of.'

'Mrs Dunbar is looking after them,' Kitty replied with a grin. 'Would you like to examine her for exhaustion?'

Naomi tossed her head. 'She should be so lucky.'

'It's the day for cleaning all the bombed-out furnishings. I've got to unlock all the rooms. Why don't you come round the building with me and we can have a natter while I do it?'

They went round the first and second floors. When they came downstairs again, Ivy was at the front door, talking to someone on the step.

'No, I'm sorry,' she was saying. 'Dunbar's isn't a hotel any longer... Yes, it's a shame... I know just what you mean. So many people have such fond memories... Well, there's the Grove over the road. They may be able to help you. Yes, straight over there.' She pointed. 'No trouble at all. Good luck.'

Ivy closed the door and, turning, saw Kitty and Naomi.

'What was that about?' Kitty asked.

'A mother looking for a last-minute venue for her daughter's wedding reception. Their local church hall has had a burst pipe and won't dry out in time for Saturday.'

'That's a shame,' said Naomi.

'Yes, it is,' Ivy agreed, 'especially as the family has happy memories of coming here for tea on special occasions.'

'That sounds familiar,' said Lily, appearing on the stairs. 'People used to like coming here for tea.'

'We've just had an enquiry about hosting a wedding reception at short notice,' Kitty told her. 'It would be wonderful to be able to do something like that. It was one of the things I was looking forward to when we took over the hotel, but of course it's out of the question now. The bailiffs skinned the old dining room and sitting room.'

'Did they take everything that was stored in the cellar?' Lily asked.

'They didn't go down there,' Kitty replied. 'If they had, they'd have waltzed off with the booze.'

'The booze!' Naomi exclaimed. 'You've still got alcohol?'

'Well, of course,' Kitty answered. 'We haven't got any guests to sell it to.' She looked at Lily. 'What's in the cellar?'

'When the war started,' said Lily, 'Mr Jeremiah got us to pack away all the best china and crystal and it was all stored in a locked room in the back.'

Kitty's heart beat faster. 'Let me fetch the cellar keys and we'll go and look.'

Two minutes later, they were all in a dark, chilly storeroom at the far end of the cellar. Lily had brought a torch and she played the beam over the stacks of wooden boxes. Kitty tried to lift a lid off. It didn't want to come and she had to strain, but then it gave way. All four of them stepped forward, Lily shining the torch on a layer of straw.

Ivy delved inside and brought out a pretty tea plate decorated with bluebells around the rim.

'I remember this set.' She spoke almost reverently.

'So do I,' said Kitty. 'And look at all these boxes. What's in here, Lily?'

'The best stuff.'

'The best what, specifically?'

'Dinner service, tea service, crystal.'

'Oh my goodness,' breathed Kitty. Anticipation ballooned inside her and she headed for the cellar steps.

'Where are you going?' Naomi asked her.

Kitty swung around to face her. 'To catch that mother of the bride and offer her a wedding reception at Dunbar's.'

* * *

Fortunately for Kitty, Mr Barnes at the Grove hadn't been able to accommodate the reception of Miss Elsie Packer and Corporal Henry Tyler, so she was able to scoop up Mrs Packer and bring her back to Dunbar's.

'I know this room doesn't look like much now,' she told the mother of the bride, showing her the old dining room, which was now their sparsely furnished parlour, 'but I promise you that you'll have a wedding reception to be proud of.'

Quite how she was going to achieve that, she wasn't sure, but she was determined to give the bride and groom the perfect occasion.

One thing that made it considerably easier was that Mrs Packer had already got the food side of it sorted out, because she and her sister, Mrs Lowe, had originally intended to do the catering themselves.

'We spoke to a very helpful young lady called Miss Grant from the Food Office,' Mrs Packer told Kitty, 'and she gave us all the information we needed about what we're allowed to have.'

'If you bring all the food here on Friday afternoon,' said Kitty, 'we'll get it ready for you.'

'Would you really do that?' Mrs Packer asked. 'At this late date, we only expected you to provide the room.'

'Nonsense.' Kitty spoke with a smile so as not to give offence. 'This is Dunbar's. We might not be a hotel any longer, but we haven't forgotten how to host a party.'

'I was expecting to spend all morning in my kitchen,' said Mrs Packer.

'Dunbar's will take care of everything,' Kitty assured her. 'All you and your guests have to do is turn up after the ceremony and enjoy yourselves.'

'We've got a cardboard wedding cake for the photographs,' said Mrs Packer. 'A very good one with three tiers and a little soldier and bride on the top. Will you make the real cake for us or should I do that?'

'We'll do it for you,' Kitty said at once. 'Bring the ingredients along and leave it to us.'

She showed Mrs Packer out and turned to face the others.

'Kitty!' Naomi exclaimed. 'You can't. You just *can't*. It's too much work – and what if it goes wrong?'

'We'll have to make sure it doesn't,' Kitty replied.

'All that work...' Naomi lamented.

Shortly after that, Naomi had to be on her way. The moment the door shut behind her, Ivy descended on Kitty.

'I hope you haven't made that Mrs Packer any promises you can't keep.'

'I haven't,' Kitty said firmly. 'As long as we all muck in and don't sleep a wink between now and Saturday, everything will be just fine.'

* * *

Kitty, Lily, Beatrice, Ivy and Abbie stood in the former dining room and Kitty could see the others trying to conceal their dismay.

'Well, it's not as though they were expecting anything glamorous if they'd originally booked their church hall,' said Ivy.

'All the more reason for us to do something special,' said Kitty.

'You're right,' said Lily. 'It's to do with expectations. What you expect from the church hall isn't the same as what you expect from Dunbar's – even if we have had the bailiffs.'

Kitty smiled at her, grateful for her understanding. She urgently wanted this to go well, not just to give Elsie and Henry a day to remember, but also because, if she pulled it off, it might lead to other special occasions being held here. Imagine that! This could be the fresh source of income she needed.

'That's the trouble,' said Ivy, sticking her oar in as usual. 'We *have* had the bailiffs.'

'Instead of thinking about all the things we haven't got,' said Kitty, 'we need to concentrate on everything we *have* got.'

'Beautiful china and crystalware,' said Abbie.

Kitty smiled to herself. Abbie had picked up the word 'crystalware' from Lily. The two of them had been carefully washing everything and Lily had showed Abbie how to rinse the crystalware in hot water and then leave each piece to dry naturally, standing upside down on tea towels.

'What's in the attic?' Beatrice asked. 'Think of all the board games and other things we found up there. They made all the difference to the children's clubs.'

'They used to be brought down for the Christmas season, didn't they?' said Kitty. 'The decorations must be up there too.'

'We can't hang tinsel,' said Ivy. 'It would look ridiculous.'

Kitty wanted to tell her to stop being so negative, but it would be rude to say it in front of the others. Maybe she'd have a quiet word later. No, she wouldn't. She needed to show Ivy what was possible, then Ivy would change her mind of her own accord. She wouldn't be able to help herself.

'I bet I know what we could use,' said Abbie. 'The long strings of little silver bells that used to be wound up the staircase in and out of the balusters. I always loved seeing them when I was little. We could loop them around the walls or across the ceiling.'

'Good idea,' said Kitty. 'Let's all go up to the attic and see what else there is. There must be other things that aren't necessarily purely for Christmas.'

'There's bunting,' said Lily. 'There's pretty bunting in different colours and I bet we can find the Coronation bunting too, with all the flags of the Empire.'

'That would be perfect for wartime,' said Beatrice.

On the third floor, where they all slept, there was a staircase behind a door, and this led up to the attics beneath the roof.

'We ought to bring all these boxes down to the third floor and store them in one of the empty rooms,' said Abbie. 'It's not a good idea to keep anything up here. If an incendiary came through the roof...'

'That'll be a job for you and me, Abbie,' said Lily, 'but not today.'

'That's right,' said Kitty. 'Today is for having a look at what we've got.'

'This is a waste of time,' said Ivy. 'The bunting will be fine, but

Christmas decorations – for a summer wedding? We'll be a laughing stock.'

'The silver bells will be weddingy,' said Abbie. 'Like church bells.'

'Maybe so,' Ivy conceded, 'but everything else…'

'Let's see what we can find,' said Kitty. She was becoming tired of Ivy's attitude.

There were boxes of baubles in various styles, all of them very clearly Christmassy. Finally, Beatrice removed the lid from a large box and took out some crepe paper decorations, the sort that opened out and clipped together at the back – and they were all shaped like bells.

'More wedding bells,' Abbie said, delighted.

They trooped back downstairs with the bunting, the strings of silver bells and the box of crepe paper bells, and returned to the old dining room.

'I think we can make it look nice,' said Lily, looking round.

'Nice?' said Ivy, and Kitty's heart sank into her shoes. Then Ivy said, 'It'll look a jolly sight better than *nice*. It'll look… festive. And I don't mean Christmassy festive. I mean special occasion festive.'

Kitty bowed her head for a moment in relief. She'd been right. Once Ivy had been presented with something tangible, she'd perked up.

After that, things went much more smoothly, though Kitty wasn't sure if 'smoothly' was the right word when there was so much to do and they were all rushed off their feet. She was glad Naomi wasn't here to see it.

'There's a real feeling of "all hands on deck", don't you think?' she asked Beatrice when they stopped for a breather. 'There's a tingle of excitement in the air – or am I being daft?'

'It's because it's a wedding,' said Beatrice. 'Everyone wants it to go well.'

'If we can make a success of this reception...' mused Kitty, then she shook her head as if to dislodge the pesky ambition that had taken up residence. 'We'll have to see how it goes.'

Between the five of them, they cleaned the old dining room from top to bottom.

'We must stop calling it the old dining room or the parlour,' said Ivy. 'It isn't going to be very impressive if we use one of those names in front of the bridal party.'

'The reception room,' Abbie said at once and the others agreed.

Kitty had the chance to use the new name not half an hour later, because Mrs Packer turned up to ask if her husband could bring along a crate of beer he'd managed to get his hands on.

'And we've got a bottle of gin as well,' she added.

Afterwards, when Kitty told the others, Lily had an idea.

'What about the Dunbar's drinks? When we hosted a special occasion, I sometimes had the job of standing just inside the doorway with a tray of sherry for people to help themselves as they walked in.'

'It would make a lovely start to the reception,' said Beatrice.

'Proper Dunbar's,' said Ivy.

Kitty almost bounced on her toes in delight. 'We'll have to work out what to charge, then I'll speak to Mrs Packer.' Inspiration stirred. 'We've got the punch bowl too, haven't we? What if we made a fruity cordial and added a splash of alcohol? We'd have to think of a special name for it.'

'Wedding Punch,' said Beatrice.

'Dunbar's Wedding Punch,' said Lily. 'You have to have Dunbar's in the name.'

'Dunbar's Wartime Wedding Punch,' said Abbie.

'Perfect,' said Kitty. 'This is getting better and better. But we mustn't be too free with the alcohol. Once it's gone, we won't be able to get any more.'

'That sounds as if you think we might need more,' Ivy said slyly. 'Thinking of moving into the world of hospitality, are you?'

'Let's see how Saturday goes before we start making plans,' said Kitty, still trying to keep a lid on her new ambition.

Ivy turned to Abbie. 'Why don't you run down to the kitchen and count the punch glasses?'

'There are—' Lily began.

Ivy spoke over her. 'Thanks, chick. That'll be a big help. It's no good having fancy ideas about punch if we can't rustle up enough glasses.'

Abbie disappeared readily.

'Sorry,' said Ivy, 'but I didn't want to say this in front of her in case she started asking awkward questions.' To Kitty she said, 'How is Mr Packer paying for the reception? It would be a shame to see a cheque disappear into the Dunbar's bank account.'

'Cash, I'm pleased to say,' Kitty was happy to report. 'They were all set to pay cash for the church hall and Mrs Packer asked me if I'd take cash too, as if I was doing her a favour by saying I would. And before you ask, yes, she does know that Dunbar's costs more than a church hall. I added a charge for us to get the food ready too.'

She'd been tempted to do the food free of charge as a goodwill gesture, but she was running a business and it had become even more important to keep that in mind once she'd been denied access to the Dunbar's bank account.

She didn't say so out loud in case it sounded gloating, but she was very much looking forward to putting Mr Packer's payment into her post office account. That would be a big feather in her cap.

* * *

Lily picked up the photograph of Daniel from the top of the chest of drawers that did double-duty as her dressing-table. This was the bedroom she'd been given when she was fourteen years old. Kitty had offered her a bigger one when she'd moved back in after Toby's death, but Lily hadn't wanted that. Her room was simply furnished, with a bed, the chest of drawers, a hanging cupboard and a washstand in the corner. There was a mat beside the bed and some shelves were attached to the wall. Essentially, the room looked the same now as it always had, but if you opened the cupboard or the drawers, you'd find more clothes than there used to be. Better quality too. Even her carpet slippers had leather soles. Daniel had been generous. Lily had wished at the time that he would spend his money on her cousins rather than on her, but she hadn't liked to say so. Besides, Auntie Nettie and Uncle Irwin might have seen it as charity.

Lily stood looking at the picture of her handsome husband and remembering the inexperienced young girl who had fallen head over heels in love. Being catapulted into a relationship had made her feel like she was an adult, but she hadn't been grown-up at all, really. If she had been, she wouldn't have been so eager to please. She wouldn't have let Daniel's mother throw so many spanners in the works.

But it hadn't been Mrs Chadwick's fault that the marriage had ended.

Until then, Lily had kept the photograph of Daniel on the top of her bedside cupboard because – well, she couldn't have said why. Probably out of habit. But she'd moved it to the chest of drawers last summer after they officially went their separate ways. It had crossed her mind that maybe she should put it away in a drawer, but somehow that hadn't felt right.

And now she'd met another man, and had made a firm decision to get on with her life. Right this moment, she couldn't remember which had come first, the man or the decision.

There was a soft tap on her door. Lily replaced Daniel's picture on the chest of drawers.

'Come in,' she called.

Kitty opened the door. 'Can I have a word?' She stepped inside and shut the door behind her. 'I wanted to catch you on your own so I could ask you something a bit delicate. It's about Elsie Packer's wedding. If you'd rather make yourself scarce for the day, I'd understand. Don't feel you have to help out. We can manage without you.'

'Oh aye?' Lily smiled. 'Now the china and crystal have been washed, and the room's been decorated, I've served my purpose, have I?'

Kitty smiled back, getting the joke, but then her hazel eyes turned serious. 'I don't want you to be upset, Lily. You've been through so much in your marriage and I don't want to thrust someone else's big day on you if you'd find it difficult.'

'I'll be fine,' Lily assured her. 'Me and Daniel – that was a long time ago. That's how it feels. As for Elsie Packer and her corporal, I hope they have a wonderful day and if I can contribute to it, then I'll be happy to.'

Kitty nodded. 'Good. I wanted you to have the choice.'

Lily looked at her. Kitty was her boss and her landlady, but most of all she was a true friend.

Lily kissed her cheek. 'Thank you for thinking of me.'

* * *

'It looks splendid, doesn't it?' breathed Abbie, standing in the doorway of the newly christened reception room.

'It certainly does.' Lily smiled affectionately at the girl, glad to see her excited.

A lot of hard graft had gone into getting the room ready. Pairs of crepe paper bells hung from the ceiling lights and in the corners of the room, while the strings of silver bells were displayed in graceful loops around the walls and also from the corners of the room to the centre of the ceiling.

'What about a table for the food?' asked Beatrice.

'There's the club room table,' said Abbie.

'There's the table in the old staff dining room off the kitchen,' said Lily.

'Imagine getting that up the basement stairs,' said Kitty. 'Let's borrow the club room table. You don't mind, do you, Beatrice?'

The table that the children used for ping-pong had received a thorough polishing using Lily's home-made furniture cream. Then, with much laughter, they'd struggled to get it out of one door and in through the other, having to turn it on its side and angle it this way and that to feed the legs through the openings, with Ivy holding each door open as wide as it could go.

Lily had spent ages pressing all the tablecloths. Two large cloths had been employed to cover the ping-pong table and hang all the way to the floor, and Abbie had pinned union flag bunting to the front and sides. The food was to be set out on this table in due course, with the cardboard wedding cake as the grand centrepiece. The real cake was an eggless sponge that Mrs Ivy Dunbar had made, whisking it until it was as light as air.

Every table and chair Dunbar's possessed had been arranged around the room in companionable clusters, the snowy table-cloths disguising the differences in style. On a table in one of the corners stood a gramophone and a selection of records, provided by Vivian. Lily had told him about the wedding and he'd made the offer of a loan. After a little thought, Lily had decided to ask Kitty.

'The gramophone belongs to Dr Shawston?' Kitty had questioned, frowning. 'The man who saved the children from drowning? How does he know about this wedding?'

'We've seen one another a few times,' said Lily and held her breath. Would Kitty press for details?

But Kitty merely said, 'It's a kind offer. Please tell him I'd be delighted.'

Vivian had delivered the gramophone yesterday evening when they had all been busy putting up the British Empire bunting in the foyer, and he'd stayed to help. Perhaps Lily ought to have felt madly self-conscious, but she hadn't. He hadn't singled her out for special attention and that had suited her. Would anyone ask questions afterwards? But no one had. Presumably everyone had taken their acquaintance at face value. It had made Lily wonder where she wanted this relationship to go, if anywhere. She had felt wary of him to start with, then friendship had begun to grow. Now... what?

During the morning, the Packers arrived with the food.

'Would you like to see the reception room?' Kitty offered.

'Yes, please,' said Mrs Packer.

'No, not me,' said Elsie. 'I want it to be a surprise when I walk in with my new husband.'

Kitty escorted Mrs Packer across the foyer and opened the door.

'*Oh*,' said Mrs Packer. 'It's *won*derful. Thank you so much.'

Next moment, Elsie was by her side. 'Just look. Oh, Mum, just look.' Tears rolled down her cheeks. 'Don't mind me. They're happy tears.'

'She's always been a one for crying at happy things,' said her mother.

'I just hope I'm not going to blub my way through the wedding,' said Elsie, her smile watery but nevertheless radiant.

When the Packers departed, Lily and the others got the food ready. She, Beatrice and Abbie were on sandwich duty. Abbie did the shrimp paste while Beatrice worked on the lettuce and cucumber, and Lily made sandwiches of salad cream and chopped cabbage.

Meanwhile, Kitty made sausage rolls and vegetable rolls while Mrs Dunbar filled fritters with celery and cheese, and used tinned salmon to make croquettes.

'Cover the sandwiches with damp tea towels so the bread doesn't dry out,' she told Abbie.

'Everyone will be here soon,' said Kitty. 'Let's pour the sherry and put it on the trays.'

Lily and Abbie were to position themselves immediately inside the reception room, offering drinks as the guests walked in.

'Your job,' Kitty said to Beatrice, 'is to stick close to the punch bowl and make sure no one swipes a quick sample before we're ready to serve it.'

'May I have a taste?' Abbie asked.

'Certainly not,' said her mother. 'There's half a bottle of port in there.'

'And two tablespoons of brandy,' Lily added with a grin.

Kitty's eyebrows shot up her forehead. 'Brandy?'

'You can't have a good punch without brandy,' Lily answered blithely. 'It's the Dunbar way.'

'Along with the beer and the gin the Packers have provided, they'll barely be able to totter home afterwards,' Kitty said wryly.

'Precisely,' said Lily. 'And they'll all remember it for the rest of their lives as the most wonderful wedding reception they ever went to.'

* * *

'And it was wonderful too,' Lily told Vivian that evening as they strolled through the streets. 'It lasted until around five and then they all went to the station together to see the happy couple on their way. They've got two nights in Southport, then Corporal Tyler has to return to his unit.' She remembered her own partings from Daniel and felt a pang for the newly-weds. 'Still,' she added, wanting to hang on to the happiness of the day, 'they'll have a first-class day to look back on.'

'It must have been hard work for you and the others,' said Vivian. 'When any sort of function goes well, it's thanks to what's going on behind the scenes.'

Lily turned her face up to his. 'It was worth it. It was just like the olden days.'

That made Vivian laugh. 'You make it sound as if Dunbar's was a thriving hostelry back in the Middle Ages.'

Lily pretended to give his arm a slap. 'You know what I mean. It was like the old place had come back to life.'

'Do you miss the way it used to be?' he asked.

Lily thought about it. 'Yes and no. It feels right in a way that Dunbar's closed its doors at the same time as everything went so badly wrong for me. If Dunbar's had carried on, and I'd had to go back to being a chambermaid, that would have been hard.'

'I can imagine,' said Vivian. 'No, that's not true. I can't imagine what it was like for you to lose your son. But I can offer my sympathy and try to understand.'

Lily recalled the way Daniel's grief had floored her. She had known exactly how he was feeling and it had been too much for her to face up to. Was it easier for Vivian to offer support because he hadn't suffered the same terrible bereavement? Or had she been weak?

'Let's talk about something else,' she said.

'Tell me more about today,' he replied at once.

Lily was happy to do so. She talked about the Dunbar's Wartime Wedding Punch, which had proved immensely popular.

'And your Gracie Fields record led to a proper sing-song.'

'I'm glad to have contributed,' he said, 'though the community singing might have owed more to the punch than it did to my record.'

'You can share the honours,' Lily teased.

The more time she spent with him, the more comfortable she felt. His having provided the gramophone and helped put up the empire bunting had only increased her feeling of ease... but the ease had a new edge to it, a spark of attraction that hadn't been there before. Or maybe it had been, but she had never allowed herself to see it.

And if she was acknowledging it now, was that because she was ready to act on it?

15

Kitty was chuffed to bits with how the wedding reception had gone, not least because the bride's cousin, who had been her bridesmaid, had taken Kitty to one side and asked if she could hold her own reception at Dunbar's later in the year.

When Kitty described the reception to Naomi, her sister seemed conflicted.

'I'm delighted it went well, obviously,' she said, 'but it worries me that it'll give you ideas.'

'Too late.' Kitty couldn't stop a huge smile breaking out. 'It already has.'

The next time she saw Mr Tulip, she told him about the reception and, next thing she knew, he had pointed another bride-to-be in the direction of Dunbar's.

'This really could turn into a new venture,' Kitty told Abbie.

'See?' Abbie replied. 'I said you should have left the decorations up after the wedding.'

'Cheeky,' said Kitty. 'You only suggested it because you liked the place looking pretty, not because you thought we'd get more bookings.'

'If this new business takes off,' said Abbie, 'who knows, I could end up working here. I could be the social secretary.'

Kitty's heart gave a little bump. 'I would love that, but we're a long way off needing somebody to do that job.'

'So I still have to go to work at the Town Hall when I leave school?' Abbie asked.

'Without question,' said Kitty. 'You're lucky to have a job with the Corporation.'

'But I could end up working for Dunbar's one day,' said Abbie. 'Daddy would love that, wouldn't he?'

'Yes, he would,' Kitty agreed. 'No doubt about it.'

She talked to Beatrice about it later on while the two of them sat together in the kitchen.

'Abbie has written to Bill to tell him all about the wedding reception,' said Kitty, 'but if Bill expects a nice fat sum of money to appear on the next Dunbar's bank statement, he's in for a disappointment. I put the cash straight into the post office.'

'Does he know about that account yet?' Beatrice asked.

Kitty shook her head. 'Not yet. I'm going to hold off from telling him for as long as I can. He won't like it one bit.'

'Perhaps... perhaps you should tell him and get it over with,' Beatrice suggested.

'It isn't just that I want to dodge his wrath,' Kitty explained. 'I also very definitely do not want to feel answerable to him.' She looked at her friend. 'You're very tactfully not saying anything.'

'I want to provide moral support,' said Beatrice, 'but it's important not to come between man and wife.'

'Wives are meant to be answerable to their husbands,' said Kitty, 'and they're meant to be happy to be so. They've never been meant to question it, and that still applies even though the men are away at war and the wives are here at home, taking responsibility for everything.'

She smothered a sigh. When the war was over and Bill returned home, was she going to have to fit back in with the old, accepted ways? Her mouth went dry. Even posing the question was a daring thing to do. Some might call it outrageous. At any rate, it was best kept to herself. Even if she wanted to discuss it, it wouldn't be fair to put Beatrice on the spot.

Instead, she changed the subject.

'Never mind me. What about you and Frank? You haven't been out together for a little while.'

Beatrice looked away for a few moments. 'I wasn't very nice to him the last time I saw him.'

'Beatrice, that doesn't sound like you.'

'I think he might have retired to lick his wounds,' said Beatrice. 'Or maybe he simply doesn't want to see me again.'

'Surely not,' said Kitty. 'The man who walked up and down Lily Street, hoping to bump into you? The man who sent you peonies because they had artificial ones in the restaurant?'

'The man I more or less accused of walking off with my life,' said Beatrice.

'Explain,' Kitty insisted.

'Same old story,' said Beatrice. 'Nothing you haven't heard before. He was the one who didn't want children and now he is very happy being the father of five. Me, I was positive about wanting a family, yet I've ended up with... a different life.'

'I'm glad you didn't say you've ended up with nothing,' Kitty told her warmly.

'I've recently trained myself not to say that, though I have to say it's a lot harder trying to train myself not to think it.'

Kitty reached out to cover Beatrice's hand with her own and gave it a gentle squeeze. 'I would never make light of your child-lessness—'

'Don't finish that sentence,' Beatrice broke in. 'I know what you were going to say. "But you have a good job... But you work with children..." I know those things. I don't need to be reminded.'

'I'm sorry,' said Kitty. 'You're right. I was going to say something of the kind.'

'I understand,' Beatrice answered. 'It's human nature to try to make others feel better. Meeting Frank again has brought a lot of things to the surface, things I thought I'd left behind. I'm finding it all rather difficult. Maybe... maybe I'm still unhappy at heart.'

'Oh, Beatrice.'

'I've got so much to be grateful for.' Beatrice sat up straight. 'Things went badly wrong for me last year, but I ended up living here with you and I've got a job that is better than anything I could have dreamed of.'

'All that is true,' Kitty said gently, 'but just because some things are good doesn't mean you're not allowed to feel that other things are bad.'

'I feel all churned up about it,' Beatrice blurted out. 'I can't seem to think straight because I'm so busy just *feeling*.'

'Just remember one thing,' said Kitty. 'I know we're all supposed to have stiff upper lips these days, but you can always say anything you like to me.'

* * *

Lily paused for a moment outside Dunbar's front doors. She drew a breath, rather a sharp one, smoothed her coat and touched her hat to make sure it was on straight. She was sure her appearance was exactly as it should be, but she felt the need to check all the same. There was nothing quite so smart as a WVS uniform. Pretending to be out on WVS duty was the perfect way to hide the development in her relationship with Vivian. Everyone was on duty at all sorts of times.

Lily was enjoying this new phase of her life and part of the enjoyment was derived from keeping it secret. Not because she was secretive by nature or because she intended to deceive her friends, but simply because she wanted to keep it private. It felt safer that way – less of a commitment. That made her sound like a flighty piece with an eye for the men, and nothing could be further from the truth. She believed wholeheartedly in loving and loyal committed relationships and yet – and yet it felt important to keep this new relationship private. She preferred the word 'private' to 'secret'. It made her feel better. Being Vivian's mistress – she shrank from the word, yet it was the only one that described their relationship – had made her happy; or perhaps not so much happy as plain relieved. It had made her feel alive again. She had forgotten what that felt like.

'You're looking better than I've seen you,' Kitty remarked to her. 'Your eyes are brighter.'

'Yes, I do feel better than I've felt for a long time,' Lily agreed.

'Good.'

Guilt caused an ache in the back of Lily's throat. She didn't want to lie to her friend, but neither was she ready to talk about what had happened between her and Vivian. It was hard enough talking to Vivian about it. All Lily wanted was to live in the moment, but Vivian was already picturing their future together. Maybe he was right to do so. After all, Lily wasn't the sort to take up with a man just for the heck of it. But she still wasn't ready to think about the consequences.

'I'm still married,' she said to Vivian, trying to pass it off lightly. 'I can't make any decisions.'

'You could if you wanted to,' he replied firmly. 'I'm happy to wait until after the war, Lily. They're already expecting thousands upon thousands of divorces to take place afterwards. A divorce now would be newsworthy, but after the war yours will be just one among many.'

Lily was taken aback and couldn't hide it.

'What's the matter?' Vivian asked. 'A post-war divorce was always on the cards for you… wasn't it?'

'Of course,' Lily agreed, but her heart hammered. She forced herself to think about it. 'I know it has to happen, but I still can't imagine it. Will I have to meet up with Daniel to plan it? Is it going to be like those divorces in novels and films, where the man does the decent thing and takes the blame? Then he goes to a seedy hotel with a young woman specifically so that a private detective can witness them entering the premises together, even though everyone knows that nothing is actually going to happen between them?' A little shudder ran through her shoulders and across her back. 'And why should Daniel take the blame? I'm the one who's carrying on with someone else.'

'Carrying on?' Vivian repeated. 'I can assure you that that's the very last thing I'm doing.'

'It's just an expression folk use,' said Lily. 'I didn't mean anything by it.'

'I should hope not,' said Vivian. 'I couldn't bear to think that, for you, this is just "carrying on" when, for me, it's absolutely and unquestionably the real thing.'

Lily's heart swelled with emotion and her skin tingled. When Toby had died, she hadn't lost just him. She had lost her relationship with Daniel as well. Now she had been given another chance at love.

'This is happening so fast,' she whispered, touching Vivian's lips with gentle fingers.

But if this relationship was really and truly what she wanted, why wasn't she rushing into it at top speed?

* * *

July came, but Beatrice couldn't stop thinking about June and the fall of Tobruk, which had stunned the whole country, not least because the Germans took over twenty thousand prisoners of war. She tried to concentrate on the good things. July meant Abbie was shortly to leave school and start work at the Town Hall. Beatrice was looking forward to the two of them walking to work together. Or maybe Abbie wouldn't want to go with her. Maybe she would meet girls her own age and pal up with them. Beatrice hoped so. She was keen for everything to go as swimmingly as possible for Abbie, who was a lovely child – no, not a child any longer. She would have to stop using that word. Abbie wouldn't thank her for it.

Beatrice was still thinking about the problem of the looker-after children possibly facing evacuation. She went to see Sister District, who was in charge of the district nurses in the area where Beatrice used to be the inco lady. Sister District was a slim woman with an upright figure and intelligent eyes. She didn't just glance your way when she spoke or listened to you; she always turned her head and looked directly at you, which was good in a way, because it made you feel listened to, but all the same it could be unnerving.

Beatrice sat in her office, pleased to see her again and hoping the feeling was mutual. Sister District asked her about her work. Beatrice resisted the temptation to launch into her real reason for coming here and talked in general about her duties.

Sister District breathed a small sigh. 'I never doubted your integrity, you know – when you were accused of theft, I mean. But I had to suspend you because it was such a serious accusation.'

'It worked out well in the end,' said Beatrice.

There was no point in mentioning just how bad things had

got for her. She'd lost her home as well as her job and sometimes people who knew of the allegation had been perfectly vile to her in the street.

'It certainly sounds as if you are doing well in your new role,' said Sister District. 'What brings you here today, Miss Inkerman? I assume you haven't popped in simply to pass the time of day.'

'That's correct,' said Beatrice, glad of the opening. She began to explain about the looker-after children, but she didn't get very far.

'Oh, them.' Sister District nodded. 'I remember you being concerned about them last year when you worked for the inco service.'

'The Corporation is considering having them evacuated,' said Beatrice, careful not to mention Miss Brewster by name. 'That way, they can't carry on being responsible for what happens at home.'

Sister District's mouth turned down at the sides as she considered this. 'I can see the reasoning behind it.'

'So can I,' said Beatrice. 'I'm sure nobody wants these children to have these duties, but it seems rather drastic to send them away. I've come here to ask for your help – or at least for your advice,' she added quickly, not wanting to be pushy. 'I've been wondering if perhaps the district nurses could take over the looking after of these invalids, so that the children would be free to be children.'

Sister District was already shaking her head. 'That wouldn't do at all. I appreciate the reason behind your desire to see these children have better lives and proper childhoods, but foisting all that work onto my district nurses isn't the answer. The nurses could go in and administer medication, if necessary, but it isn't their job to do the shopping or the cleaning. As for things like bed baths, our service provides those for people who are temporarily ill, not for permanent invalids. That's the family's responsibility.'

Beatrice suppressed a sigh. 'I thought it was worth asking.'

'I feel sorry for these children, I really do,' said Sister District, 'but district nurses are there to provide nursing care, not domestic support. If the mothers of these children don't have adult relatives who can step in, then I'm afraid the work is bound to fall on young shoulders. I'm sorry, Miss Inkerman.'

'Thank you for seeing me, anyway,' said Beatrice.

'What about the WVS?' suggested Sister District. 'Have you tried them?'

'No,' Beatrice answered. 'They will help out when someone is ill or is convalescing after an operation, and they'll always help out in a time of crisis, but what I'm looking for is permanent support.'

'But it wouldn't be permanent, would it?' Sister District looked thoughtful. 'It would be permanent if my district nurses took it on, but you're talking about children being evacuated, aren't you? That makes it a wartime situation, and that makes it temporary in my book.'

Beatrice's eyes widened. Had she been approaching this in the wrong way?

* * *

Sister District had given Beatrice a lot to think about and it made her feel better, more positive. As tempting as it was to go dashing round to the local WVS office and speak to Mrs Ford, the branch organiser, it would be far better to hold her horses. She talked it over with Kitty in the kitchen while Kitty worked her way through the ironing pile and Beatrice did some household mending.

'I think the best way to approach Mrs Ford might be for me to write up a report,' said Beatrice. 'I've learned how to write reports since I've been at the Town Hall.'

'Miss Brewster has been good for something, then,' Kitty said with a smile.

'Credit where it's due, yes,' Beatrice agreed.

'You'll have to make sure you give Mrs Ford all the information and leave nothing out,' said Kitty.

Beatrice nodded, well aware of the importance of this. 'I quite like the idea of it, actually. I haven't forgotten how, when she met me, I was in disgrace because of that accusation of theft hanging over my head.'

'It was a hard time for you,' Kitty acknowledged.

'I'm not blaming Mrs Ford,' Beatrice said quickly. 'I was lucky she agreed to take me on as a member of her WVS group, but you're right: it was hard not being allowed to do anything on my own and always having to have another WVS lady with me. If I can put together a good report, it will show Mrs Ford what I'm made of.'

'She's already found that out over the past year,' said Kitty. 'You don't have anything to prove as far as she's concerned.'

'Thank you for saying that,' Beatrice replied, touched. 'I know you're right, but I still want to impress her.'

The doorbell rang. Beatrice was in the middle of sewing a button onto a blouse of Abbie's. She was about to set it aside, but Kitty had just finished folding the final pillowcase, so she went upstairs to answer the door. She returned a minute later.

'It's Frank,' she said.

'Did you tell him I was here?' Beatrice asked.

'Of course I did. You need to speak to him, Beatrice.'

'I'm not ready,' she answered.

'By which you mean you're still tying yourself in knots,' Kitty replied. 'Tell him that. Honestly, I think it's the right thing to do.

He's obviously interested in you and you ought to talk to him. Who knows, it might help clear your mind.'

Beatrice seriously doubted it, but she went upstairs and found Frank waiting for her in the foyer. As always, she was struck by what a fine figure he cut. Just a few minutes ago, she'd been feeling good about herself and the possibility of impressing Mrs Ford. Now she was back to being unsure of herself and what she should do.

Frank gave her an uncertain half-smile. 'You don't look pleased to see me.'

About to say, 'Of course I am,' Beatrice stopped herself. She remembered what Kitty had said. She made herself say, 'I honestly don't know whether or not I am.'

'Crikey,' said Frank. 'That's honest. Rather too honest.'

'I don't mean to be rude,' Beatrice said quickly, wanting to make amends. 'I'm trying to be honest, especially after what I said the last time I saw you. I want you to understand the position I'm in. I want you to see it from my point of view.'

'I'm listening,' said Frank. 'I want to understand.'

Beatrice struggled to find the words. It wasn't just a matter of choosing them. It was also having the courage to utter them.

When she didn't speak, Frank said, 'For me, meeting you again has been an extraordinary experience. I never imagined I would see you again. I'll be honest. I was very happy being married to my late wife and I continue to be very happy with our children. I'm not going to pretend I spent years pining for you. But now that I've found you again...' His chin dipped down for a moment, making him appear embarrassed. 'I don't want to say the wrong thing. After what you said to me last time about how I've ended up with the life you wanted for yourself, I've barely been able to think of anything else. There's a part of me that would completely understand if you never wanted to see me again, but even as I say those words, I'm terrified of giving you that idea if it hadn't occurred to you before. Sorry, sorry, I'm rambling. I'm so nervous about seeing you. All I can say is that meeting you again has brought romance back into my life. That probably sounds a mad thing to say when you've done nothing to encourage any such thing. I just want you to give me a chance.' He shook his head. 'My tongue has run away with me. If you want to shut me up, you should probably say something now.'

'This seems to be easier for you than it is for me,' said Beatrice. 'Every time I try to think about meeting you again, all I can picture is your children – the family you supposedly didn't want.'

'Come and meet them.' There was great warmth in Frank's voice. 'I mean it, Beatrice. Come and meet my children. Get to know them. I would be proud and happy to introduce them to you – and you to them.'

Beatrice's hands felt clammy. 'No.'

'No?' he asked. 'Or not yet?'

'Stop trying to push me,' said Beatrice. 'I have to do this at my own speed.'

He surprised her by smiling. 'At least you've acknowledged that you're doing it, as you put it. That gives me the hope I came for. Thank you, Beatrice.'

16

Kitty was sitting at a table in the reception room, writing to Bill, when the doorbell rang. She heard Ivy answer it and a few moments later Naomi appeared, dressed in her WVS uniform. She bent over Kitty to give her a kiss before she sat down.

'Writing to Bill?' she asked.

Kitty nodded. 'It's mostly about Abbie, probably repeating all the things Abbie has already said in her own letters.'

Naomi shrugged. 'That doesn't matter. Abbie is everything to Bill.'

Kitty hesitated before she said quietly, 'It sometimes seems like the one thing left that we have in common.' In truth, it *was* the only thing, but she couldn't bring herself to say so out loud, not even to Naomi.

'Have you told Bill about the wedding receptions?' Naomi asked.

'There's no point in trying to withhold the information,' Kitty answered in a dry voice. 'Abbie and Mrs Dunbar will both have told him all about them. We've held four now and there are three more in the diary.'

'Has Bill asked what you're charging?' Naomi asked.

'Yes, but I ignored the question.' Kitty tried to make light of it. 'Instead I extolled the virtues of Dunbar's Wartime Wedding Punch. With luck, he won't twig that there are no wedding payments listed on his next bank statement.'

Naomi raised her eyebrows. 'And if he does?'

Now it was Kitty's turn to shrug. 'Then I'll have to come clean, won't I? But I'm holding off as long as I can. I'm not going to go looking for trouble.'

'Don't...'

'Don't what?' asked Kitty.

'Well, don't forget that, at the end of all this, at the end of the war, Bill is going to come home and... well, I know things have been hard; I know he has made things hard for you; but don't... don't store up the bad bits or you'll make it worse in the long run.'

Kitty looked at her in surprise. 'Are you telling me to swallow what Bill has done?'

'Don't sound so needled,' Naomi answered. 'I'm just reminding you that the war won't go on for ever and there's nothing to be gained by building up problems.'

Kitty was silent. Should she tell Naomi the truth of what was in her mind and her heart? That she had been aware of all that was wrong in her marriage for a long time, but keeping Dunbar's afloat had expanded her thinking. Now she didn't just think of Bill's shortcomings and what an impact they had on her life. She also thought about her new responsibilities and how well she was managing. Instead of wringing her hands over Bill's behaviour, she thought with pride of her own achievements. She also turned cold inside every time she thought of how she no longer had feelings for him. What did the future hold for them?

Should she, could she, share any of that with her sister? But the door opened and Ivy appeared with a tray of tea, and the moment slipped away.

The three of them chatted for a while, then Naomi went on her way. Kitty quickly finished her letter, licked a stamp, stuck it on the envelope and took it to the pillar box. When she came back, she went up to the third floor. There were times when she missed the family flat. Small rooms along a narrow landing didn't exactly create a cosy atmosphere.

As she walked along the landing, Ivy appeared from her bedroom.

'There you are,' she said. 'We need to have a word. I meant to grab you earlier, but your sister arrived.'

'Is anything wrong?' Kitty asked.

'No. Why, should there be?'

Kitty opened the door that had been set up as a little sitting room for the Dunbars. When they had first talked of leaving the family flat and moving upstairs, Kitty had briefly, just for a flash, entertained the hope that there might be a sitting room just for her and Abbie, and a separate one for Ivy, but it would have been churlish, not to say plain unwelcoming, not to have it as Ivy's room as well, especially after the way Ivy had given up her own furniture so they could accommodate lodgers.

They sat down.

'It's the girls,' said Ivy, referring to Miss Tennant, Miss O'Brien and Miss Gregson. 'The end of July isn't far off and they'll be leaving soon to go back to their jobs in London. I assume you will want to replace them with more lodgers.'

For a moment, Kitty indulged in sentimental thoughts of the family flat. 'Yes, we better had. It's all about bringing in the income.'

'Do you want to advertise or would you rather leave it to me?'

'If you're happy to take it on...' Kitty knew this was what Ivy was angling for.

Ivy sat up straight, looking pleased with herself. 'Good. And there's another thing. It's more than time to stop carrying the chairs downstairs every time there's a wedding reception and then fetching them back up again afterwards. You know I'm right, Kitty. It's a heck of a lot of work.'

'But I like having chairs up here,' Kitty protested.

'Because this room is so comfy?' Ivy asked with a hint of sarcasm – more than a hint.

'Because I want to provide Abbie with a proper home.' Kitty looked round rather helplessly at the inadequately furnished room.

'Of course you do.' There was no sarcasm now, just understanding. 'But we can't carry on carting chairs up and down all those stairs, especially if there are going to be more functions. The same goes for that dratted ping-pong table. Do you remember Lily suggesting the table in the old staff dining room off the kitchen? I've had a look at it. It's not as wide as the ping-pong table but it's longer, just what you need for setting out a buffet. Getting it up the basement stairs to the reception room will be a nightmare, but once it's there, it can stay for good. And there's nothing to say we can't use the room ourselves as a sitting room, if we want to. As for Abbie, I wouldn't worry. As long as she's got her mum here, Dunbar's will always be her home.'

* * *

The day Abbie left school, she arrived home clearly happy and excited. Kitty felt emotional. She had wanted to go and meet Abbie at the school gates and walk home with her on her last day, but you couldn't inflict that sort of attention on a fourteen-year-old, so she had stayed at home, anxiously awaiting her daughter's return.

'I can't believe my baby has left school,' she said.

Abbie groaned. '*Mum*, I'm not a *baby*.'

'You'll always be your mum's baby,' Lily answered with a grin.

Abbie flashed Kitty a look. 'As long as you don't call me that in public.'

'I wouldn't dream of it,' Kitty answered, but her heart still felt full.

The following morning, Abbie looked every inch the office junior in a dark skirt and white blouse, which was what she'd been instructed to wear. Kitty admired her appearance while not letting herself gush, much as she was dying to.

When Abbie set off to walk to the Town Hall with Beatrice, Kitty longed to stand on the pavement and watch her precious daughter disappear along Lily Street, but she restrained herself. For a moment, she ached for the little girl who had loved nothing better than to be the centre of parental attention, but she knew it was more important to focus on the bright young lady her daughter had grown into.

Knowing how Bill must be feeling today at having to miss out on this special milestone, Kitty settled down to write him a letter about how smart and pretty Abbie had looked as she went off to her first day at work. She might not have time for her husband these days, but she would always have time for Abbie's father.

It wasn't long before she had other things to write about. The end of July brought a series of air raids. Middleton was hit, as was the station at Royton, and more than three hundred incendiaries were dropped over Thornton.

The end of the month also brought changes to rationing. A new clothes rationing year started, but the number of points everyone was allowed had gone down. Syrup and treacle were removed from the preserves ration and put on points instead.

'I can't work out if that's a good or bad thing,' said Kitty.

'At least they've put the cheese ration up,' said Beatrice.

'Only for a few weeks,' said Ivy. 'It's come to something when an extra bit of cheese is a treat to be grateful for.'

'We deserve a treat now that sweets and chocolate have gone on the ration,' said Beatrice.

August brought heat. Dogs panted in the shade and waves of heat rose from the pavement. Sunlight brightened all it touched and in the grey landscape of wartime rubble, colours appeared more vivid.

Kitty had got used to Abbie coming home at six o'clock instead of four. Abbie proudly handed over her wage packet each week and Kitty gave her some spends.

'Make it last,' she said each time, making sure she had a smile on her face as she said it.

To Ivy she said privately, when they were sitting together in the reception room, 'I want her to be careful with money, but I don't want to labour the point in case it pushes her the other way.'

'Just because money slips through Bill's fingers like water doesn't mean Abbie will be that way inclined,' said Ivy. 'You can trust her. She's got a good head on her shoulders.'

The doorbell sounded.

'Typical,' said Ivy. 'As soon as we sit down for a cuppa.'

'I'll go,' said Kitty. She gently stubbed out her cigarette in the ashtray so she could re-light it later.

She opened the front door to find Mr Barnes from the Grove, along with three more of Lily Street's hoteliers.

'Goodness,' she said. 'This looks like a deputation.'

'That's because it is,' Mr Barnes replied bluntly. 'Well, are you going to let us in?'

Kitty was on the verge of standing aside to do just that, but she stopped herself. She had faced a lot in the past year and it had toughened her. She looked at the men in front of her. Not one of them wore a smile.

'No, I don't think I am, Mr Barnes,' she said in a pleasant voice. 'Not if this is a deputation. Something tells me you aren't here to ask me to join Lily Street's fire watchers.'

'We're here,' said Mr Barnes, 'about this wedding reception service you've set up. It seems you're doing well out of it.'

'Yes, I am, thank you. Not that it's any of your business.' Kitty allowed her gaze to scan the displeased mouths and hard eyes in front of her.

'On the contrary,' said Mr Barnes, 'it is very much our business. You've already compromised the good name of the Lily Street hotels by becoming a storage institution—'

'I've done no such thing,' Kitty retorted, a sharp note entering her tone. 'One of the conditions attached to the change of use of the building was that Dunbar's must still look the same from the outside as it has always done – precisely so that the rest of Lily Street didn't get a bad name. In any case,' she added, 'the storage facility has been up and running for a year. It's a bit late to complain about it now.'

'We're not here about the storage business, Mrs Dunbar,' said Mr Clements from Fairhaven, which was a few doors down from the Grove. 'We're here about your wedding receptions.'

'What about them?' Kitty was truly baffled.

'You're taking business away from the rest of us,' Mr Barnes declared, his face so tight with annoyance that his lips barely moved, 'and we won't stand for it. We have written a letter,' and he flourished an envelope, 'requiring you to cease and desist.'

That made it sound formal, even legal, and Kitty's heart fluttered. But he'd said '*We* have written', which didn't make it sound like a solicitor's letter.

'Well?' Mr Barnes thrust the letter towards her. 'Aren't you going to take it?'

Kitty folded her arms. 'No, I'm not, Mr Barnes. You've told me what it contains, so there's no need for me to read it.'

The men looked as if they didn't know whether to be astonished or vexed. Then Mr Rossiter from the Belvedere spoke up.

'*And* you've taken in hotel residents.'

'Oh, you mean the lodgers. They're living in the family flat. You all have a family flat, don't you, in your hotels? Well, that's where my lodgers are, so you can't call them hotel residents. This is their billet and they've been here for a few weeks now, so it's a bit late in the day for you to take exception – not that you have any reason to do so,' she added quickly.

'We shall complain to the Corporation,' said Mr Barnes.

'You do that,' Kitty flung back at once. 'Address your letter to Miss Fay Brewer in the Welfare Department. That's Fay without an E. She's the one who asked us to offer the young ladies a billet. I'm sure that if you're all thinking of offering your own family flats as billets, Miss Brewer would be only too delighted to inform the billeting officer on your behalf. Now, unless you have more complaints, kindly excuse me.'

She shut the door on them and, turning, leaned her back against it. It took her a moment to realise that Ivy was standing in the reception room doorway.

'That was—' Kitty began.

'I know,' said Ivy. 'I heard every word. I was all set to barge in and help you, but you didn't need help. You managed perfectly well on your own.'

'Thanks.' Kitty's smile was a bit shaky, but it was still a smile. 'I did, didn't I? Those rotters!' she exclaimed as vexation came bubbling up. 'Fancy ganging up on me like that. Well, I'm not having it.'

'What are you going to do?' Ivy asked.

'For a start I need to go to the Town Hall and see Fay Brewer and warn her she might receive a letter of complaint against Dunbar's.'

'I'm sure she won't,' said Ivy. 'Those idiots had their knickers in a twist about so-called hotel residents. They wouldn't dare approach Miss Brewer for fear of being expected to give up their own family flats.'

'You're probably right,' said Kitty. 'Even so, having bandied her name about, I owe her an explanation. I'll go and see her tomorrow.'

In the event, however, she saw Fay Brewer that same evening. Every so often Miss Brewer dropped in for a session of the Time Off Club, and this was one of those evenings. Kitty drew her aside and poured out the story of what had taken place that afternoon.

'Well, really!' Fay Brewer exclaimed, her hazel eyes seeming to darken. 'What bullies. I'll go and sort this out right now.'

'Honestly, I'm sure you don't need to do anything,' said Kitty.

'I disagree. Not that it is any of these men's business but I will explain to them, in words of one syllable if necessary, that the agreement you have with the Corporation is that Dunbar's is now used for storage and that your two big front rooms on the ground floor are used for meetings, and that includes social functions. Well, it does,' she added breezily. 'What are the Time Off Club and the Gentlemen's Club if not social gatherings? And you have the Corporation's blessings for both of those. A wedding is just a different sort of social gathering.'

'We've got a post-funeral get-together booked in as well,' Ivy put in.

'There you are, then,' said Miss Brewer. 'I shall make them

feel very ashamed of themselves for wanting to disrupt funeral arrangements. You mentioned Mr Barnes. He's at the Grove across the road, isn't he? Who are the others and which are their hotels?'

'I'll come with you,' said Kitty.

'No need. In fact, it would be better if you didn't,' said Fay Brewer. 'I shall march through the Grove's front doors and ask Mr Barnes what makes him think he can interfere in Corporation business.'

Off she went. Kitty and Ivy looked at one another.

'I swear that feather in her hat is perkier than usual,' said Kitty.

Miss Brewer returned forty minutes later, smiling cheerfully.

'Did you lay the law down with Mr Barnes and the rest?' asked Kitty.

'I did better than that. I've set their wives on them. I started at the Grove, but Mr Barnes was out on ARP duty, so I went to Fairhaven and Mr Clements was out also, but Mrs Clements was there with her friend Mrs Rossiter from the Belvedere. To cut the story short, the wives had no idea their husbands had been plotting against you and they were mortified when I spilled the beans. As for the weddings, Mrs Rossiter immediately said that in wartime there are more than enough to go round and what on earth did Mr Rossiter think he was up to? Then Mrs Clements said that she'd heard good things about a delicious punch you've been serving.'

'Dunbar's Wartime Wedding Punch,' said Kitty.

'I shouldn't be surprised if you find her on your doorstep tomorrow, thoroughly cheesed off with her husband and hoping you'll share your punch recipe.'

Kitty laughed. 'You're a marvel. I never imagined things would take this turn.'

'I can't take the credit,' said Miss Brewer. 'I was all set to lambaste the men. Next time I find myself in a similar situation, I'll head straight for the wives.'

Kitty admired the way she made light of her success. 'I'm grateful. You've been a brick ever since the day I met you. What you did this evening went above and beyond the call of duty, as the saying goes.'

'But there's a price to pay,' Miss Brewer said in a serious voice.

'What's that?' Kitty asked.

'The next time you make a batch of Dunbar's Wartime Wedding Punch, you have to save a glass for me. I'm keen to know what all the fuss is about.'

* * *

The wives of the four hoteliers who had complained turned up on Dunbar's doorstep the next morning, Mrs Rossiter armed with a sponge cake fresh from the oven and Mrs Barnes carrying a twist of tea. They invited themselves in before Kitty could do the honours and soon all five women were seated around two small tables pushed together in the reception room.

'We didn't want to come empty-handed,' said Mrs Rogers from Rosebank, 'not after the way our husbands behaved.'

'The sponge is delicious,' said Kitty, 'but there was really no need to bring the tea.' It was a little white lie. Truth be told, with four unexpected guests, she was glad of it.

'Nonsense,' said Mrs Rossiter. 'After the way those men behaved...'

'You do understand, don't you,' said Mrs Clements, 'that they dreamed up that stupid complaint behind our backs?'

'But it's turned out well in the end,' Kitty said with a smile. 'Look at us now.'

'That's what we thought,' said Mrs Barnes. 'Tea and cake and sensible conversation without a complaint in sight. We never came to see you before because, first of all, we were giving you time to settle in, and then Dunbar's shut down.'

'And when it reopened for storage,' said Mrs Rossiter, 'we were afraid it would lower the tone.'

'I hope you feel that hasn't happened,' said Kitty.

'It hasn't,' Mrs Rogers confirmed.

'But by the time we realised that, especially with our husbands muttering away in the background,' said Mrs Clements, 'we were used to leaving you alone and never gave it another thought.'

'Until yesterday evening when we found out what our husbands had been up to,' said Mrs Rossiter. 'I gave my Ernest what for, I can tell you.'

'And we've been hearing about your special punch,' said Mrs Rogers.

'Who told you?' Kitty asked.

Mrs Barnes rolled her eyes. 'My husband saw some of your guests leaving, looking rather happy, shall we say? He couldn't get through the front door fast enough. He raced across the road to ask about the reception.'

'And heard about our punch,' said Kitty. 'I still have a bit of alcohol on the premises from the hotel days, but once it's gone I can't replace it because this isn't a hotel any longer. That might make your husbands feel better.'

'They don't deserve to feel better,' said Mrs Clements and they all chuckled.

The conversation moved on and by the time her neighbours left, Kitty felt the day had got off to the best possible start. She smiled at the thought of yesterday's forthright men ending up eating humble pie, and she enjoyed telling Ivy about it when she came home from a morning spent queuing up at the shops.

'So you stood up to them and then their wives put them in their place. Serves 'em right,' said Ivy. 'You've got WVS this afternoon, haven't you? I'll make you a sandwich to have before you go.'

Kitty went upstairs to get changed, proud to wear her uniform. There was no end of work for the WVS because so much of what they did was linked to welfare. What would happen with Beatrice's idea to involve the WVS in helping the invalid mothers of the looker-after children? Kitty hoped her friend would succeed. Those children meant so much to her. She was working hard on her report for Mrs Ford.

When Kitty reported for duty, she was assigned to the task of cleaning the mobile laundry. She was in the middle of mopping the floor when the sound of an explosion made her look up, startled. An explosion, but no air raid warning?

She jumped out of the vehicle and ran inside, hearing a telephone bell ringing in the office. The sound cut off and a couple of minutes later, Mrs Ford appeared. She didn't need to ask for silence. Everyone gazed at her.

'There's been an explosion, as you no doubt heard, and there is considerable damage. At least one house has been destroyed. Mrs McFarlane, please could you be in charge of getting the mobile canteen ready? Mrs Peters, could you gather together any first aiders who are here? Excuse me one minute,' she added as her telephone rang again. When she came back from answering it, she told her listeners, 'It was thought to start with that it might have been a gas leak, but we now know it was an unexploded bomb. Unexploded no longer,' she said in a dry voice.

Kitty gave a little shudder. The ARP wardens and the rescue men were always meticulous about hunting out UXBs after a raid so that the bomb men could deal with them, but some weren't found, and then...

Jobs were swiftly allocated. Everyone knew what was required. Kitty was to go as a general assistant to respond to whatever needed doing at the scene.

'It sounds awful,' Miss Turnbull murmured as she passed Kitty.

'Yes, it does,' Kitty agreed.

When she reached the site, it looked like an earthquake had struck. An explosion had destroyed a house on a corner plot. The house faced – used to face – onto James Street, and the next two houses along were also badly damaged. The side of the destroyed house was on Rackham Street, and the next three houses had also suffered considerable damage. On the corner, the road itself and the pavement had vanished into a crater. As for the house on the corner – well, there was no house on the corner. There wasn't even a big pile of rubble and timber and pieces of roofing. There was nothing more than a mound of debris, but as Kitty stood and looked further afield she saw clumps of brickwork, half a door, roof tiles, the wooden frame of an armchair, all the bits and pieces that had been blown far and wide and that were now all that remained of the house. But the greatest part of it must have been reduced to dust.

'Mrs Dunbar?'

She turned. It was Frank Marsden. His face was grey, which could have been a layer of dust or might just as easily have been shock.

'You're a heavy rescue man, aren't you?' said Kitty.

He nodded. 'A bad business, this. We're going to need cranes on caterpillar tracks.'

'Do you know what happened?' Kitty asked. As a heavy rescue

worker, Frank was more likely than anyone else to know. 'People are talking about an unexploded bomb.'

He nodded again. His light-blue eyes seemed to gaze far into the distance, then they snapped into focus as he looked at Kitty. 'The house on the corner was damaged a year ago by a bomb.'

'Oh, so this damage isn't new, then?' Even as Kitty spoke the words, she knew she was wrong. The smell of cordite was fresh and strong here.

'Last year's damage made the house uninhabitable,' said Frank. 'What no one knew at the time was...' His voice faltered, but he continued, '...was that a second bomb had got buried. It's been lying in wait ever since.'

'How terrible,' Kitty whispered.

'It's finished the job on this house and... well, you can see the rest.' He wiped the back of his hand across his mouth. 'I must get on.'

As he walked away, Mrs Peters signalled to Kitty and she went over to her. Mrs Peters turned to an ARP warden.

'This is Mrs Dunbar. She'll assist you.'

The ARP man nodded to Kitty. 'I'm Mr Stone. We've got nine dead so far, six of them children—'

'*No,*' said Kitty.

'—and we need to make a list of all the missing.'

Kitty went hot and cold all over and her scalp prickled, but she pulled in a deep breath and prepared to do her duty calmly and efficiently.

'It was the best way to help the folk of that community,' she said later at home, not exactly making light of it, but not dwelling on it either. She wanted to protect Abbie from the details, though heaven knew, the wartime children knew far more than they ought to.

She went on WVS duty the next morning and heard that of

the eight missing people, six had been found dead deep in the rubble and the other two had simply vanished. She felt ill. Sometimes a corpse was complete. Other people were blown to pieces – literally. And sometimes the pieces were so tiny that there was nothing left to be picked up.

She went home with a heavy heart, where she found Ivy looking perky and excited. Good. This was what she could do with. She looked expectantly at her mother-in-law.

'You'll never guess who I bumped into this morning, Kitty,' said Ivy. 'That nice Mr Marsden. You didn't tell me his house had been damaged in that explosion yesterday.'

'Was it? I didn't know—'

'Anyway, he needs a temporary home for himself and his children, so I've offered him our flat. They're moving in later today.'

17

'You've done *what?*' Beatrice asked, shocked.

'Not me,' said Kitty. 'It was Mrs Dunbar.'

'She's invited Frank and his family to move in?'

Part of Beatrice's mind hoped that if she said it out loud, Kitty might stare and frown and shake her head as she said, 'Good grief, no. Whatever made you think that?'

But Kitty said no such thing. She said in a resigned voice, 'She thought she was helping.'

'Helping Frank,' said Beatrice. She wasn't comfortable with it, but she could understand.

'Helping the two of you,' said Kitty. 'You and Frank. It's no secret that he's taken you out. You haven't seen one another recently, so she... thought she'd help things along.'

Beatrice could have died of mortification right there on the spot. Mrs Ivy Dunbar thought she was helping things along, did she? Heat swept up the back of Beatrice's neck and across her face. Mrs Dunbar knew that Frank and Beatrice had been acquainted years ago, but she had been told nothing of the whys and wherefores of their separation, and now she had decided to try her hand at matchmaking. Beatrice could have throttled her, but of course she couldn't utter a word, because how could she explain how utterly inappropriate it was to have Frank and his children under this roof without telling the story of their ill-fated engagement?

Besides, it would be deeply ungracious to let it be seen that the last thing she wanted was to have Frank here at Dunbar's. Ungracious and ungenerous. Probably unpatriotic too, given that he had been forced to leave his house because of an explosion caused by a Jerry bomb.

So she would have to put on her best face, but it wouldn't be easy with her heart pitter-pattering and every nerve-end she possessed jangling beneath her skin. Having Frank in close proximity was the very last thing she wanted.

And it was close proximity, too. The flat didn't have a kitchen and Mrs Ivy Dunbar was going to cater for the Marsden family, the same way she had catered for the Town Hall lodgers.

Beatrice had been curious about Frank's children, of course. Part of her had very much wanted to meet them even though she had declined to do so – and thank goodness she had. Imagine if Frank had paraded her in front of them as his new lady-friend – and even if he hadn't said it in so many words, the children would have known – only for them all to end up under the same roof like this. It would have been intolerable.

Should she be grateful not to be in that position? But it didn't make up for the self-consciousness and discomfort of having Frank here.

But... but it was impossible not to feel her spirits being lifted by the presence of the Marsden children.

At twelve, Rowena was the oldest. Beatrice already knew

something of her because Frank had talked about not wanting to burden her with responsibility for the younger ones. Even so, she did boss them about. She was a slender, dark-haired, dark-eyed girl with a pointed chin and it was immediately clear that she was keen to hang about in the kitchen and enjoy some adult female company.

'She needs a mother,' Mrs Ivy Dunbar remarked in an offhand tone, but there was nothing off-hand about the glance she darted at Beatrice. It might only have been a glance but it pinned Beatrice to the floor.

'All children need a mother,' Kitty responded in a mild voice. 'Have you heard what is happening to the sweets and chocolate ration later this month? It's going up from two ounces per person per week to four ounces, but it's only temporary, for seven or eight weeks, something like that. Then it's going to be three ounces until further notice.'

But Ivy Dunbar wasn't going to be diverted as easily as that. 'That's interesting,' she said. She looked at Beatrice. 'You'd better tell the Marsden children.'

'Why me?' Beatrice asked innocently. 'I wouldn't remember the details, but I'm sure you would.'

'That Herbie has a sweet tooth,' said Mrs Dunbar.

Herbie was the second-oldest, dark-haired and blue-eyed like his father. He and sandy-haired Leslie, the next in line, were lively, good-natured lads whose main aim in life was to collect more impressive pieces of shrapnel than their friends. As far as they were concerned, the best thing about moving into Dunbar's was the proximity of the vast bomb site in the adjacent road, which was a source of endless adventure and new chums.

Georgie, the middle girl, was every bit as lively as her brothers. In looks, she was a younger version of Rowena, though nothing like as neat. The smallest Marsden was Josephine, known to the family as Josie-Posy. The others made a pet of her and helped her with her shoelaces, her hair ribbons, her reading and with cutting up her meat. Rowena undid her knitting for her when she made a complete hash of it and Herbie polished her shoes.

'No one ever did any of those things for me when I was the youngest,' Georgie grumbled.

'You'd have spat in their eye if they'd tried,' Les replied with a grin and Georgie grinned back.

When Beatrice, Kitty, Lily and Mrs Dunbar were working in the reception room, preparing for a twenty-first birthday celebration, Mrs Dunbar looked round to make sure the door was closed, then delivered her opinion of Miss Josephine Marsden.

'They make a baby out of her, they really do. She's six, for heaven's sake.'

Lily shrugged. 'She's a sweet child.'

Mrs Dunbar snorted. 'I'd be sweet an' all if I had you lot flocking around me, tying my apron, running my bath and lighting my cigarettes.'

'We could chew your food for you as well,' Kitty said with a grin.

'They're making a rod for their own backs, that family,' said Mrs Dunbar. 'You mark my words. They're spoiling that child. What she needs—'

Beatrice hastily turned away and bent over the cutlery on the snowy tablecloth.

'—is a mother.'

* * *

Beatrice avoided it for as long as she could. Then she got fed up of avoiding it and decided to get it over with. It had to happen some time and she was only making it worse for herself by ducking out of it.

She had to have a serious conversation with Frank.

Of course, it wasn't all that simple. They needed to speak privately and preferably with nobody else being aware of it, especially Mrs Ivy Dunbar.

As things stood, they spent a limited amount of time together, always with others. As much as Mrs Dunbar might have wanted to throw them together, even she couldn't magically make the kitchen table comfortably seat six more people. At breakfast-time, she sent up trays of cereal and toast using the dumbwaiter which had once been used to provide room service, with a maid removing the tray and taking it along to the appropriate room. Now it was the children who vied with one another to fetch and carry from the dumbwaiter, and Frank naturally ate with his children in the flat.

At the other end of the day, the children had their tea in the kitchen when they came home from school, leaving the adults and Abbie to eat together later, with suitable arrangements being made around everyone's war work. On top of this, Frank worked shifts, which meant he wasn't at the table every evening.

One sultry evening, when Beatrice was due to go on WVS duty, she hovered beside one of the windows in the reception room. Frank was due back from work shortly and she intended to catch him on Lily Street. She couldn't help but remember the occasion when he had walked repeatedly up and down the road, anxiously awaiting the opportunity to bump into her.

Ah, there he was. Beatrice straightened her hat, grasped the handle of her bag and hurried for the front door. Outside, she walked briskly along the street towards him. She smiled – not a huge smile; she didn't want to look delighted; but a pleasant smile. As she drew close, she slowed and he did the same.

After a brief exchange of greetings, Beatrice said, 'I can't stop. I've got to get to the WVS. But we need to talk.'

'We do indeed,' Frank agreed at once. There was warmth in his voice and his light-blue eyes showed how pleased he was.

Beatrice put on her best business voice. 'I suggest we meet up somewhere away from Dunbar's.'

'I could take you back to our favourite restaurant,' Frank offered.

Crikey, she couldn't have that. 'I just want to talk. Privately.'

'How about the foyer of the Royal Exchange?' Frank asked. 'Once the audience has disappeared inside, we can find a quiet corner.'

They made arrangements. Frank seemed inclined to stay and chat, but Beatrice didn't want to be sucked into a friendly situation. She excused herself and went on her way. Colour tingled in her cheeks and she hoped no one else would notice or, if they did, she hoped they would put it down to her hurrying through the heat.

She knew she shouldn't do it, but she couldn't help it. She looked back over her shoulder. There he was, at the foot of Dunbar's steps, and he was looking at her. He touched the brim of his hat in polite salute.

She shouldn't have looked.

* * *

Beatrice sat behind a small circular table tucked into a corner, waiting for Frank to reappear with their drinks. She had never had a drink in public with a man before. Did that make her pathetic? Boring? Women even went into pubs without a male escort these days and it was now regarded as acceptable. Perhaps it was time to stop being so old-fashioned.

The thought was reinforced when Frank set down her sweet sherry in front of her and sat in the seat opposite. He took a moment to look around, obviously noting their position in the farthest corner.

'Anyone might think you're ashamed to be seen with me,' he remarked, but he smiled as he said it.

'I'm not ashamed,' Beatrice insisted, hating to be put on the defensive, 'but I value my privacy and – and—' Yes, why not get straight to the point? 'Having you and your children living in Dunbar's places me in an awkward position. You must appreciate that.'

'I'm not sure that I do,' said Frank.

Beatrice blinked. How could he not see it? Surely he felt the same. The conversation she had planned in her head relied upon his agreeing with her.

'The last time I saw you before you moved in,' she went on, struggling to gain the upper hand, 'I told you I needed time on my own to think about...'

'About us,' said Frank.

'Yes,' she replied, then amended it to, 'To think about whether I want there to be an us.'

'If anything, I would have thought that having my family at Dunbar's would help you make up your mind.'

Was he being deliberately obtuse? Beatrice tried again.

'I find it unsettling to have you there.'

A serious, intent expression came over his face. 'You find it unsettling to be with my children?'

'No, of course not. They're delightful.'

'I like to think so,' he said with quiet pride. 'It means a lot to me to hear you say so. But if it isn't their presence you find difficult—'

'I never said "difficult",' Beatrice objected.

'All right: unsettling, then. If it isn't them, then it's me.' But he didn't sound as if it bothered him. If anything, it made him appear rather pleased. 'Should I be flattered?'

'Stop it. Stop trying to make something more out of this. I'm trying to hold a serious conversation.'

'So am I,' said Frank. 'So far I've gleaned that my children are a delight and that I'm an unsettling presence.'

'It's not just you,' Beatrice blurted out. 'It's Mrs Dunbar senior.'

A frown tugged at Frank's forehead between his eyebrows. 'Now I'm lost.'

'Haven't you noticed? She's matchmaking, or trying to.'

'Between you and me?'

Beatrice nodded. 'She wants to help things along if she can. That's why she invited you to move in.'

Would Frank be outraged? Embarrassed? Would he declare his intention to find other digs for his family? To Beatrice's consternation, he threw back his head and laughed.

'That's priceless, that is,' he declared.

Beatrice scowled. He was enjoying this far too much.

'It isn't priceless at all,' she said stiffly. 'It's embarrassing. Don't you find it embarrassing?'

'Not at all. It's rather sweet. Good for her.'

'I wish I hadn't mentioned it. Please don't let her know that you're aware.'

But Frank didn't seem to be listening. 'Well, fancy that! If I hadn't been intent on rekindling my old romance with you, my family wouldn't now be living in Dunbar's.' He leaned forward. 'I'm enormously grateful for the hospitality. Have you any idea how tough it is to find digs for a family of six? If we hadn't been offered the flat in Dunbar's, we might well have been split up. I wouldn't have had a choice.' For a moment, he looked shaken. 'It means everything to me to keep my children with me. They are my world. Mrs Dunbar senior might have had her own private reasons when she made her kind offer, but she has made a huge difference to my family's life. Until our own house is fully repaired, Dunbar's is our home.'

18

In the early hours of the morning, Lily crept up the steps at the front of Dunbar's. Why was she being so careful? Guilt? She had nothing to feel guilty about. She wasn't being unfaithful. She was separated. Standing outside the front doors, she automatically ran her hands over her WVS uniform, smoothing it. Not that there would be anybody up and about at this time of night to take note of her appearance.

She inserted her key into the lock, turned it and opened the door just enough to slip through sideways. It was what everyone did in the blackout. She closed the door with the tiniest of clicks. Kitty always left a night-light in the foyer and its gentle glow guided Lily to the staircase.

She went on cat-feet up to the first floor... the second... the third, and into her bedroom. When she closed the door, she huffed out a breath she hadn't been aware she was holding. She uttered a little laugh. Sneaking about like this didn't come easily to her, but there was no denying it had its exciting side. And it was oh, so very lovely, such a relief, to have some joy in her life.

But the joy was squashed flat when she arrived home a couple of nights later. As usual she was wearing her uniform. She closed the front door behind her and stood still for a moment before silently making her way across the floor to the foot of the stairs. She put her foot on the bottom tread and placed her hand on the smooth wood of the banister rail. Before she could take another step, the light clicked on.

She gasped and her heart all but jumped clean out of her chest – but there was nothing to worry about. This was exactly why she wore her WVS clobber for her romantic trysts.

Mrs Ivy Dunbar was on the first floor landing leaning over the banister rail, her work-worn hands grasping it with such force that her knuckles gleamed white. Her face was all angles and points, her skin tight with anger. Something inside Lily faltered. There could be no mistaking her fury, but at the same time Lily rejected the very idea, because why would Mrs Dunbar be angry?

'Where have you been?' Mrs Dunbar demanded. Although she pitched her voice low, it still contained energy and power.

'I've just come back from WVS duty,' said Lily.

'That's interesting. What were you doing tonight?'

'I was at the club for foreign servicemen. In the kitchen. I only ever work in the kitchen.'

'That's even more interesting,' Mrs Dunbar replied, 'because that's where I was on duty – and you weren't there.'

Lily stared.

'And it's not the first time, is it, that you've worn that uniform to go out of an evening? You dress yourself up to look all respectable so nobody will ask where you're going or what you're doing; and if anybody should be up in the middle of the night when you finally drag yourself home, no one will question where you've been, because you're in uniform.' Mrs Dunbar tossed her head, her mouth twisting in scorn.

'I...' Lily began but she couldn't think what to say next.

'Don't you try and make excuses, lady,' Mrs Dunbar snapped. 'You can't wangle your way out of it. Do you think I was born yesterday? I know what you've been up to. A couple of weeks ago I noticed a discrepancy between the duty roster and when you seemed to go on duty – "seemed" being the operative word. I've been keeping an eye on you ever since. You're a liar, Lily Chadwick.'

Lily finally tried to defend herself. She ought to be able to build up a fine old fury at having been spied on, but how could she when Mrs Dunbar was in the right? All she managed to say was, 'I'm not a liar.'

'Oh yes you are. Putting on that uniform for your own shabby purposes is a lie if ever there was one. You're a disgrace to the WVS and you deserve to be drummed out. You're a liar and a tart – and you should be drummed out of Dunbar's as well.'

* * *

As Kitty came downstairs from the third floor, she heard an argument in progress along the landing in the vicinity of the dumbwaiter. The children were arguing over who was going to carry the breakfast trays to the flat. Kitty took a couple of steps in that direction to sort it out, then stopped herself. It was Frank's job, not hers, to organise his children. If she did it this time, she might end up doing it next time as well.

Instead she went to the family flat. The door stood wide open. She rapped on it with her knuckles.

From somewhere, Frank's voice called, 'Hello? Come in.'

Kitty stayed outside. She called cheerfully, 'Morning, Mr Marsden. I think you've got a bit of a squabble on your hands out here,' and then she walked away without waiting for a response.

Downstairs in the basement kitchen, the sight of Abbie

tugged at Kitty's heart. When the two of them had occupied the family flat, they used to come downstairs together, but now Abbie ran down on her own. It never occurred to her to wait for her mother.

Ivy had made a summery version of porridge, using barley flakes soaked in water, which she heated gently along with milk, grated apple and a tiny sprinkling of sugar. She dished up and put the bowls on the table.

'Here's yours, Kitty... Beatrice...'

Ivy set down Lily's bowl with a clatter. Kitty expected a 'Whoops' or a 'Sorry' but Ivy simply put down the next bowl.

'Abbie... and me.'

'The Marsden children love using the dumbwaiter,' Kitty remarked. 'They were arguing this morning about collecting the trays.'

'They think it's fun,' said Abbie. 'I used to love the dumbwaiter when I was little.'

'Did you sort out the quarrel?' Ivy asked Kitty.

She shook her head. 'Not up to me.' She grinned at Abbie. 'I have enough to do keeping my own child in check.'

'*Mum*,' Abbie objected.

'It's Mr Marsden's job to oversee his children,' said Kitty.

'What they need—' Ivy began.

Kitty spoke over her. 'Some of us were discussing this at the WVS the other day: the way that neighbours are more inclined to muck in and help a widower with his children than they are to help a widow with hers. I suppose the feeling is that a mother is always expected to manage, but there isn't the same expectation of a father.'

'That's because children are the mother's responsibility,' said Ivy. 'No one would seriously expect a father to look after his children in that way. It's his job to be the breadwinner and the head of the household, not to make sure they comb their hair or have clean handkerchiefs.'

Knowing that from there it would be just a short step to the Marsden children being in need of a mother, Kitty created a diversion. She put her spoon in her empty bowl.

'That was delicious, Mrs Dunbar. Thank you.'

The others added their thanks, Lily in a voice that was barely audible. She had hardly lifted her eyes during the conversation. Abbie cleared the table while Ivy got up to make the toast. She looked round from the grill.

'Who's having butter and who's having jam?'

These days, you had one or the other, not both. One of Ivy's wartime duties was in the jam-making centre, where the women grated carrots to produce 'orange peel', bulked out strawberry and blackcurrant jam with rhubarb, and concocted all sorts of vegetable jams, like marrow and green tomato, which was surprisingly enjoyable, certainly much more palatable than parsnip jam.

After breakfast, Abbie and Beatrice set off for the Town Hall. Lily went out too with her library books under her arm.

'The library won't be open for ages yet,' said Kitty.

'I could do with a spot of fresh air,' Lily replied.

'Are you all right? You look a bit peaky.'

'Just tired,' said Lily.

'Late duty,' Kitty said, understanding.

'And I didn't sleep much when I got home,' Lily added.

'We'll all benefit from a jolly good sleep when the war is over,' said Kitty.

She went back down to the kitchen, where Ivy was unloading the Marsdens' dirty dishes from the dumbwaiter. Together they washed up and dried. When they'd finished, Kitty was about to run along, but Ivy put her hand on her arm.

'Hang on a minute. I need to have a word.'

She pulled out a chair and sat at the table, looking expectantly at Kitty, who did the same.

'Has something happened?' Kitty asked.

Ivy's lips narrowed. They were thin to start with and now they all but vanished. 'I think we can safely say that something's happened.'

Kitty didn't like her tone, which was a mixture of foreboding and malice. Sounding a little sharp herself, she asked, 'What is it?'

'It's that Lily girl.'

The rudeness took Kitty's breath away. 'Don't call her that. It sounds... derogatory.'

'Pardon me for speaking as I find,' Ivy answered with a sneer.

'Don't talk in riddles. Just tell me.'

'All right, then.' Ivy leaned forward. 'Lily Chadwick is a tart.'

'A—?'

Ivy nodded grimly. 'You heard. I caught her coming in last night in the small hours—'

'She'd been on late duty.'

'She flaming well hadn't. Oh, she dressed the part, I grant you. She had her uniform on, but I know full well she never went on duty. It isn't the first time either.'

Kitty could hardly scrape her thoughts together. 'Are you suggesting—?'

'I'm not *suggesting* anything. I'm telling you for a fact. She's been out gallivanting and I bet I know who with: that doctor, the one who rescued the children.'

'She's entitled to go out if she wants to,' Kitty said in a tight voice. 'It's not as though she's still married.'

'Tell that to the registrar,' Ivy said scornfully.

'Lily is separated. I know there are some young wives who behave as if they're single, but Lily is separated.'

'Oh, so it's all right with you that she's sleeping with this bloke?'

Kitty's mouth dropped open. 'How do you know they're sleeping together?'

'Well, if he was taking her dancing, I doubt she'd be wearing her uniform.'

'Plenty of folk wear uniforms all the time these days,' said Kitty, but her pulse had quickened.

'And do they all tell lies about being on duty when they're not?' Ivy raised her thin eyebrows. 'She might have pulled the wool over your eyes, Kitty, but she can't do it to me. Don't take my word for it. Go and look at the WVS duty rosters. And then there's the fact that I challenged her last night and she didn't deny it. She couldn't.'

Kitty caught her breath. She could hardly take this in. 'If Lily is having an affair with Dr Shawston, that's her business and she's obviously taking pains to be discreet about it.'

'Discreet?' Ivy scoffed.

'Yes.' Kitty felt herself to be on firmer ground. 'She's an adult.'

'Not in the eyes of the law. She's under twenty-one.'

'She's old enough to be married and separated,' said Kitty.

'You might call her separated. I call her still married.'

'She's old enough... old enough to have lost her only child,' said Kitty. 'That alone makes her an adult in my eyes.'

'So she's a discreet adult, is she?'

'She's entitled to a private life,' said Kitty, 'and she's obviously gone to some trouble to keep it private.'

'And she's failed,' Ivy answered ruthlessly. 'I've found her out and now I've told you.'

'I say it's none of our business,' Kitty declared.

'So you're condoning it?' Ivy challenged her.

'I didn't say that.'

'Aren't you forgetting something?'

'What?' Kitty demanded.

'Estranged or otherwise, Lily is married to Daniel Chadwick and now she's set herself up as Dr Shawston's bit on the side—'

'Don't be crude,' Kitty exclaimed.

'She lives here at Dunbar's,' Ivy ploughed on in a tone of righteous censure. 'She's a member of this household. I think she's a tart. You think she's a "discreet adult". We'll have to agree to differ about that. But I'm shocked at you, Kitty Dunbar, if you think it's suitable to have Lily Chadwick living under the same roof as our Abbie.'

* * *

Well, it had been bound to happen, Lily acknowledged. The moment she saw the uncomfortable look on Kitty's face, she could tell that Mrs Ivy Dunbar had spilled the beans. Lily felt ashamed – and angry. It was none of anybody else's business what she did in her private life. It wasn't as if she had flaunted it.

It took her a moment to understand that the person her vexation was directed at was herself. As much as she cared for Vivian, as light-hearted as she felt in his company, there was a part of her tucked away deep inside that was still little Lily the working-class orphan, who had grown up drinking in the comments of Auntie Nettie's neighbours as they had passed judgement on Cissie Binns, who had tried to make out that she'd been on a visit to her sick auntie in Blackpool when everybody knew she'd run off with the window cleaner, only he'd changed his mind and she'd had to come slinking back; and Flo Flackwell, who wasn't above a spot of slap and tickle with the rent man; not to mention Agnes

Tolworthy, who was getting more than cod fillets from the fishmonger.

And now here she was, Lily Chadwick, who had lost her baby and ditched her husband and ended up falling for the charms of a handsome doctor who wasn't at all bothered that she had a wedding ring on her finger, and what did that say about him?

No, that wasn't fair. Vivian truly cared for her. Lily had no doubt about that. As far as he was concerned, her marriage to Daniel was over. And he was right. It was very sad and unfortunate, but her marriage was over. There was no reason at all why she shouldn't find happiness elsewhere. She wasn't hurting anybody. And she had bent over backwards to keep it secret.

Until Mrs Ivy Dunbar had got involved. It gave Lily a creepy feeling to think of Mrs Dunbar spying on her. She didn't want to use that word even in her head, but what other word was there when Mrs Dunbar had watched her leave Dunbar's in her uniform and then checked the duty rosters? Lily wanted to be outraged – and she was – but she also wanted to crumple beneath the weight of her shame.

And now here was Kitty obviously wanting to take her to task.

Lily had just started cleaning the reception room when she heard the door open behind her. All the breath had instantly been sucked out of her body and she hadn't wanted to look round, certain it must be Mrs Ivy Dunbar. She'd gritted her teeth and turned round – and it was Kitty.

Several expressions chased one another across Kitty's face – discomfort, sympathy, anxiety, determination. Well, Mrs Dunbar had taken the wind well and truly out of Lily's sails when she'd confronted her, but Lily wasn't going to let herself be walked all over a second time.

'She told you, then,' she said stiffly.

Kitty nodded. 'I'm sure that doesn't come as a surprise to you.'

Lily shrugged. If there was one thing she knew in that moment, it was that she couldn't bear to be chucked out of Dunbar's. She felt vulnerable. Dunbar's was her safe place.

'Mrs Dunbar called me a tart,' she said.

'Oh, Lily, I'm sorry.'

'It's not your fault. You didn't say it.' Lily lifted her chin. 'Unless you're about to say it now.'

'It isn't up to me to tell you how to behave,' Kitty answered. 'You make your own choices. I know there are plenty of girls these days who are, shall we say, giving their boyfriends something to remember them by before they go overseas.'

'This isn't like that. It's a proper relationship with a man who's here all the time.'

'I can appreciate the appeal of that, especially after everything you've been through,' said Kitty. 'Lily, I'm not just your landlady or your boss. I'm also your friend and I care about you. The last thing I want is for you to be hurt again. If ever you want to talk about your situation, I'll always listen.'

'Thank you,' Lily whispered, deeply touched.

Kitty straightened her shoulders. 'I need to make sure you understand my position. My first responsibility is to my daughter.'

Dread rolled inside Lily's stomach. 'You want me to move out.'

'I want you,' Kitty said in a steady voice, 'to keep your secret. I don't want there to be any gossip about you. Mrs Dunbar won't say anything to anyone, I can assure you of that. What matters to me is that Abbie is protected from this. She isn't old enough. Do you understand?'

Lily burst into tears.

* * *

Tears welled up in Lily's eyes in sheer relief every time she pictured Kitty's willingness to turn a blind eye. The tears spilled over when she told Vivian. They were in his flat near Manchester Royal Infirmary. He had rooms in a men-only building. Each floor was looked after by a landlady, short for landing-lady. The landing-ladies took care of their gentlemen by cleaning their flats, doing their laundry and, if required, seeing to their shopping and catering.

There were no rules governing female visitors and Lily felt respectable, if rather daring, being escorted by Vivian to his front door. When she left in the dead of night, she crept down the stairs, scared to use the lift in case it chose that moment to break down. Even so, she didn't know what she'd do if she heard somebody else's footfalls on the stairs. It simply wasn't possible to feel at ease leaving a man's rooms at that time in the morning.

Now, as she snuggled up to Vivian on his ancient sofa, she couldn't hold her emotions in check as she repeated Kitty's words.

'Hey, hey, don't cry.' He tenderly dabbed at her cheeks with his handkerchief, at the same time holding her closer with his other arm. 'It's good that she's on your side – on our side.'

'It would have been just awful if she'd made me leave Dunbar's. She'd have been within her rights to tell me to go,' said Lily. 'Anyway, all she cares about is that Abbie doesn't find out, but we're already keeping it a secret, so that won't be a problem.'

Vivian didn't reply. Lily pulled away a little so she could tilt her face to see him properly. He looked thoughtful.

'What?' she asked.

'Are you happy keeping our relationship secret?'

'It isn't a question of being happy or unhappy. It's the way it has to be.'

'Because technically you're a married woman,' said Vivian. 'I know that, and I know we have to preserve your reputation – but I still wish we didn't have to maintain the secrecy.'

'Well, we do,' Lily said gently, 'and that's all there is to it.'

'I notice that you don't say that you too wish we didn't have to keep the secret.'

Lily sat up. 'Are you trying to make me feel guilty?'

'Of course I'm not.'

'Because you're succeeding.'

In one fluid movement, he was kneeling on the floor in front of her, holding her hands in his.

'Lily, my darling, is it so wrong of me to wish you weren't married to another man?'

'I'm separated,' Lily said softly. Then, in an effort to lighten the mood which had suddenly become serious, she added, 'You should be glad I'm married. If I was single, I certainly wouldn't be having an affair.'

Vivian cupped her cheek. 'If you were single, I wouldn't want you to.'

Lily leaned forward and kissed him. It was the only way she could think of to put a stop to the conversation.

19

Summoned by Miss Brewster, Beatrice felt a twist of anxiety. Had her formidable colleague received permission to have all the looker-after children evacuated? Had she sent for Beatrice to help her finalise her plans? Beatrice was still working steadily on her report for Mrs Ford, but there was a lot to do. It was proving to be time-consuming because she needed to visit every housebound mother and persuade her to share personal information about all the assistance she required but without explaining to her why these details were needed. In a few cases, the mums were happy to talk, just glad of the company, but others were less so, and some were downright suspicious.

'Why are you asking?' was the question posed again and again, in various tones of voice.

Gradually, Beatrice had cobbled together a suitable reply. It was essential not to get hopes up by making even the vaguest reference to the possibility of help. Instead she concentrated on the children.

'I'm trying to ascertain which are the most common jobs children are called upon to do in these circumstances... No, I'm not here for the truancy officer...'

Her report was building up steadily, but she still had other mothers to visit, and she couldn't do it in work time, which was another reason it was taking longer than she had expected at the outset.

And now Miss Brewster had sent for her. Did this mean she was too late? What if the invalid mothers had already been issued with lists of what the children were to take with them when they were sent away? What if – what if Beatrice was to be given the job of delivering the lists?

'Good morning, Miss Inkerman.' Miss Brewster glanced at her in a way that suggested Beatrice had taken her time getting here, which was categorically not the case. 'Sit down. You're going to come to the magistrates' court with me *as an observer,*' she added with a sharp look, 'in an adoption case.'

'Adoption?' Beatrice perked up, not just because time hadn't run out for the looker-after children, but also because she was genuinely interested.

'Yes, indeed. Adoption rates are rising.'

'That's good,' said Beatrice. 'All those children needing families.'

Miss Brewster's lips tightened. 'Many adoptions these days are of irregular babies. Do you know what that means?' Without waiting for a reply, she answered her own question. 'An irregular baby is what you get when a woman has a child and her husband is not the father. It seems to be all too common these days. I believe that Army Welfare Officers sometimes suggest to the husbands that it might be better for the long-term stability of the family as a whole if they take on the cuckoo in the nest as their own.'

Beatrice wasn't sure what to make of this, but she remarked, 'I can see the reasoning.'

'Part of which is undoubtedly that the army doesn't want its men distracted by thoughts of divorce.'

Beatrice couldn't help saying, 'How cynical.'

'How realistic,' Miss Brewster replied. 'But that's by the by. I mentioned it only because an irregular baby is at the centre of the case where I am to advise.'

'And I'm to accompany you,' said Beatrice, hoping to prod Miss Brewster into revealing further details.

But Miss Brewster was not to be drawn.

'For the purposes of training and observation only.'

* * *

Walking into the magistrates' court building behind Miss Brewster, Beatrice couldn't help noticing the smartly dressed people – gentlemen in pin-stripes, with watch-chains looped from the little pocket in their waistcoats, and lady-clerks looking crisp and efficient in neatly pressed jackets and skirts. It made her all the more aware of not being as well-dressed as she would have liked. It ought not to have mattered, but it did.

Miss Brewster announced their arrival at the reception desk and a clerk showed them upstairs to a small side room.

'If you would please wait in here, ladies,' he said. 'The room where the hearing is to take place is just across the corridor. The magistrate in charge of the matter is Mr Brent-Williams and he will be assisted today by Mrs Ames, a lady-magistrate.'

Miss Brewster gave the man a gracious nod without a smile. 'Thank you.' Her tone suggested she was giving him permission to leave the room.

They didn't have to wait long for the magistrates to appear. Mr Brent-Williams was a craggy-faced man with dark eyes and an imperious manner. Mrs Ames was a stout lady with a pair of reading-glasses dangling from a silver chain around her plump neck.

Mr Brent-Williams was obviously in charge. He made that clear from the moment he appeared. Even though he politely held the door open for his colleague, he somehow inserted himself into the space ahead of her the moment she was inside the room. Did that mean Mrs Ames was a trainee like herself, Beatrice wondered, though it was difficult to imagine somebody with such poise being a trainee.

'I am Mr Brent-Williams and this is Mrs Ames,' said Mr Brent-Williams, his glance darting swiftly between Miss Brewster and Beatrice.

Miss Brewster took a step forward, hand outstretched. 'How do you do, sir? I am Miss Brewster from the Welfare Department. I am pleased to have this opportunity to share my expertise and perhaps help guide your thinking.'

She made no attempt to introduce Beatrice. A flush of uncomfortable colour seeped into Beatrice's cheeks. Drat Miss Brewster! And was that a trace of pity in Mrs Ames's eyes? That made it worse.

'You'll be sent for when you're required, Miss Brewster,' said Mr Brent-Williams. 'This matter has turned out to be far more complicated than expected at the outset, not to mention highly distasteful.'

Complicated? Distasteful? What on earth was this about? Beatrice tried hard to look as if she knew all about it.

When the two magistrates left the room, Miss Brewster finally got around to telling Beatrice why they were there.

'It's an adoption matter,' she said. 'I mentioned to you earlier that it involves an irregular baby.' She gave a delicate little shudder and the word *distasteful* skittered across Beatrice's mind.

'This one was a foundling – I take it you know what one of those is?'

'An abandoned baby,' said Beatrice, her heart swelling with sorrow for the poor little mite. What a way to start your life.

'A girl,' said Miss Brewster, 'known as Bessie Beech.'

'That's a pretty name,' Beatrice said with a smile.

'It's a silly name.' Miss Brewster huffed out a sharp breath. 'A prospective adoptive couple quickly came forward, but just when they were about to receive permission to have the child, the real mother crawled out of the woodwork, wanting the baby back. That was when the truth came out about the father not being her husband. Anyway, she wasn't allowed to have the child, but her parents have decided that they'd like it.'

'Her,' Beatrice said quietly.

'Pardon me?'

'Her. Not it,' said Beatrice.

Miss Brewster gave her a hard look that suggested Beatrice was too soft-hearted for this job. 'Mr Brent-Williams has asked me to attend today to give my advice concerning the child's best interests.'

Beatrice frowned. 'I didn't know you were involved in a case of this sort. I mean to say, you've never mentioned it.'

'I wasn't aware that I am required to inform you of my workload, Miss Inkerman,' was the stony reply. 'But it so happens that I am not associated with the case, beyond having read the relevant documents so as to understand the background.'

Beatrice was shocked, though she did her best to hide it. Was it normal practice for a baby's fate to be decided in part by someone who had not been involved all along? How... cold.

Presently, the clerk returned to show them to the room across the corridor, where Mr Brent-Williams was holding his meeting. As they left the side room, four people in the corridor looked round at them. A serious-looking, middle-aged man with a moustache stood with a good-looking woman with conker-brown hair. Standing slightly apart from them was a beautiful girl with green eyes and another middle-aged woman, this one with clever eyes and jet-black hair that fell in fashionable waves to her shoulders.

Beatrice could see the anxiety in all their eyes. 'Are they witnesses?' she whispered to the clerk.

He gave a discreet shake of his head. 'They're here to lend their support to Mr and Mrs Atkinson, the young couple who wanted the baby in the first place.'

Then shouldn't they be in the room with them? But it wouldn't be appropriate to ask, and there wasn't time anyway. They entered the opposite room. It had a long, polished table down the centre, with three chairs on each of the long sides, and two at each end. At the end that was furthest from the door sat Mr Brent-Williams and Mrs Ames. In the three seats with their backs towards the corridor were a smartly dressed older lady whose costly coat boasted a fur collar and cuffs. Her husband, equally expensively dressed, was silver-haired, although his eyebrows were dark. In the third seat was a sober-suited, professional-looking man.

Opposite them, occupying two of the three chairs, was a couple in their twenties. The wife had golden hair that fell in a tumble of curls, and blue eyes. Behind his glasses, her husband's hazel eyes were warm and kind, and made his face look gentle.

The older couple looked... Beatrice couldn't pin down a word to describe her instinctive reaction to them. All she knew was that she felt an immediate liking for the young couple, the Atkinsons. Then she spotted the difference between the two couples. The young pair looked nervous, which made her warm to them, but the older couple – the grandparents – looked confident and sure of themselves. Beatrice immediately put herself on the side of the young Atkinsons.

At the end of the table closest to the door, there were two seats. The clerk held one for Miss Brewster. Before she sat down, she gave Beatrice, who was about to take the chair beside her, a nudge.

'Over there, if you please, Miss Inkerman,' she said coolly. 'I'm the one giving evidence.'

Beatrice felt her face colour. Mr Atkinson rose to his feet and pulled out the chair beside his. Beatrice sank into it, wishing she could carry on sinking until she had fallen through the floor.

'Miss Brewster,' said Mr Brent-Williams, 'thank you for attending this meeting. I understand you have acquainted yourself with the facts of this case. These are the child's grandparents and these are the child's former prospective adoptive parents.'

Mrs Atkinson gasped. '*Former*—?'

Mr Brent-Williams glanced sharply at her. 'I cannot in good conscience refer to you in any other way, Mrs Atkinson, not with matters as they stand.' To Miss Brewster, he said, 'I have read the reports provided by your colleague Mrs Fitch and by Warden Everett about the Atkinsons; and I have read the report compiled on behalf of Mr and Mrs Prescott,' and he indicated the grandparents, 'by their legal representative. I would now be glad to hear your opinion on the subject of natural family versus adoptive family.'

Miss Brewster waited a moment, as if savouring the moment.

'I am not the welfare officer for this case,' she said, 'but I am happy to provide my professional opinion, which is based upon years of experience, on the question of the two sorts of family.'

She started by describing – in far more detail than Beatrice personally considered necessary – her experience with Manchester Corporation. Eventually, she came to the point.

'It is my professional opinion, based upon years of working in the Welfare Department, that a child is almost always better off in its natural home, by which I mean the home of the people he or she belongs to by birth.'

Mr Atkinson stirred in his seat, but before he could speak, Mr Brent-Williams raised a hand to stop him.

'You are not here to comment or ask questions, Mr Atkinson.' Looking down the table at Miss Brewster, he said, 'You said "almost always". Tell me what you mean by "almost", if you please.'

'Obviously there are exceptions,' Miss Brewster replied. 'Some families are so objectionable that there can be no question as to their suitability. I am a great believer in certain things. One is that small children are better off in the home with their mothers rather than in a nursery – unless the mother is completely unsatisfactory, of course. Another belief I hold is that a child should, where possible, grow up in its family home with its blood relatives. I cannot speak more plainly than that.'

Beatrice caught her breath, and she wasn't the only one. She was aware of the Atkinsons doing the same. She wanted to leap to her feet and declare that Miss Brewster was just plain wrong. She wanted to assure the Atkinsons that she could tell they were decent people with a lot of love to give.

'Thank you for your professional opinion, Miss Brewster,' said Mr Brent-Williams.

Miss Brewster stood up and Beatrice followed suit. The clerk opened the door and they left the room. Beatrice lowered her gaze so as not to meet the eyes of those waiting outside. What would they think if they knew Miss Brewster had come down heavily on the side of the grandparents? And would they assume that she, Beatrice, was in agreement?

'There,' said Miss Brewster as they went down the stairs. 'I trust you have learned something today, Miss Inkerman.'

Oh, she'd learned something all right. She'd learned the importance of not being so full of yourself that all you cared about was your own opinion. She'd learned that, no matter how experienced Miss Brewster was, she was definitely someone Beatrice had no wish to emulate.

* * *

Lily sat on her bed, staring at Daniel's writing on the envelope in her hand. Her fingers trembled and the words shimmered slightly. What had made him write to her? Had he decided he wanted a divorce now instead of waiting until after the war? Had he met another girl? Lily was in no position to criticise or take umbrage if he had.

She hadn't seen him or heard from him since they'd bumped into one another in the street back in the spring. Now it was September and here was a letter from him. She was desperate to open it, but scared too, only she couldn't think what she had to be scared of. All the same, her heart was racing fit to burst.

Oh, she was being ridiculous. There was only one way to find out what Daniel wanted. She opened the envelope, removed the pages – pages, plural – and unfolded them. Taking a breath that failed to calm her nerves, she started to read.

My dearest, loveliest Lily,

Am I still allowed to call you that? It's how I think of you, how I've always thought of you. No matter what becomes of us, you will always be my lovely Lily. I have tried to forget you, tried to move on, but my heart just won't, can't, doesn't want to, plain refuses.

I am more sorry than I can express that I wasn't there with you when Toby died. It was not through any fault of my own that I was absent, but I will feel guilty about it until the day I die. You needed me and I wasn't there. As your husband, it is my job to protect you and hold you close, and I wasn't there. I never got to see nor hold my son. That has left an emptiness inside me that feels as if it will never fill up again.

I can appreciate now how very hard it must have been for you to be confronted by my grief in all its raw newness after you had spent weeks having to cope on your own. We were out of step with one another from then on. Faced by the loss of a much-wanted baby, what chance did we stand? Such a loss might bring other couples closer together, but with us it had the opposite effect.

Ever since I saw you in the street earlier in the year, I have been unable to stop thinking about you. Seeing you gave me the oddest feeling, the richest feeling – a mixture of recognition and seeing you as if for the very first time.

Do you ever think of that first time, Lily? You were standing just inside that doorway, holding a tray of drinks. You smiled at each guest – such a pretty smile. From the moment I saw you, I couldn't take my eyes off you. You were the loveliest girl I had ever seen. You still are.

When I saw you at the end of May, I had to return to duty the next day. Otherwise I might have come banging on Dunbar's door, desperate to speak to you. Since then, whether at sea or on dry land, I have thought of you, dreamed of you, all the while.

Why haven't I written to you before now? Because I was frightened. I'm still frightened. What if you say no? What if you don't want to see me again? What if all my dearest, most important hopes are in vain?

I will lay out my hopes so you know exactly what I want, what I wish for with all my heart.

I want you, Lily, my loveliest Lily. I want our marriage. I want us to grieve together and I want us to look to the future together. I want you to be my wife again. If you will resume our marriage, I swear to you that I will love and cherish you for the rest of our lives.

When you receive this letter, I will be at sea, so you needn't worry that I will appear on your doorstep. In fact, I won't return to England for some time, as I have something to do in America, like I did once before, if you recall. Please think over what I've said and write to me. You have plenty of time to do so. It is possible I might not return to Britain until next year.

I want to assure you that it is perfectly safe for you to write to me at the family home. If you're thinking my mother might destroy your letter, I promise you she won't. I have made it abundantly clear to her that if she interferes between the two of us, she will not see me again.

I was wrong in the way I sometimes treated you last year, Lily.

I was so sure that you and my mother would become friends if you were left to your own devices, but I was wrong. At the time I hated to think of it in terms of taking sides, and so I didn't, which left you, my darling wife, feeling unsupported. To be blunt, I should have had words with my mother. I know that now and I will never sit on the fence again.

Please write back, Lily. A simple 'yes' or 'no' is all it needs to be, but you know that 'yes' would transform my life. I hope you feel it would transform yours too.

With all my love, always
Daniel

* * *

Kitty watched over Beatrice with interest, while trying not to be obvious about it. It was clear that she'd grown fond of the Marsden children. She gave them access to the club room when it wasn't needed for her clubs.

'It keeps them occupied,' she said mildly when Ivy remarked on it. Trust Ivy!

Later, Kitty tried to steer Ivy away from making comments in the future.

'Leave her alone. She'll make up her own mind.'

Ivy blew out a stream of tobacco smoke. 'Seems to me she's already made it up – or as good as. She can't resist those kids. It's clear to anyone with eyes in their head that she's dying to be a mother.'

Kitty couldn't deny it. She had witnessed Beatrice gently trying to wean the older children off helping Josie so much and encouraging the little girl to be more independent.

'Josie is a perfectly capable child,' Beatrice told Kitty. 'It's just that the others see her as the baby of the family and she's more than happy to sit back and be waited on hand and foot.'

'Tell the others to leave her alone and come and wait on me instead,' Kitty answered with a laugh. 'Seriously, though, I can see how much you like them – and they like you too.'

Beatrice nodded. 'They're dear children. Don't look at me like that.'

'I'm not looking at you like anything,' Kitty protested.

'Yes, you are. You were hearing Mrs Dunbar's voice in your head saying, "They need a mother." I know you were, because I could hear it too.'

Kitty smiled sympathetically, but she wasn't sure what to say.

Beatrice sighed. 'I feel torn. I like having the children here, but I also feel wary about the situation with Frank. I don't want to cause any upset. He and the children have nowhere else to go until their house has been repaired.'

'I'm sorry that my mother-in-law has put you under pressure,' said Kitty.

'But if she hadn't been interested in trying to throw me at Frank, where would the Marsdens have gone? There can't be any doubt that the children would have been split up. I hate feeling that I'm under a microscope, but I can't be sorry that Frank has been able to keep his family together.'

'So many families have been separated by this war. Abbie was evacuated for only a short time, but Bill and I hated it when she was away.' Kitty touched her friend's arm. 'Are you all right?'

Beatrice nodded. 'Frank is being the perfect gentleman. He's keeping to the flat mostly and leaving me be.'

'That must make it a bit easier for you.'

'I suppose so. I'm grateful to him for that.'

Kitty chuckled. 'Imagine what Mrs Dunbar would make of it if Frank used this opportunity to woo you with flowers. He could serenade you in the foyer every day when you come home from work. He could—'

'He could what?' Beatrice asked, playing along.

'Nothing.'

She'd been about to say that he could get his children to sit at Beatrice's feet for bedtime stories, but even though she was larking around, that would be a bit too near the knuckle.

* * *

Kitty felt anxious about Lily. The girl was pale and withdrawn, her blue eyes troubled and her brow clouded. Had something

new happened? Kitty checked with Ivy that she hadn't been
turning the screws on Lily.

'Of course not,' Ivy stated flatly. 'You said to leave her be and
that's what I've done – even though you're wrong.'

That stung, but Kitty chose not to react. There was no point in
falling out with Ivy.

She waited for Lily to return from WVS duty that afternoon,
gave it a few minutes, then followed her up the stairs and
knocked on her door. After a pause, it opened. Lily had clearly
just swiped tears off her face.

'Oh, sweetheart.' Without another thought, Kitty stepped over
the threshold and took Lily in her arms. 'Is there anything I
can do?'

Lily moved away from her, shaking her head. 'No, nothing.'

'I can listen,' Kitty said gently. 'I think you need someone to
talk to. You're obviously deeply upset.' When Lily didn't reply, she
added, 'When Mrs Dunbar caught you coming home from being
with Dr Shawston, I...' How best to say this? 'I didn't judge you –
and I'm not about to judge you now either.' Treating Lily as
gingerly as she would a stray cat she wanted to tame, she reached
for the girl's hand. 'Come on. Sit with me on the bed.'

Lily sat stiffly beside her. Kitty ached to take her in her arms.
She seemed so fragile.

Looking straight ahead and not at Kitty, Lily said, 'I had a
letter from Daniel.' It came out as a whisper.

That was the last thing Kitty had expected. 'I see.' She waited
before she asked, 'What did he say?'

'He... oh, Kitty!' Now Lily turned to her. 'It was a love letter.
He wants us to get back together.'

'And what do you want?' Kitty asked her.

Instead of answering, Lily went off on a different tack. 'When I
saw his writing on the envelope, I thought maybe he wanted to

seek a divorce right away. I thought perhaps he'd met somebody else.' She fell silent.

'Like you have,' Kitty said softly.

'I never went looking for a new relationship,' Lily declared. 'It just happened.'

'I know.'

'Whatever Mrs Dunbar thinks.'

'It doesn't matter what she thinks,' said Kitty. 'What matters now is what *you* think and what you want to do.'

'I don't want anybody to get hurt,' said Lily.

Kitty sighed and slipped an arm around Lily's slender shoulders. 'It's inevitable that somebody is going to get hurt.'

'I know,' Lily whispered.

'What did you think when you read Daniel's letter?'

'Do you remember when I said that Daniel and me and our marriage felt like it had happened a long time ago? Well, it doesn't feel that way any longer. It feels like all the understanding that we didn't have last year when we needed it so badly has finally come about. He said we were out of step with each other last year, and that's true. That's how it was.'

'Does that mean...?' Kitty stopped herself. 'I don't want to push you into anything, Lily. This is your decision and you need to think long and hard about it.'

Lily looked directly into her eyes. 'No, I don't,' she said.

* * *

Lily was in no doubt as to what she had to do, but that didn't mean it was going to be easy. In fact, she dreaded it and her throat tightened when she pictured it. She was due to see Vivian that evening. Their usual routine was to have a meal out or go to the pictures, after which he would take her back to his rooms. She had never let him collect her from Dunbar's, no matter how much he wanted to. It was as though he sometimes forgot she was a married woman, albeit a separated one, but she had never forgotten. Or maybe he just chose to disregard it.

Now, Lily wondered what to do for the best. She had to talk to Vivian in private, which meant in his rooms, but she couldn't spend the whole evening before that with him as if nothing was wrong. That meant she had to go to his rooms before he was ready to set off to meet her. The regular beat of her heart seemed to stumble at the thought, but she couldn't put it off.

She set off in plenty of time, feeling self-conscious every step of the way. It was one thing to slip into the building with Vivian late in the evening in the pitch-dark of the blackout, but it was quite another to walk inside in the golden glow of a glorious September evening. Anyone might see her, a brazen girl entering a place where the accommodation was for men only.

As she approached, two young men were leaving the building. She put on a spurt and they held the door for her to enter. Did they exchange a speculative glance? Lily made a point of not looking. She ran upstairs to the first floor, where Vivian had rooms overlooking the back of the property.

She felt more like turning tail and fleeing, but she rang his doorbell and waited. The door opened and there he was, speaking to somebody over his shoulder. Lily froze. It had never occurred to her that he might have company. Then he turned his head and saw her. The surprise in his expression was quickly followed by delight.

He reached out to draw her inside. 'Come in, come in.'

She wanted to hold back. Whoever was in there with him, she didn't want to see them and she didn't want them to see her. She said, 'I don't want to interrupt,' but before she knew it, Vivian had drawn her across the threshold.

'You remember Dr Barry, don't you?' he asked.

'Yes,' said Lily, 'from the night we rescued the children.'

Dr Barry was sitting on the sofa. He came to his feet. 'Mrs Chadwick, how nice to see you again. Well, Shawston, I'd best be off.' He picked up his hat.

It couldn't have been more obvious that he was leaving on her account. Lily felt embarrassed, although she had no desire for him to stay. She wished he hadn't been here at all. Did he know about her and Vivian?

Vivian saw his friend out and shut the door behind him. Then he turned to Lily with a smile, the light in his eyes showing how pleased he was to see her. Her heart dipped, but what had she expected?

'This is a surprise,' Vivian said. 'Not that I'm not delighted to see you. This is a dream come true for me, you feeling comfortable enough to turn up at my digs like this. Let me take your coat.'

He fussed around her, offering her a seat, a drink. They always sat together on the sofa, cuddled up close. Lily knew it would be wiser to sit in the armchair, but it would have felt like a snub. It would have felt like trying to take the easy way out, using her actions to drop a massive hint instead of having the courage to utter the words.

She sat on the sofa and Vivian flung himself down beside her, pulling her into his arms. Lily wriggled free before he could kiss her.

'Vivian, there's something we have to talk about.'

He answered, 'That sounds ominous,' but he said it like it was a joke.

Lily had planned what to say, but now all the words flew out of her head.

'I'm sorry,' she said. 'I – I can't see you again.'

His head jerked back. 'Can't? Why not? Is this something to

do with the mother-in-law at Dunbar's finding out about us? It's none of her business what you do.'

'It's not that.'

'Then what? Why can't you see me?'

Lily swallowed. 'I've heard from Daniel – my husband. He wrote to me. He wants us to try again.'

Vivian went very still. 'And you want to?'

'Yes.'

In a swift, fluid motion, he was on his feet, looking down on her. He pushed a hand through his hair, mussing it.

'You said your marriage was over by mutual consent. You said you were just waiting for the war to end to get divorced.'

'And it was true when I said it. I never lied to you.'

'But the first time your husband snaps his fingers—'

'It's not like that,' Lily exclaimed.

'You'll forgive me if I disagree.'

'Vivian, I'm sorry, I truly am.'

'Are you? Is this what you've been hoping for all along? That your husband would want you back?'

'I never thought for one moment—'

'Is that why you got together with me? So word would get back to him and make him jealous?'

'What? *No!*'

He dragged in a shaky breath and blew it out again. 'Sorry. I shouldn't have said that, but this has come out of the blue. Lily, you've told me what happened last year. How do you imagine you can possibly recapture what you and your husband had before your baby died? You can't go back to how things used to be. Life doesn't work that way.'

'Believe me, I'm well aware of that,' said Lily. 'I know things will be different now for Daniel and me. We both know it.

Nothing will ever bring our son back. Last year, that meant we couldn't bear to be together, but now... now we want to try again.'

'You're going to "try"? That doesn't sound as if you're certain of what you're doing.'

'I am certain. We both are.'

'I can give you certainty. Wait here.'

Vivian disappeared into his bedroom. When he returned a few moments later, he was carrying a ring box. He opened it and held it out.

'Here's certainty,' he said. 'A diamond flanked by a pearl on each side. It originally had a sapphire on each side and I thought how appropriate that was because of your blue eyes, but then I remembered hearing once that pearls mean tears. I know you must have shed thousands of tears for Toby and I wanted you to know that I will never forget the pain you went through and are still going through. I had the sapphires exchanged for pearls as my way of ensuring you could always carry a little piece of Toby with you. This is the certainty I'm offering you, Lily. A lifetime of love and hope and happiness, and my help to carry the memory of Toby. I'm looking ahead and I want you by my side for always. That's my certainty. *You* are my certainty. I realise that receiving your husband's letter must have shaken you up. That's only to be expected. But he wants to turn back the clock and that can't be done. I'm looking to the future and the certainty I am offering you is a marriage of love, respect and undying devotion. Now *that* is certainty. That's real certainty.'

20

Beatrice's report was ready at last. She had prevailed upon the mothers of all the Time Off Club children to be open with her about the extent of the responsibilities their children carried, from running errands and beating the rugs to standing in shopping queues or doing the dishes, from turning the mangle and fetching medicine to emptying the commode and robbing Peter to pay Paul.

As she had drawn up her report, Beatrice had fought back tears more than once. Weeping wouldn't help these families. She'd been swamped by memories of her own childhood, and young womanhood too. There was no task these children were called upon to do that she herself hadn't performed from an early age.

Her life seemed to be crammed with memories these days – memories of being a girl taking care of her mother and their home, memories of Frank and her fateful decision to part company with him. It felt as though her whole life was centred around her past. That wasn't what she'd anticipated when she'd had the great good fortune to be offered the post in Welfare. She'd felt then as if she had a whole new life to look forward to.

Anyway, this was no time to dwell on herself. She had a duty to these special children, not just because of the work that had been thrust upon them, but also because she was the one who had drawn attention to them by setting up her Time Off Club and persuading the mothers to let the children attend school in the mornings. If she hadn't done those things, Miss Brewster wouldn't have got a bee in her bonnet and dreamed up her evacuation plan.

Beatrice went to make an appointment to see Mrs Ford in her office. Every time she set eyes on the branch organiser, she was reminded of how she had started off here under a cloud. She couldn't help wondering if the headmistressy Mrs Ford had the same memory every time she saw her too.

'An appointment?' said Mrs Ford. 'My diary's in the office. Come through.' She scanned the diary on her desk. 'Tomorrow afternoon? No, you work full-time, don't you? I'll be here tomorrow evening. Can you manage that?'

It was a Time Off Club evening, but Beatrice was sure Kitty would be happy to take charge for her. She made the appointment.

'What is it to do with?' Mrs Ford asked.

'I've produced a report for you.' Beatrice passed it across the desk.

Mrs Ford's eyebrows climbed up her forehead. 'Have you indeed?'

'It's about some children, some families, I'd like the WVS to assist, if possible. This gives all the background information.'

Mrs Ford flicked through the pages. 'You have been busy, haven't you?'

'It's important,' Beatrice answered. 'Will you have time to read it before our meeting? Should we choose a later date?'

'Tonight's my bridge evening,' Mrs Ford told her, 'but I'll make sure I read your report before I go out. We'll discuss it tomorrow evening.'

* * *

You had to get out of bed pretty early in the morning to be up before Mrs Ivy Dunbar, but Lily managed it with no trouble. She was too anxious to stay in bed. She'd given up trying to kid herself, though she'd had a jolly good go at it the first few times. But she was way beyond that now.

Drawing her dressing gown around her, she tied the belt and opened the door a crack so that she could listen. She didn't hear anyone moving about, so she slid out onto the landing. There was a bathroom here on the third floor, but she didn't dare use it, just in case. As she tiptoed down to the floor below, her head felt swimmy, though that was nothing compared to how her stomach felt.

She made it to the bathroom just in time, not even waiting to pull the light-cord before flinging herself towards the lavatory, where she hung over the pan and heaved her heart out.

Afterwards she slumped over the basin to splash her face. There was no doubt about it. It was exactly the same as when she'd been expecting Toby. Her body felt the same. She'd been scared that time too, because she'd been unmarried. She'd felt sure Daniel would make an honest woman of her without hesitation, but she'd still been scared. Daniel, of course, had married her immediately and willingly, though his mother liked to make out that he'd only been doing the decent thing and wouldn't have taken Lily on otherwise.

And here she was now, pregnant again, and the father wasn't her husband. How could she ever have let herself become involved with Vivian? Stupid question. She knew exactly how. He was handsome and attentive. He'd shown her nothing but understanding. Any girl would have leaped at the chance to go out with him, but he had wanted only her and she hadn't been able to resist. His moving declaration when she'd told him it was over had broken her heart. As for when he'd produced the engagement ring – she could hardly bring herself to think of it. That he'd had the setting changed to include pearls for Toby had brought home to her what a very special man he was.

But she had already made her decision, the only choice she could possibly have made. Daniel was the man for her. He was right to say they had got out of step with one another. That described it exactly. Losing a child was the hardest, cruellest thing parents could possibly have to face together – and she and Daniel hadn't faced it together, which had made it far worse. But Daniel's thoughtful, insightful love letter had changed everything. It had righted everything. It had brought them back into step with one another, which was precisely where Lily wanted to be, now and always.

And now – and now she was carrying Vivian's child. What was she supposed to do? Ask Daniel to divorce her so she could marry her baby's father? But that wasn't what she wanted. She didn't want to be married to Vivian. She wanted to be married to Daniel. She wanted to return to their marriage. She longed for them to have a second chance. She wanted that with all her heart. She had never before felt so certain of anything.

Daniel.

Vivian's baby.

Daniel.

Vivian's baby.

* * *

Mrs Ford's office door stood open. She was on the telephone. Beatrice waited outside, hoping the call wouldn't end with the branch organiser jumping to her feet and hurrying past her, saying, 'Sorry – an emergency.'

Mrs Ford caught sight of her hovering and beckoned her inside, pointing to the chair on the other side of the desk. As Beatrice sat down, she caught sight of her report. She didn't know what she would do if Mrs Ford said no.

'Yes, I will... Thank you... Goodbye.' Mrs Ford replaced the receiver in its cradle and looked at Beatrice. 'Your report, Miss Inkerman,' she said without preamble. 'Most interesting and rather worrying. I had no idea that some children have to take on these responsibilities.'

'I think that nobody realises unless they see it happening,' said Beatrice. 'I missed a great deal of schooling because of taking care of my mother and our home.'

'So you have a personal interest in the matter.'

'As well as a professional one,' Beatrice answered, wanting to make this clear.

'Of course: you work in the Welfare Department.' Getting down to business, Mrs Ford continued, 'You said you were hoping for WVS support.'

'Yes, please,' said Beatrice. She squeezed her hands into fists in her lap, but this was no time to be bested by nerves. She had prepared what to say and she owed it to the Time Off Club children and also to herself to state her case calmly and in full. 'The WVS routinely looks after people who need to convalesce at home after an operation or an illness. When it's the lady of the house who is bedridden, it doesn't just mean providing nourishing light meals and changing the bed. It includes doing the shopping and the housework, maybe collecting the children from school, all sorts of things.'

'Go on.' Mrs Ford's tone suggested she knew what was coming next.

This was the moment. 'I'd like to ask the WVS to take on the domestic jobs done by these children with responsibilities. That's the official name for them. If the WVS would step in, then the children could have proper childhoods and an uninterrupted education. It would make a huge difference to them.'

Mrs Ford glanced down at the front page of Beatrice's report. Beatrice sensed she was giving herself a moment to think.

Mrs Ford looked up. 'You're asking an awful lot, Miss Inkerman. This is a commitment of considerable proportions.'

'I know,' Beatrice answered, 'but, you see, there's nobody else to do it. Other families in this situation might have relatives who could help out, but the families I'm interested in don't have anybody. The district nurses won't step in. They'd administer medication to a patient who couldn't do it for themselves, but they wouldn't do the shopping or the washing. That's not their job, and the Welfare Department doesn't provide services like that.'

'It sounds as if they should,' Mrs Ford commented.

'I agree.' Beatrice couldn't help letting her frustration show. 'But right now, such services don't exist, which is why these children have to take the responsibility onto their young shoulders.'

'And you want the WVS to take on this role.' It wasn't a question.

'Yes, I do,' Beatrice declared. 'Goodness knows, we've taken on any number of welfare jobs since the war started. We provide mobile canteens and mobile laundries. We turn out at the drop of a hat to provide tea and sandwiches for hundreds of soldiers at a time who are on their way through from one place to another. We find jobs for evacuated children when they leave school if they haven't got a home to come back to here. We keep the British Restaurants running. We drive around with pies and sandwiches for the land army every day. We have clothing exchanges and social clubs. We go house to house collecting salvage. We support the work of the Citizens Advice Bureau. We collect feathers to fill pillows for evacuees and rosehips for vitamin C syrup. We visit the elderly at home and the sick in hospital. Good heavens, we've even been known to provide impromptu choirs for weddings and funerals.'

Beatrice stopped, aware of having got thoroughly carried away.

Mrs Ford gave her a wry look. 'That was quite a speech, Miss Inkerman.'

'And every word of it was true,' Beatrice replied. 'You know what folk say. "If you need something doing, ask the WVS." There's nothing the WVS isn't capable of tackling. What I'm asking for is wartime assistance. There's a move afoot in the Town Hall to have these children with responsibilities evacuated so that they won't have the responsibilities any longer. Can you imagine the guilt and worry the children will feel if they're sent away? If the WVS will help the mothers for the duration, then their children can stay put, get a regular education and play out in the street with their friends, like children are supposed to.'

Mrs Ford looked thoughtful. 'This is long-term care.'

'For the duration of the war,' Beatrice specified. 'I know it isn't a permanent answer to the problem, but it's the best one I can think of for now.' She hardly dared ask, 'What do you think, Mrs Ford?'

'This will need to be discussed at committee level and I will have to consult the other branch organisers,' said Mrs Ford. 'But I wish you and your proposal well, Miss Inkerman. As someone recently remarked to me: if you need something doing, ask the WVS.'

* * *

Although her instinct was to hug her secret to her for as long as possible and try to avoid looking into the future, Lily forced herself to confide in Kitty. If Kitty wanted her to leave Dunbar's, then the sooner Lily knew the better, even though the fine hairs on her arms stood up in fear at the very thought. She had to come clean.

'Kitty, please could I have a word in private?' she asked in the most ordinary tone she could muster.

They were in the kitchen and Kitty started to pull out a chair.

'Not here,' Lily said, alarmed. Anyone might come down the stairs. Worse, anyone might stop on the stairs and listen in. Or was her situation making her oversensitive? She shouldn't think ill of others. Probably that was her own guilt skewing her judgement.

'Let's go up to the reception room,' said Kitty.

They went upstairs and shut the door behind them before choosing one of the smaller tables.

Lily swallowed hard. She started by reminding Kitty about Daniel's love letter.

'Have you made a decision between him and Dr Shawston?' Kitty asked.

For a moment, Lily was surprised that Kitty's up-to-date knowledge was so far behind. 'Yes. I did that at once. I didn't even have to think about it. Daniel's letter made me remember all the reasons why I loved him – why I *love* him. I still do and I always will. It's a great shame about Vivian, but there it is.'

'How did he take it?' Kitty asked.

'It was horrible,' said Lily. 'He was desperately hurt. He – he wanted us to stay together for always. He...' Her voice fell to a mere breath. 'He had an engagement ring.'

'Oh, Lily. Did he produce the ring before or after you told him you want to go back to Daniel?'

'After,' said Lily.

'It might have been better if he'd kept it to himself,' said Kitty, 'but I know I only think that because it would have made things a little easier for you.'

'You're a good friend,' said Lily, 'but... you might change your mind when you hear the rest.' She squared her shoulders. 'I'm having a baby. Vivian's baby.'

Kitty went pale. 'Does he know?'

Lily shook her head. 'He has no idea.'

'Are you going to tell him?'

'No,' Lily answered at once.

'You sound very sure of yourself.'

'Think about it,' said Lily. 'What if he said, "Great. Now you have to marry me"? But I don't want to be married to him. Daniel is the only man I want. I know that now. I can't marry Vivian. It wouldn't be right.'

Kitty nodded. 'What about Daniel?'

A great wave of anxiety washed over Lily. It was all too much. 'I've made such a mess of everything, but I really believed my marriage was over and done with.' Tears poured freely and she tried to dash them away.

Kitty wrapped her arms about her. 'Hush, Lily, hush. One thing at a time. You've been very brave to tell me.'

It had to be said. 'I'll understand if you want rid of me.'

'Do you want to leave Dunbar's?' Kitty asked.

'Of course I don't, but that's probably just me being stupid. It was one thing when you turned a blind eye to me and Vivian, but you can hardly pretend this isn't happening.'

'I have to think about this,' said Kitty, 'but I'll say now what I said that other time. My first priority is Abbie. I care about you, Lily, and I want to help you, but my child's welfare is more important than anything.'

* * *

Miss Brewster's features were so tight with fury that her whole face had shrunk. 'This is a disgrace, Miss Inkerman,' she declared, eye glinting. '*You* are a disgrace. You have gone behind my back and made your own arrangements. You – a nothing, a nobody – have dared to pull the rug out from under my plans. You have acted above your station and let down the whole Welfare Department.'

'This couldn't have been done without the agreement of the Welfare Department,' said Beatrice. 'The WVS approached them with this alternative plan and the powers that be preferred it to the evacuation idea.'

Miss Brewster's eyes narrowed so much that they almost closed. Only those sharp glints could be seen through the slits.

'You needn't imagine you will ever receive any further training or advice from me,' she declared.

Beatrice wanted to say, 'Thank heaven for that,' but she forced herself to reply, 'I've learned a lot from you, Miss Brewster.'

Yes, and a lot of it had been valuable, but she'd also learned how one person's entrenched views could have a sour effect. If Miss Brewster had washed her hands of her, then Beatrice was grateful to be set free.

'I've also learned a lot from the WVS,' Beatrice added, forestalling her angry former mentor. 'I've learned that there's a solution for everything. I've learned that when something needs doing, women just get on with it.' After a moment she added, 'If I think something is wrong, then I have an obligation to do my best to put it right.'

'That's something else you picked up from the WVS, is it?'

'No, Miss Brewster,' said Beatrice. 'It's something I learned from working with you.'

And she left the room.

* * *

Kitty expected to have to think about Lily's bombshell for some days, but actually she decided very quickly what needed to be done.

Lily was horrified when Kitty told her.

'You *can't!*' she exclaimed. 'Please don't do that.'

'*I'm* not going to,' Kitty replied steadily. '*We* are.'

'No,' Lily said determinedly. 'Absolutely not.'

Kitty looked at her. 'Do you seriously want me to hold this conversation with Mrs Dunbar and Beatrice without you being there?'

'I don't want them to know.'

'Of course you don't. I understand that. But you know perfectly well that the only way to prevent it would be for you to leave Dunbar's and never come back.'

Lily sighed. 'I know. I just hate the thought of...' She stopped.

'Of being judged by Mrs Dunbar?' Kitty asked.

'Yes,' said Lily. 'And I don't want Beatrice thinking badly of me either.' Another sigh. 'Still, it's a bit late for that, isn't it?'

'Beatrice is one of the kindest people I've ever met,' said Kitty. 'She'll be shocked, but she cares about you and she isn't the sort to turn her back on a friend. You know that, don't you?'

'Yes,' said Lily.

'We ought to get this conversation out of the way soon,' said Kitty. 'The longer we leave it, the more you'll dread it.'

Lily gave her a look of such anguish that she almost agreed to postpone it, but she stuck to her guns. They would get it over with this evening. None of the four of them had WVS commitments and Abbie was going to the pictures with a chum from work.

Accordingly, Kitty asked Beatrice and Ivy to come to the reception room that evening.

'Have you put more weddings in the diary?' Beatrice asked, walking in.

'Yes,' said Kitty, 'but that's not why we're here. Have a seat at one of the tables for four.'

No sooner were they all sitting down than Ivy asked, 'What's this about? Something's wrong, I can tell.'

Kitty took charge. 'We have to discuss a serious situation. Lily has something to tell you.'

Voice trembling, Lily said, 'I had a letter from Daniel. It was a wonderful letter, full of love and understanding. He wants us to reconcile – and so do I.'

'That's the best news I've heard in a long time,' said Beatrice.

'Going to ditch the boyfriend, then, are you?' Ivy asked crisply.

'She already has,' Kitty replied calmly, placing a hand on top of Lily's in a gesture of support.

'What?' Beatrice looked puzzled.

'Lily was seeing Dr Shawston for a while,' said Kitty, 'but it's over now. The main thing is that she knows her own heart. She's been through so much unhappiness. For a time she thought that Dr Shawston was the man for her, but now she has realised that she still loves Daniel.'

'I never stopped loving him,' said Lily. 'The feelings were always there, but they were trapped under a layer of ice.'

'I'm pleased to hear it,' said Ivy. Kitty wished she could have sounded less grudging and more pleased, but at least she had said it.

'I think it's utterly romantic,' said Beatrice, 'and I'm very happy for you, Lily.'

'Thank you,' said Lily. 'Daniel doesn't know yet. He wrote immediately before he went on another crossing. I wrote back to him but he won't receive that until he comes home, which might not be for ages, because he has some sort of work to do in America. It happened once before. He was given a job to do by his father, who works for the War Office.'

'He'll be beside himself with joy,' Beatrice said generously. 'It's what you both deserve.'

'Unfortunately,' said Kitty, 'it isn't that simple.' She glanced at Lily, but the girl's eyes were awash with tears, so Kitty went on, 'Lily has recently found out that she is going to have a baby.'

Beatrice's eyes widened; Ivy's hardened.

'A baby,' Beatrice whispered.

'The doctor's baby,' Ivy said, her tone bitter.

'Yes,' said Kitty.

'But...' Beatrice said, and then didn't say anything else.

Ivy looked at Lily. 'So what are you going to do? Go crawling back to the boyfriend?'

Lily sat up straight. 'Please stop calling him that. And no, I'm not going back to him. I can't. I don't want to spend my life with him.'

'I see,' Ivy sneered. 'He was good enough for a bit on the side, but not for the rest of your life.'

'Mrs Dunbar,' Kitty said firmly. 'That's enough.'

'Is it?' Ivy retorted. 'I'm not the one you should be saying that to. *She's* the one who—'

Lily slapped her hand down hard on the table, making the others jump, but it silenced Ivy.

'I know exactly what you think of me, Mrs Dunbar. You don't need to spell it out.' Lily looked at Kitty. 'I'm sorry. This conversation was a big mistake.'

'No, it wasn't,' Kitty maintained. 'You've made your opinion very clear, Mrs Dunbar, but now it's time to set that aside and concentrate on the future – Lily's future.'

'I assume this future involves a mother-and-baby home,' Ivy said in a hard voice, 'and an adoption she'll have to keep secret from her husband for the rest of their lives.'

'It's very difficult,' Kitty said quietly, 'but what else is she to do?'

Leaning towards Lily, Beatrice asked, 'Are you sure you can't go back to Dr Shawston?'

Lily shook her head. 'Not feeling the way I do about Daniel. Vivian already knows I don't love him now. He knows I want to resume being married to Daniel. If he asked me to get a divorce and marry him, he'd know that, on my side, it was purely for the sake of the child.'

Ivy snorted. 'There are plenty of women who get wed to provide a father.'

'But does the man know in advance that that's her reason?' asked Lily. 'Because Vivian would. And...' Closing her eyes, she shook her head. 'I couldn't marry him, not now.'

'Lily would like to stay here with us at Dunbar's for the time being,' said Kitty.

'Dunbar's has been my home for a long time.' Lily spoke with a quiet dignity that made Kitty proud of her. 'It's my refuge. Dunbar's took me in when I needed it most.'

Ivy clicked her tongue. 'Dunbar's did no such thing. Dunbar's is a building. It isn't capable of doing anything. Kitty took you in.'

'Yes, she did,' Lily replied, 'and I'll always be grateful to her for it. I'll never forget walking through those front doors, wanting my old job back and my old room, only to be told that Dunbar's was no longer a hotel. All the old staff had gone and Kitty didn't know me from Adam, but she let me stay and she gave me work. Not everyone would have done that.'

'What we need to talk about now,' said Kitty, 'is Lily staying here.'

'You've got to be kidding me,' said Ivy. 'Letting her stop here would bring shame on Dunbar's.'

'Not while nobody knows her condition,' said Kitty.

'I would never bring shame on Dunbar's,' Lily declared. 'When it's necessary for me to leave, I'll go without a murmur. But to stay on here while... while I get used to things would mean everything to me.'

'What about Abbie?' Ivy demanded. She glared at Kitty. 'How can you countenance keeping Lily here?'

Kitty glared right back. 'I would never hurt Abbie. You know that.'

Pushing back her chair, Lily stood up. 'I'm having a baby and I'll have to give it up for adoption. I'll very likely end up keeping it a secret from my husband for the rest of my life. There's a lot of things I don't know, but there's one thing I know for certain: I can't stay here if you're going to snipe at me every chance you get, Mrs Dunbar. I know that getting involved with Dr Shawston was a big mistake, but at the time it felt like the right thing to do and it made me happy. I don't need you to rub my nose in it.' She looked at Kitty, her expression bleak. 'Perhaps I should move out.'

'Don't do that, Lily,' said Beatrice. 'Mrs Dunbar, I'm the one unmarried woman present. I'm what is politely referred to as a maiden lady and I rather think that gives me the greatest reason to be upset and offended by Lily's predicament. And I *am* upset – but I'm upset for her, not for me. Life is complicated. The war has brought everyone's emotions to the surface. I know that in former times, I would have made certain judgements about Lily's current situation, but in former times, Lily's situation wouldn't have arisen. I'm sorry. I'm not making much sense.' Beatrice gazed around at the three of them, her brown eyes earnest. 'What makes sense to me is how dear Lily is to me. I want to help her. We all know your opinion, Mrs Dunbar, but won't you please set it aside for the sake of a girl I'm perfectly sure you care about, who needs our support?'

21

It was the beginning of October and the leaves were turning. Beatrice couldn't stop thinking about Lily's position. The poor girl. Beatrice was well aware that plenty of folk would despise Lily for getting involved with Dr Shawston – just look at Mrs Ivy Dunbar – but in her heart of hearts, Beatrice felt a twinge of envy. After separating from Daniel, Lily had met someone else. Of course, it had all turned out to be very tricky and complicated, and all sorts of heartache lay ahead, but all the same, Lily had met another man and had opened her heart to him... just as the young Beatrice had thought she would herself have the chance to do after she had given Frank his marching orders.

If only her younger self could have known what a devoted family man Frank would turn out to be. Frank's words about plenty of men not being all that keen on fatherhood until it actually happened to them still had the power to cause a painful pang in Beatrice's chest. He had uttered the statement in an almost throwaway manner when surely he ought to have spoken with gravity, ending with a sincere apology to Beatrice for not having known this when they were engaged.

Oh, she had to stop dwelling on it. Her thoughts had been flowing around and around in the same old circle ever since Frank's reappearance in her life. Having him and his family living under the same roof hadn't helped.

Beatrice thought once more of Lily. She was some years younger than Beatrice had been at the time of her engagement to Frank, yet she had faced up to her situation and made her decisions... while Beatrice, twenty years after making her own life-changing choice, was still second-guessing herself. What did that say about her?

It was high time she took a leaf out of Lily's book. She had to make a firm and binding decision about her future and close the door on her past for keeps.

* * *

Beatrice would have liked to talk over her situation with Kitty and draw on her moral support, but it felt important for her to do this on her own. It would be a way of making up for all the years of sorrow, pain and regret. Was it weakness that had left part of her stuck in the past? At any rate, she was determined not to be weak now. She knew what she had to do.

It was difficult to get Frank on his own because, when they were both at home, so were the children. Even on the occasions when they left Dunbar's at the same time to set off for work, Beatrice always had Abbie with her.

Then she and Frank happened to cross on the stairs. Beatrice stopped, so he did too, looking at her with a smile that brought warmth into his light-blue eyes.

Aware of how voices could carry up or down the stairs, Beatrice spoke quietly. 'Frank, I'd like us to have the chance to talk.'

'So would I,' he replied immediately. She wanted to tell him to keep his voice down.

'Somewhere private,' she added.

His eyes twinkled. 'We could lock ourselves in the club room.'

'We should go out. I'd like to be right away from everyone else.'

'Fair enough.' Frank nodded. 'I'll take you out for a meal one evening. How about that?'

'I thought perhaps we could go back to the foyer in the Royal Exchange,' said Beatrice.

'And sit in that corner again, away from the public gaze?' Was he teasing her? 'If that's what you want, your wish is my command.'

He seemed pleased and relaxed at the prospect while Beatrice's insides were tying themselves in knots.

'When should we go?' he asked. 'I'll enjoy walking there with you on my arm.'

'I'd rather meet there.'

'Don't be a goose,' he chided. 'Sorry – but really. We'll go together. We've nothing to be ashamed of.'

'I'm not ashamed.'

'Good. Then we'll go together.'

Should she put her foot down? Or would that be churlish? A lifetime of putting others first made her hold her tongue.

She carried on up the stairs, only to find Josie on the landing.

The little girl looked up at her. 'Are you going to marry my daddy?'

Beatrice's breath got lodged in her throat. She looked back at Frank, expecting him to share her shock, but he merely shrugged.

'Don't look at me,' he said. 'I haven't uttered a word.' He began to turn away, but then he stopped and looked up at her. 'But children can be very perceptive.'

* * *

'Here we are again,' Frank said easily, holding the door open for Beatrice to walk through.

He led her along to the same small table as before, where she was surprised to see a little RESERVED card and a bud-vase with a rose – at this time of year! It must have cost a fortune. Her gaze flew to Frank's face.

Before she could speak, he said, 'I couldn't take a chance on our table not being available, could I? May I help you with your coat?'

Beatrice turned and let him slide her coat from her shoulders. She switched her handbag from one hand to the other as she removed her arms from the sleeves. She was wearing her tweed skirt, a blouse with a Peter Pan collar and a cardy she had knitted. All of a sudden she felt dowdy when she compared her appearance to Frank's sleek suit and the evening dresses worn by the ladies who had come to tonight's concert. Her heart dipped. She looked more like she should be in the back-office totting up the takings, not sitting out here in the well-appointed foyer.

Frank hung up their things on a nearby coat stand.

'Sweet sherry?' he asked in a voice that managed to be both intimate and casual and probably gave the impression to an observer that they were at least close acquaintances if not actually an old married couple.

Frank soon returned with their drinks. Beatrice was nervy enough to knock hers back in one but she merely took a modest sip and put her glass down in front of her.

'Mrs Dunbar told me you'd had a success at work with the children you're specially interested in,' Frank said. 'She said you've stopped them having to be evacuated.'

Beatrice hadn't come here to discuss that, but there was no

way of avoiding it, not for an innately polite person such as herself. She explained the new arrangements and Frank listened attentively.

'Didn't I say to you when we met up again that time in the rain that you must be the spiritual mother to the children you work with?' he said at the end.

'As I recall,' Beatrice answered, 'you said it and then forgot all about it until I reminded you on another occasion.'

'Since then, it hasn't slipped my mind again,' said Frank. 'All I mean to say is that you've obviously found work that suits you.'

'As a substitute for not having a family of my own, you mean?' Beatrice replied, needled.

'I only meant to pay you a compliment and to express pleasure to think of you being in what seems to be the right job for you.'

'Sorry,' said Beatrice.

'No apology necessary,' said Frank, 'especially not between two old friends like us.' He leaned forward and lowered his voice. 'I'd very much like us to be more than friends.'

'That's what we need to talk about,' said Beatrice, trying to hang on to control of the conversation but knowing that it had already passed into Frank's hands.

'I've done what you wanted, Beatrice. The last time we went out together, you said you wanted to proceed at your own speed. I've given you ample time to do all the thinking you need to do. I've kept out of your way while I've been living in Dunbar's. I haven't taken advantage. I hope you agree.'

'Well – yes.' Quite honestly, any prickly moments had been caused by Mrs Ivy Dunbar, not by Frank, but she couldn't say that. 'It hasn't been ideal having you in such close proximity, but—'

'Hasn't it? Really? What should I make of that, I wonder? Could it be that you've enjoyed my family's presence in a way you weren't necessarily ready for?'

'I've enjoyed having the children at Dunbar's, certainly. They're a delight. You must be very proud of them.'

'I am.' Frank's face positively glowed with pleasure. 'That means a lot coming from you, Beatrice. I very much wanted them to make a good impression. You say it wasn't ideal having me in close proximity, and I respect that – in fact, I specifically aimed to keep out of your way – but I couldn't help but be pleased for you to have the chance to get to know my children and for them to get to know you. Ever since we resumed our acquaintance, that was something I wanted, though I wasn't sure how to make it happen. For them and you to live under the same roof has been a dream come true.'

'Frank, stop, please,' said Beatrice.

'Stop what?' He looked honestly taken aback. 'Stop being happy that you've had the chance to get to know my children? They like you, Beatrice, all of them.'

'I believe you'll find they like the two Mrs Dunbars and Mrs Chadwick and Abbie as well.'

'Of course they do. You've all made them welcome,' said Frank. With a chuckle, he added, 'You've all made my life so much easier. Seriously, Beatrice, don't underestimate their fondness for you.'

'I didn't come here to talk about your children.'

'Maybe you should have,' Frank answered at once. 'They're a part of me. Ever since we met again, you've – well, struggled is the only word for it – you've struggled with the fact that I'm a father of five. You even told me that I'd got the life you'd wanted. Well, now that life can be yours, too, Beatrice. You've lived alongside my children for some weeks now and I know you like them because you've said so. And I've told you that they like you too. Can't you please set aside your grudge against me?'

Her mouth dropped open. 'I don't bear a grudge.'

'Of course you do, but it's time to let it go. You don't have to be jealous of my family any longer. You can be a part of it. Nothing would make me happier. And I think we both know that nothing would make you happier. I'm confident I can speak for the children when I say they'll be happy too. Marry me, Beatrice.' He laughed. 'Marry me, marry all of us. Please.'

Emotion prickled at the backs of her eyes. 'I'm sorry, Frank. I can't.'

'But – is it – is it the children?'

'Frank, I adore your children.'

'Well, then.'

'But I don't adore you, Frank, not any longer. You were the sun and the stars to me twenty years ago and it broke my heart to part from you, but I had my reason and I stood by it. I carried a torch for you for a long time, and that torch lit up again when we met by chance and started seeing one another... or I thought it did. It would be oh, so easy to accept your proposal so I could have my own family, but the truth is that I don't love you now, and as much as I might relish being a mother to your children, I couldn't marry a man I don't love.'

Frank looked bewildered. He made a couple of attempts at speaking before the words finally emerged. 'Well, this isn't what I expected. You're making a mistake, Beatrice. Think about it. Say you'll think it over.'

'I've done nothing but think about it ever since the day you walked up and down Lily Street waiting for me to come home.'

'Are you saying it's over?'

'Over? How can it be over when it never really got started again?'

Frank blew out a breath. 'Well, that's me told.' He cleared his throat. 'I suppose we'd best move out of Dunbar's, then.'

'Don't do that,' Beatrice said at once. 'Please stay on until your house has been repaired and is ready for you to move back into.'

Frank looked at her. 'It's been ready for the past three weeks.'

22

October was drawing to a close and a campaign had opened in North Africa, which the news reporters were calling El Alamein. It had sounded exotic the first few times Kitty had said it, but by now it was ordinary and familiar and everyone was saying it.

On this Saturday afternoon, Abbie had set off to catch the bus to Withington to see Martha, who had the day off from Ingleby's. Ivy was out at the WVS and Kitty, Beatrice and Lily had quietly arranged to spend some time together so they could talk privately, which meant freely.

Kitty was reminded of how she had referred to the three of them as family in front of Naomi, and how Naomi had obviously felt miffed. If anything, Kitty, Lily and Beatrice were even closer now than they had been back then, and the sense of family was stronger. Kitty was aware, too, of all the things she hadn't shared with her sister in recent weeks. She'd never gossiped about Beatrice and Lily behind their backs. Naomi would have loved it if she had, but Kitty wasn't one to betray confidences.

Dunbar's was a quieter place these days now that the Marsden family had moved out. Kitty had been astonished when

Beatrice had told her that Frank had kept mum about their house being ready to move back into.

'It's not often that I'm lost for words,' Kitty had told her friend, 'but I really don't know what to make of that.'

Beatrice had done a one-shouldered shrug as if it was of no consequence, but Kitty wasn't fooled.

'He intended to stay here until he'd reeled me in,' said Beatrice.

'Oh, Beatrice, that sounds so calculating. I'm sure Frank cared for you. In fact, I know he did.'

'I know it too,' Beatrice had replied, 'but he should still have been honest about his house. I don't like to think he was manipulating me.'

And there hadn't been any more that could be said. Beatrice was clearly torn as to what she ought to think and Kitty didn't blame her.

The Marsdens had moved out the weekend after Beatrice had dashed Frank's hopes. One by one, the children had all said, 'Thank you for having us,' as if they were going home after a party, and Josie had thrown her arms around Lily's waist, adding in a choked voice, 'And thank you for saving Rowena's life,' whereupon the other children had clustered around the little girl, saying, 'Don't cry, Josie-Posy.'

Frank had shaken hands with each of them, doing nothing to single out Beatrice unless he gave her hand a secret squeeze. If he did, he didn't provoke a reaction.

Then the children had snatched up bags and cardboard suitcases. A stiff breeze blew in through the open double doors. The children clattered down the steps, lugging their belongings, and Frank gave directions to the drivers of the pair of taxis he had ordered. The children scrambled inside and Frank had stood for a moment in the road with the door open in front of him. He raised his hat to all of them and Beatrice had slipped her hand inside Kitty's, moving closer so that their arms pressed against one another's. Then Frank got in and slammed the door and the two motors had driven away.

Kitty and the others had gone back inside. Ivy had immediately headed for the basement door, declaring her intention of putting the kettle on, but Beatrice had pulled Kitty towards the reception room.

Kitty had caught Lily's eye. 'Tell Mrs Dunbar we'll be down for tea in a few minutes.'

She followed Beatrice into the room and shut the door. Beatrice stood in the middle of the room, with her back to Kitty. Her whole body was rigid with tension, her shoulders practically up as high as her shoulders. Slowly she rolled her shoulders and dropped them – or possibly forced them down – before moving her head in a manner that suggested she was lifting her chin.

At last she turned to face Kitty. She looked staunch, but then Kitty saw her eyes and went straight to her.

'Beatrice, I'm so sorry.'

'So am I,' Beatrice answered. 'Not about Frank – I made the right choice there – but about the children. Oh, Kitty, I'll miss them so much.'

'I know you will,' Kitty whispered, hugging her.

After that, Kitty had been prepared for Beatrice to be quiet for a day or two afterwards, but Beatrice behaved exactly as normal, though that might have been a conscious decision so as not to give Ivy anything to comment on.

Kitty had asked Ivy not to find new lodgers for the time being.

'As if I would,' Ivy had retorted, 'with what's going on in this house.'

'Kindly stop making barbed remarks about Lily's situation,' Kitty said.

'Did I mention her name?'

'You didn't need to.' Deciding it was time to put her foot down, Kitty said, 'If Abbie finds out the truth of Lily's condition because of something you said, then you and I will have a serious falling-out.'

'I would never do anything to harm Abbie.'

'Of course you wouldn't. It's time you treated Lily with some consideration. She's in a desperate situation and she needs our support. You've had your say – more than once – and from now on, I want you to be kind.'

'Are you telling me how to behave?'

'I'd like to think I don't have to,' Kitty had replied in her calmest voice, but she'd made her point and since then Ivy had not only dropped the snide remarks but had also been noticeably kind to Lily.

All the same, Kitty hadn't invited her to be part of this afternoon's cosy chinwag. Kitty, Beatrice and Lily had been through a great deal together before Ivy came to live here and it had given them a special closeness. Although Ivy had reined in her attitude towards Lily, Kitty wanted Lily to feel completely comfortable this afternoon, because they were going to talk about the baby.

Kitty and Beatrice sat together at one of the tables in the reception room, waiting for Lily, who was due back at any minute from a WVS shift.

'Are you all right, Beatrice?' Kitty asked.

Beatrice sighed, then, lifting her chin, she adopted a bright tone. 'I have to accept my life the way it is and devote myself to my work. I'm very lucky to have a job I love. That's what I have to focus on now. After all, it was my main focus before Frank came back into my life, so really nothing has changed.'

Kitty's heart felt sore on Beatrice's behalf. It was too simplistic to claim that nothing had changed. The interval with Frank and his children had clearly made a difference, but there was nothing to be gained from saying so. Beatrice was going to devote herself to her welfare work with children and Kitty dearly hoped for her sake that it would be enough.

Damn Frank!

The two of them glanced up at the sound of the front door opening.

'Here she comes now,' said Beatrice.

'She'll probably want to change out of her uniform first,' said Kitty, but Lily came straight in and sat down.

'You aren't going to believe this,' she said. 'I can scarcely believe it myself.'

'What is it?' Kitty asked.

'It's Vivian,' said Lily, looking from Kitty to Beatrice and back again. 'When I was leaving the British Restaurant, I bumped into Dr Barry. He's Vivian's colleague and he was there the night of the rescues. I was going to dash off, but he'd already seen me and he asked how I was. Then he told me...' She pressed her palm over her mouth, then let it drop away. 'He said Vivian has joined up.'

Kitty and Beatrice both exclaimed in surprise.

'I know,' said Lily. 'I couldn't take it in either. Dr Barry said that Vivian thought it was for the best. The army always needs more doctors. He said Vivian was very cut up after I... after we split up.'

'Poor fellow,' said Beatrice, 'but at least this means you needn't worry about seeing him around.'

'That must be a weight off your mind,' said Kitty, 'or it will be once you've had a chance to think about it. You're probably too shocked at the moment.'

Lily looked down at her hands in her lap. 'To think he was so upset that he couldn't bear to stay here.'

'Now don't start feeling guilty about that,' Kitty advised firmly.

'You aren't responsible for his decisions.' She took a chance on adding, 'I can guess what Mrs Dunbar would say if she was here.'

'What?' Beatrice asked.

'She'd say that if a man chooses to get involved with an estranged wife, then he's hardly in a position to complain if she wants to return to her husband.'

Lily's watery smile turned into a little laugh. 'That sounds like Mrs Dunbar all right.'

'Don't feel bad about it, Lily,' Beatrice said encouragingly. 'You've got plenty to worry about without that.'

Lily lifted her chin as she looked at Beatrice. 'Are you saying that because of what you've found out for me?'

'No, it was just a general remark,' Beatrice answered, and Lily nodded.

'Why don't you tell us what you've learned about the adoption process?' Kitty requested after a minute. Clearly Lily wasn't about to ask.

'Nobody thought twice about my questions,' said Beatrice, 'because of my job. Also, it's worth saying that a lot of girls and women are in need of this information these days, which makes it even easier to come by. What it comes down to is this. There are various adoption agencies, and also some of the mother-and-baby homes organise adoptions. If the baby is going to be adopted, a shortened form of the birth certificate is made out after it's born, and this is replaced by a new certificate at the time of the adoption. The name of the woman who gave birth doesn't appear on the new certificate, for obvious reasons. Then it's up to the new parents if they want to tell the child he's adopted. The advice given to adoptive parents is to say that the real father was killed in action and the real mother died in an air raid. It's a way of giving the baby a respectable background.'

'Very convenient,' Lily whispered.

'There must be many children whom that particular fiction applies to these days,' said Kitty. 'It's common knowledge that there are plenty of babies whose father isn't the mother's husband.'

'They're called irregular babies,' said Beatrice. 'Miss Brewster told me that.'

'I'm having an irregular baby,' Lily said softly. Then she said in a clear, steady voice, 'I don't care what label other people use. To me, it's a baby.'

'Of course it is,' said Kitty.

'And I'm going to keep it.'

'*What?*' Kitty and Beatrice spoke at the same time.

'I'm not going to hand over my baby to someone else,' said Lily. 'I thought I'd have to because... because I'd have to keep it secret from Daniel. But the more I think about it, the more determined I am to keep it.'

'Lily, that's a very big decision,' said Beatrice. 'A huge decision.'

'Don't you think I'm capable of making it?' Lily asked crisply. 'My first baby died and I will not, absolutely will not, give away my second, no matter what anybody says, no matter what the world thinks is the right thing to do. I love my child and I'm going to keep him or her.'

'What about Daniel?' Kitty asked.

Lily was silent.

With an anxious glance at Kitty, Beatrice said, 'Miss Brewster also told me that, if a wife writes to her husband in the services and tells him there's a baby that the husband knows can't possibly be his, the Army Welfare Officer might encourage him to take on the child for the sake of the stability of the family as a whole.'

'Except that Lily can't get in touch with Daniel,' Kitty pointed out. 'He'll be in America for however many weeks and she doesn't know when he'll be back.' She looked sympathetically at Lily. 'But the question remains. What about Daniel? Are you choosing the baby over him?'

'I've made my decision,' said Lily. 'The rest is up to him. My child is the most important thing now. If Daniel doesn't want us, then I'll do my best on my own. But I am *not* going to give up my child.'

* * *

Abbie's bedroom door was ajar. Kitty had always left her door open a little ever since she had first been put into her own room, and now Abbie automatically left it that way. So it was easy late that night for Kitty, wide awake, to slip inside her daughter's room while she slept. The blackout curtain ensured the bedroom was shrouded in inky darkness, but the light from the landing let a soft glow inside, just enough for Kitty to make out her slumbering child. She had always loved watching Abbie sleep. She'd thought she would grow out of it once Abbie wasn't a toddler any longer, but she never had.

After the emotional discussion earlier with Lily, Kitty's deep love for Abbie felt like a second skin. She fully understood how much it mattered to Lily to keep her baby. She couldn't imagine her own life without Abbie and she was determined to support Lily in every way possible, but it wasn't going to be easy, not without exposing Abbie to adult matters for which she was too young.

'We won't worry about that yet,' Kitty had reassured Lily. 'The most important thing at present is for you to have a period of calm and stability so you can get your thoughts in order.'

As for the future, Lily was potentially facing life as a divorced mother, something which would stigmatise not just her but her child as well. People would always look down on them. Perhaps she would pass herself off as a war widow. That would be the kinder option. But all that was some way off yet, although Kitty knew it would come around soon enough.

Something else that would come around, probably sooner than she was ready for, was her own future. People were talking about El Alamein as a turning point. A victory in North Africa could turn the tide of the war. If it did, it would still be a long time before the war ended; but what about afterwards?

Setting up the storage business had shown Kitty how capable she was and how much she loved being her own boss; and now that she was regularly hosting special occasions in the reception room, she loved it even more. She wasn't the sort to blow her own trumpet, but she knew she was good at it – more than good.

But the fiasco of being denied access to the Dunbar's bank account had left a bad taste in her mouth; and discovering that Bill was dipping into the account when the fancy took him, to this day made annoyance sweep through her body. She knew that her lost love for Bill would never be rekindled.

She loved Dunbar's, but she didn't want to work for Bill. She wanted to work for herself. But that was way off in the future – if it ever happened at all.

For now, she, Lily and Beatrice had one very important thing in common. They were all where they needed to be – at Dunbar's.

* * *

MORE FROM MAISIE THOMAS

The next instalment in The Wartime Hotel series is available to order now here:

https://mybook.to/WartimeHotel3BackAd

ACKNOWLEDGEMENTS

Welcome back to Dunbar's! I'd like to start by saying a huge thank you to all the readers who have walked through the doors of Dunbar's with me and made friends with Kitty, Beatrice, Lily and Abbie. I hope you have enjoyed this second book and finding out what happens next. Life is never easy for my characters, but they can always rely on one another.

Many thanks to my agent, Camilla Shestopal, and my editor, Francesca Best, whose insightful comments helped to make this a better book. Thanks to Hayley Russell, Rachel Odendaal and the whole team at Boldwood; also to Shirley Khan, the series copy editor, and Anna Paterson, the proofreader.

Thanks to everyone who worked on the large print and audio versions. Love and a big hug to the wonderful Julia Franklin, who narrates the audiobook.

Thanks to fellow authors Rose Warner, Eva Glyn and Kirsty Dougal for their support for *A New Home at the Wartime Hotel*; and many thanks to all the book bloggers and reviewers who helped get the series off to such a great start, including Karen Mace, Yvonne Gill, Karen Louise Hollis, Book55, Mummab, Kath Evans, Meena Kumari, Helen Hopwood and Beverley Ann Hopper.

ABOUT THE AUTHOR

Maisie Thomas is the bestselling author of the Railway Girls series. She is now writing a new saga series for Boldwood, set in wartime Manchester.

Sign up to Maisie's mailing list for news, competitions and updates on future books.

Visit Maisie's website: www.susannabavin.co.uk

Follow Maisie on social media here:

facebook.com/MaisieThomasAuthor

x.com/maisiethomas99

ALSO BY MAISIE THOMAS

A New Home at the Wartime Hotel

Hopeful Hearts at the Wartime Hotel

Sixpence Stories

Introducing Sixpence Stories!

Discover page-turning historical novels from your favourite authors, meet new friends and be transported back in time.

Join our book club
Facebook group

https://bit.ly/SixpenceGroup

Sign up to our
newsletter

https://bit.ly/SixpenceNews

Boldwood

Boldwood Books is an award-winning fiction publishing company seeking out the best stories from around the world.

Find out more at www.boldwoodbooks.com

Join our reader community for brilliant books, competitions and offers!

Follow us
@BoldwoodBooks
@TheBoldBookClub

Sign up to our weekly
deals newsletter

https://bit.ly/BoldwoodBNewsletter

Printed in Dunstable, United Kingdom

67625739R00170